The River Child

Jo Tuscano

ODYSSEY
BOOKS

Published by Odyssey Books in 2021

www.odysseybooks.com.au

A Cataloguing-in-Publication entry is available from the National Library of Australia

ISBN: 978-1922311474 (pbk)

ISBN: 978-1922311481 (ebook)

This novel is dedicated to the memory of Elspeth Marta Rudloff

29 July 1969 – 7 September 2018

I am indebted to my sisters, Helen Williams and Susan Mayne, who were
the first readers of my manuscript and gave me feedback and
encouragement, and also to my agent and editor Irina Dunn, whose
meticulous work brought this novel to life.

Chapter One

The day Elise Boatman disappeared seemed at first to be no different from any other day. Morning came, replete with pink orange hues after days of relentless rain. The air was thickly textured with sounds and smells that signalled the safety of routine: showers steaming, pots banging, and bacon spitting under a not so clean grill. The staff at the guesthouse woke, reluctantly shed their night-time fantasies, and climbed into their dull, daily personalities like small-part actors readying for the stage. It was a Thursday, the fifth week of the long school holidays, 1971. The day my mother blew the perfect smoke ring.

Cotton coloured clouds scudded across the sky, the skin of the day stretched over us, and just before eleven-thirty my mother's screams shattered the stillness. She ran from the garden into the kitchen. She was sweating, shaking, her words tumbling out in short, breathy spurts.

'Elise is missing,' she said. She doubled over, panting, as if the effort of getting those three words out had spent her energy.

The news spread quickly, hearts banged with panic and heads swam dark with imagination. A delivery truck rumbled down the guesthouse drive into the village and soon everybody knew. Phone lines buzzed. The villagers ran up the hill to the guesthouse. My mother's screams were contagious; other women and men shouted Elise's name. The staff abandoned their posts. Walter Heather, the maintenance man, dropped his tools and swore.

A sergeant from the village arrived within a short time.

An hour later, the police, police rescue, and emergency services arrived on the island.

And after a day had passed and there was no sign of the girl, thoughts about finality crept in, hovering like a net ready to fall, menacing, catching everyone, entwining them all—the staff, the guests, the family, and the onlookers. All were bound together by the thoughts that surface when a child goes missing; thoughts about the searing chasm where a life should have been and the gaping hole of missed opportunities. The celebrations, graduations, weddings, and grandchildren that would never be. The room that would be left untouched for years; the teddy bear on the pillow yellowing over time, its remaining marble eye dull with dust.

On the other side of the door, on that morning, I heard my grandmother Edwina and my mother Margaret talking in strained voices. My grandmother's voice was strangled high with panic.

'No,' she said. 'Walter Heather is odd, I grant you. And there were rumours, but none of them were true. If it was anyone, it'd be John Newmark. The children know to keep away from him when he comes to visit Olivia. Perhaps I should have said more. Keep away from Mr Newmark, he's overly fond of children. I've always said it, you know I have, Margaret. Perhaps that simply wasn't enough. Perhaps I should have explained.'

'Yes, perhaps you should have,' my mother replied. A pause. My mother's voice again, deliberately slow. 'Perhaps you should never have employed Olivia in the first place. John comes to see the children here occasionally. Supervised visits, of course. He's on the island right now.'

My grandmother made a grunting noise.

'They'll be looking at anyone who has a record. The police will interview him first, then. Olivia's a good employee. Not her fault she married a man like that.'

My grandmother opened the door. Startled at seeing me there, she gave me a pointed look.

'Siobhan, how long have you been standing outside this door?'

'I just got here,' I told her, hoping she wouldn't notice the redness creeping over my face and feeling relieved that I had practised the art of wide-eyed innocence over a long period.

Her face softened momentarily. She believed me, of that much I was sure. It wasn't the first time I'd lied to her.

On that first day, rumours surfaced. Memories sharpened, then blurred, then sharpened again, small details adding layers of importance to the unfolding tension. Those who had only tenuous connections to the child suddenly found themselves talking to police. They were needed. They were contributing. Neighbours vied with each other, swapping small pieces of information to bolster their sense of significance, all too ready to be linked to something so tumultuous.

Her favourite colour's blue. I know, I knitted her a jumper last year.

She played with my little one quite a bit. We only live ten houses away.

She just loved my strawberry tarts. She ate three last time her mother visited.

Bob Patterson, a local councillor, was sure he had seen her with someone in the main street that day. It looked like her, he told us, but the rain made it difficult to see well. He was concerned about the rising water levels from the river that lay just beyond the guesthouse gardens. The police divers were battling poor visibility. It's stopped for now, but if the rain comes back, the river will flood, he told my grandmother. It will make finding her body difficult. Bloody dangerous, in fact.

'They're not looking for a body. They'll find her,' my grandmother said.

At eleven years of age, I knew about danger. Growing up on a river, I understood flooding and the havoc it could cause. The river was easy to understand; its rhythms informed my life. What I didn't understand was the conversation I overheard from outside the door. I knew to stay away from John Newmark, who was the estranged husband of Olivia, my great aunt's carer. John Newmark was overly fond of children. I had always thought that the warnings about John Newmark had meant that children should stay away from him because he loved children so much that he would spend all day in conversation with them and neglect his duties. He had done building work for my grandmother in the past. I didn't understand what John Newmark had to do with Elise's disappearance. Did they even know each other?

As the day wore on, the police canvassed two possibilities: drowning and abduction. Everyone on the island would be interviewed. It was then that the small community began to turn on itself. A thin membrane of disquiet snaked through the most solid of marriages. Wives scrutinised their husbands. They asked subtle questions that would elicit information about their husbands' whereabouts on the day the three-year-old disappeared. They checked through pockets and wallets. Then they shook their heads in shame for even thinking that their husbands might prefer a three-year-old and yet they made contingency plans in their heads, did quick mental calculations on how they would live and what they would tell their children if the worst that they imagined happened. Standing in their sons' bedrooms, they surveyed the tarnished sporting trophies on makeshift shelves and reassured themselves that a normal, healthy teenage boy would have no interest in a girl so young. Despite this, they inspected beds, ripping off sheets and bundling them into washing machines while wincing at the stains that told them of their sons' retreat into private worlds where mothers were not welcome.

Despite the islanders' speculations, for most of the small population there was the secret relief of knowing that islanders did not turn against each other. If Elise had been abducted, it was not by one of their own. Never. They could be part of the drama without really worrying. It had to be a mainlander. Mainlanders were a breed apart; years of separation from Rachley Main town had resulted in islanders almost believing that mainlanders and islanders had distinctly different gene pools. The behaviour of those who lived on the other side of the river only confirmed what Rachley Islanders suspected. Divorces, affairs, scandals, public displays of drunkenness and immorality did not happen on the island. And then there was the Newmark thing, a mainland family.

'Mainlanders,' they said, shaking their heads.

Down in the village, circles of furtive whisperers stood on street corners, shackled together in shock. Abduction was the word of the day.

They haven't found a body, have they? Somebody's taken her. A child. How could they?

Dreadful business.

It's positively sick.

They should bring back the death penalty.

On that first day, the frenzied search for Elise began inside, then outside, spreading to the guesthouse, the part we called Our House, while unbeknown to us all, Elise lay deep in the water, not yet found, not yet mourned, the wheels of grief not yet in full motion. Police, police rescue, and emergency services scoured the island. The rain returned. By the end of the first day, rumours swirled and swelled so much they exploded under the weight of their own absurdity. Children formed search groups and ran furiously around the town. Bob Patterson's wife ran home and changed before she emerged in a khaki pantsuit and a hat edging dangerously close to a topee, as if she were hunting big game instead of a small, blonde girl. The police asked Walter Heather to present himself at the station. Routine questions, my mother told me. He was away for hours. What could he possibly want to take Elise away for?

My grandmother did not join in the search. Her obesity rendered her sedentary most of the time. She had a guesthouse to run. She sat by the phone, running her hand up and down the cord as though it might deliver good news if she rubbed hard enough. At one point, she yelled at the cook and threw her tortoise-shell hairbrush against the wall. My grandmother informed the staff they were not to speak to the guests about the missing girl. The guests were removed from what was happening, still ordering champagne and oysters delivered to their rooms, answering their doors in terry-towelling bathrobes with Gables Guest House monogrammed in bright purple on the pocket. As the news spread, more of them wandered down to reception.

'Found that girl yet?' they'd ask.

There was talk of the punts being suspended. Crossing was too difficult. The moorings were now underwater. If the rain continued, our lifeline to the mainland would be severed. Rachley Island, an inland island, would be cut adrift to fend for itself. Our island was a strip of land twenty-five kilometres long and eleven kilometres wide. Across the waters on the western side, a distance of a quarter of a mile separated us from the mainland. On the other side, to the east, there was almost a kilometre between us and the coast. There, people ate salty chips and flicked sand from their towels, detached from our despair. They listened with vague interest to news reports about a missing child up north near the border of New South Wales and Queensland and then turned to their lotto results with deep sighs.

At four o'clock, there was still no word. No sighting. Nothing from the police. My mother poured herself a straight gin and downed it.

'Come on,' she said. 'Come with me.'

My mother and I ran down to the river, the sludge squelching under our gumboots. The rain had stopped, but the sky told us there was more rain to come. We could only get so far as the flooding had made it impossible to get near to the bank. We stood, staring out across the swampy picnic ground, at the bins, the swings, the wooden tables lying in a flat, brown stew. The see-saw had come adrift. It floated on the surface, tangled in branches and crayfish nets. In the distance, a police boat disappeared around a bend.

My mother and I walked without speaking and then we both stopped. We stopped and stared out over the river. We were in line of sight of Billy's tree.

'How much can one family bear?' my mother asked.

I didn't answer. I didn't have to. My mother stuck a cigarette between her lips and left it there without lighting it. A sick feeling washed over me. Billy's tree. It was now part of the river markers, along with Simon's Boatshed, the flood marker poles, the crayfish nets, the punt wharf. Three years previously, Kerrie-Anne Boatman and I had found her brother Billy hanging from the river red gum. We had gone down to the river and had seen his green boat floating aimlessly in a slow circle. And then we saw him. It didn't look like Billy at first; his face was puffed and swollen, his arms hung limply, sticking out slightly on both sides as if he were carrying two heavy loads. He hung from a thick rope, a grotesque mannequin in brightly coloured clothing, his slack body shimmering in the wet. His toenails were painted bright red. I remember the sounds of that day: two-way radios crackling; the police helicopter above, dipping and rising, deciding where to land; people running down to the river. Bob Patterson was one of the first on the scene, his breath a rotting compost of morning eggs, bourbon, and stale tobacco. He was wearing the T-shirt he'd been wearing for weeks leading up to the local council elections. *Bob for the Job*. He gave out his business cards to the police. Campaigning, even here, some of the locals said. Bob turned his florid face away from Billy's swinging corpse. He lit a cigarette. Jesus, he said, shaking his head. He sidled up to one of the police officers.

'He was a fuckin' poofta, ya know,' he said.

The officer said nothing.

'He fucked men, you know,' he said, slightly louder. 'Used to do it at the abandoned army barracks over on the east side.'

Still, the officer didn't react. My brother spat into the wet earth, just missing Bob Patterson's foot, and then turned his back on all of them. The police rescue climbed the tree, slackened the rope, and the body was lowered slowly to the ground just as Sarah Boatman, her face blanched with shock, swept down the riverbank, her arms flailing, her mangled grief so raw that people turned away. Her screams were drowned out by the helicopter above. My mother arrived and told me to go home, but I didn't want to go home so I ran, down into the village until I reached the turn-off tree, the place where Boatman and I always parted before taking different routes home. I kept on running until I couldn't run anymore.

I went to Billy's funeral with my mother and brother. The village cemetery is tucked into the side of a hill that runs down to the river. You'll have a spectacular view, Billy, my brother had said as he threw a handful of dirt into the grave. The village children, too young to comprehend, played games amongst the headstones; who could find the oldest person buried there, the youngest baby, the strangest family name. It was the first funeral I ever attended and I remember being shocked when people started throwing dirt into the hole. My brother didn't throw his dirt in like the others. He stood still, his arm stretched out, his fist closed. He let the dirt trickle out slowly. I held my breath until he'd finished. He said they should have put Billy back in his boat, taken it to the coast, and let him go back to the water.

After the funeral, I went back down to the river. The willows on the bank seemed to bend even lower over the river, as if in deference to what had happened. People still moored their small boats along the river's edge. A thick patch of oil floated in a near perfect circle. Casuarinas spread out their arms over the ripples. Willow leaves skimmed the surface of the water, small eddies spun and danced in the sunlight. Cords of vines lay in dark green ropes. Mosquitoes hung thick in the air.

On the day we went down to the river to look for Elise, my mother stood still. When she spoke, it was almost a whisper.

'Not again. It can't happen again. First Billy and now...'

'Elise isn't dead, Mum,' I said. My voice cracked. My mother took my hand.

'I know,' she said.

She screamed out Elise's name and then she bent down and picked up a piece of cable, grey and speckled with mud. She walked down as far as she could to where the flat sheet of water began. She bent forward and struck out at the river, thrashing the cable cord down on its surface, over and over. Gasping for breath, she kept going, her mouth set in a grim line. I said nothing. Finally, she stood, breathing in short rasps.

'Xerxes whipped the water,' she said.

I didn't reply.

'Come on,' she said. 'Keep looking.'

In the late afternoon, I was disturbed when I tried to recall Elise's face and found I was unable to do so. I didn't understand why the police had asked me what Elise was wearing on the morning she disappeared. They asked me about the colour of her eyes. My mother said children could be unreliable witnesses and therefore the police had to check that my description was credible. I remembered what Elise had been wearing. I recalled the colour of her eyes.

'Blue,' I said.

'Green,' my mother said.

I looked up at my mother. She saw the torment on my face. I had failed Elise once already that morning and now I was failing her again.

'Blue-green,' my mother said and planted a cigarette in her mouth as if it were a full stop. 'Yes, blue-green.'

Olivia Newmark threw up in the guesthouse garden on the first evening of Elise's disappearance. It was five o'clock, still light, but rain spattered the windows and dark clouds were forming. Olivia was employed as a private nurse for my grandmother's sister Esther. Like other wives on the island, she too had questioned her husband as to his whereabouts when the girl went missing. Olivia, however, had a reason. Almost two years before, when Olivia's family had lived on the mainland, her husband John had been arrested. In the middle of a breakdown and after too many bourbons at a party one night, he was found behind a garden shed with a very young girl. His pants were around his ankles. The child was crying. Olivia's husband was crying as well. In the days that followed, before he was charged and taken away, the local teenagers threw rocks at the windows of Olivia's house. They spray-painted *Pedo, Rockspider, Kidfucker*

on the driveway. Underpants Man, they screamed as they cycled away.

'This is a family neighbourhood,' the women on the street told Olivia. 'We won't tolerate such things, nervous breakdown or not.'

Ronny Boyle from two streets away took the entire contents of his sister's underwear drawer and threw them over the Newmark's rose garden. For a whole day, the roses were cocooned in the small domes of pink bra cups. White lace panties hung off thorns. Olivia plucked the undergarments off the rose bushes late at night. She did not leave the house during the day for a week. The next week, the 'For Sale' sign stood like a badge of disgrace on Olivia's lawn. She moved her family, minus her husband, to the island and gained employment as my great Aunt Esther's carer.

Olivia, like the rest of the staff, joined the search, mumbling frantic prayers as she ran all over the property. Her estranged husband had visited her the day before. Olivia permitted these visits for her children's sake. She always stayed in the room while John spent time with the children. He's done his time, she told us. He's learned his lesson. Please, not again, she prayed. Not Elise. Not anyone.

In the late afternoon, Bob Patterson and his wife arrived and were ushered into the dining room where we had assembled. Bob drew himself up to his full height, ready to speak. A self-styled leader, he felt the need to disseminate information: what the police were doing, when the divers would be given clearance to search the river again, how the Boatmans were holding up, and what we could do in the meantime. He boomed unselfconsciously, flattening anybody else's attempts at dialogue. His wife interjected on a number of occasions, her voice a respirator rasp of Alpine Menthols and Cedel Fresh Breath. As he talked, the rain fell heavily, the noise rattling the windows, forcing him to increase his volume.

Bob filled the room with his voice. His wife winced and hugged her drink; she gave him a look that only another long-suffering wife could understand. A small, brown walnut of a woman, she rolled after her husband in her protective shell, never quite cracking. As the night unfolded, the councillor drank until his voice suddenly became so loud that his wife spilled her cocktail in surprise.

It was during the delivery of Bob Patterson's speech that everyone's eyes were drawn to the garden outside, to the sight of Olivia retching hideously, clutching the top of a topiary bush trimmed into the shape of a heart. Olivia seemed to be chanting, and then a yellow-green curtain of vomit fell from her mouth over the small, green bushes. It splashed down onto her white nurse's shoes. She looked up and saw her captive audience and, too sick to care, she let forth another arc of watery waste and coughed until there was nothing but a long rope of sticky saliva that plopped onto a leaf in a glistening glob. Her hand covered her mouth, and she stumbled into the garden behind, leaving a trail of undigested droppings behind her. My grandmother told my Aunt Sunita to tell Olivia to go home.

My grandmother drew the blinds and motioned for me to bring another tray of drinks. My mother shifted her weight onto one foot, and then curled one knee behind the other, her slimness and boniness making her look for a moment like a water bird about to peck at a morsel in the sand. She dragged on her cigarette, but instead of holding down the smoke for some length, she blew it out quickly, as if she desired to be rid of it. She filled her highball glass, adding the ice-cubes carefully as if they were diamonds.

'Summer started late,' my grandmother said. 'Not good for business. There's talk of us being cut off and the punts suspended. If the rain doesn't stop, the river will do its worst. And this Elise thing. It could well ruin us.'

My mother was putting on a brave face. Sarah Boatman, Elise's mother, had rung. Sarah was my mother's best friend. Sarah's other daughter, Kerrie-Anne, whom I called Boatman, was my best friend. My mother cried into the phone. When she had finished her conversation with Sarah, she motioned for me to come into the laundry room. It had always been our routine to do the washing after dinner. Years later, I realised that the simple act of doing the washing, the continuation of a ritual in the middle of devastation, was one of the small acts keeping her sane.

At night, with cigarette firmly clamped in her lips, we'd hang out the washing, pegging my grandmother's and my aunt's huge, white bloomers on thin, tight wires in the laundry room as the rain had not abated. On the line outside, I used to see them drying, floating and fluttering like sails against a blue ocean sky, stretched out with the wind behind them, belly full. Stained with cycles of blood, stretched with time and childbirth, they were continually bleached and mended. She'd peg the whites; I'd do the coloureds. There was no integration policy in the Montrell laundry. Strict apartheid made sure the two sides never met. We'd hum Vivaldi or The Messiah as we pegged along the line. My mother wasn't a churchgoer, but she said Handel never went to church either. Handel and Bach were her staples, and they became mine as well. To me, they were definite; they had patterns that repeated, that commanded you to listen. It was music with authority; it knew where it was going. It made me feel safe.

I liked to press my face into damp, white sheets, squashing them up against my nose, feeling the coolness and breathing in the cleanness. Clean, wet sheets stirred my senses in ways that others might be stirred by the smell of coffee, oranges, or jasmine bushes. Cigarette smoke has the same effect. My mother's smoking both alarmed and fascinated me. She didn't smoke like other people who inhaled and exhaled in a matter of seconds. The smoke seemed to stay down there forever before she slowly released it like escaping gas, bits at a time. Just when I thought there was no more to come, a small stream of grey-blue would jettison itself from the thin, coral-coated lips. Her smoking was our barometer to her moods. The way she smoked told us about fear, anger, and reckless happiness. My mother said little and revealed even less. She moved through life with an elegant melancholy, the perpetual cigarette dangling from her mouth, humming the classics and reading women's magazines in the evenings, her gin and ice-cubes in a highball glass by her side. I once saw a photo of my mother on a carnival ride. Her hair was sticking straight up on end, one dangling earring was flying out like a comet, the other was lost to the wind and wildness of the day, her face was joyful and free. These were my first clues, the first small hints that pointed to the person she used to be.

'There are certain things I'll take with me to the grave, Siobhan,' she was often heard to say, and because I was a child, I laughed and made lists of what I thought those things might be. Perhaps her blue beads and the hat with the daisies or the pincushion in the shape of a cat.

I tried putting on a brave face on that first night. Knots of guilt gripped my stomach. I lay in my bed, checking off the sounds that shut the house down for sleep, but no longer found them soothing. The nightly patterns had always been a comfort, but now they rang hollow. I listened to the cook banging pots in the kitchen. I tried saying the cook's unpronounceable Russian name aloud to take my mind off what was happening. Sch-liap-nik-ova. Schliap-nikova. Schliapnikova. The sound of Aunt Esther snoring in the room next door floated into my head. I could hear my brother Brenton's radio, loud and static, the *click-clack* of the calculator as my grandmother did the accounts, and the jangle of my Aunt Sunita's gold bangles as she paced up and down the hallway.

It's all right, they'll find her. It's a small island; she'll be somewhere. They haven't found her body, so she's out there somewhere. The police are searching even at night. She'll be safe and well.

Gradually, the noises of the night faded as staff, guests, and family retreated to their rooms to sleep. Doors slammed in the guesthouse, the tread of feet in the hallways above grew soft and distant, and muffled conversation floated down the stairs. The guests were not real for me; they came and they went and they blurred into each other. They were unseen ghosts of stairs, doors, and landings. It was only when I cleaned their rooms that they took on the shapes and smells of reality; they had people things: brushes, combs, luggage, soiled clothes, and family holiday photos strewn on unmade beds. Finally, there was total quiet, but my thoughts could not keep still, rattling aloud in my head. I shuffled around in my bed, trying to get comfortable. My cousin Jamilla, who had come to stay for the school holidays, was sleeping opposite me. She complained I was keeping her awake.

Just wait a few days, my mother said. Every time the phone rang, my grandmother ushered me out of the room. It rang constantly after Elise's disappearance. Sometimes it was Beatrice, my grandmother's youngest sister, offering to help.

My grandmother told her to stay where she was.

Nothing seemed real in those first few days. Solid truths became slippery. Sarah Boatman turned up in our kitchen on day two. My own version of events blurred until I no longer could construct a sequence of the day before. I repeated the story of what happened over and over on that first day, but by the second day, it became more like what I wanted it to sound like and less like the reality. In cloudy panic, nothing was what it was. If someone had asked me if a tree was really a tree or a bucket was really a bucket because that's what they've always been, I might have said no.

And on the third day, he rose again from the dead. Corinthians 1:54 gave me no comfort. Reverend Landers had organised a special prayer service. He prayed for the Boatmans, for the police and emergency service people, for those in the community who were searching. He chose his words carefully when he prayed for others who had been affected by Elise's disappearance. My mother's hands gripped the back of the pew in front of her. The veins between her knuckles stood out. I looked down at my own hands and at the finger that had recently bore the cut. Blood sisters, Boatman had told us. Elise, Boatman, and I had pressed our cut fingers hard into each other's, so the blood crossed over. Bonded for life.

The small church sweated in the heat, in the crush of bodies pressed into the pews. I knelt, stunted and speechless, my mother beside me as the congregation intoned the prayer. And on the third day, she rose from the dead. I knew by then that wouldn't happen. Prayers for Elise were no help. Reverend Landers told us not to abandon hope. In the pit of my stomach, I knew she was gone, and I had to take some of the blame. Down in the village, bubbles of grief floated to the surface of everyday life, where they dissipated in ripples that spread quietly through the small community. No one was left unscathed. My mother muttered to herself all day, smoking continuously. My grandmother said life must go on. The staff crept softly around, afraid of interfering with the process of grieving, but having to communicate with the family, nevertheless. They spoke in respectful tones about towels, washing, broken taps, and blocked toilets as if the items themselves had died. My grandmother, torpid with the heat, sat in her armchair on the veranda in the evenings, sucking in the slight breeze, silent. My brother locked himself in his room and turned the music up loud. The guests came and went. Life beat to a muted rhythm; we were going through the motions only. Olivia prayed aloud to Saint Hyacinth, Patron Saint of Drowning; nobody else would give voice to what everybody feared. The police had no reason to think Elise had been abducted. They had checked all punt crossings with the Rachley Punt Company and no staff on board had seen a child matching Elise's description. That information pressed down on our family as we sat in our chairs, immobilised.

'A family can only stand so much,' my mother said.

'It's as if the Boatmans are cursed,' my grandmother replied.

My mother banged an ashtray down on the table where the wreckage of an uneaten breakfast lay limp and cold.

'It's not the Boatmans I'm talking about,' she said.

It took me days to psyche myself up to visit Elise's grave and yesterday I went for the first time since her funeral. It was 1999, and it had taken me twenty-eight years to go there. The grief of so long ago had left its invisible markings on me. Strange, sombre brush strokes painted under flesh and bone. They seeped in under the skin, so deep that no one knew they were there. If I rubbed hard enough, they would come to the surface, but unlike the silver stretch marks on my body, they could not be treated cosmetically. I wrapped up my grief, tied it, sealed it and stored it away where no one could find it. No autopsy of my heart would ever reveal it, so carefully was it concealed. Sometimes my memories popped out of their packages without my permission, responding to songs and scraps of conversations about Elise, presenting themselves in full force, without warning. It took every effort to bind them up again. It is why I never had children; I didn't trust myself after what happened.

The headstone was simple. There was no angel or clasped

hands. I felt no connection to the grey, flecked stone. She would always be with the river. That's how it felt to me.

The therapist said it's not my fault. You were a child yourself, she told me. You can't blame yourself for Elise's death. She wanted to talk about my mother. I agreed only because all my friends were going to talk about their mothers, so it seemed like a good idea at the time, but I really wanted to talk about Elise. After some time, we did talk about her and gradually my guilt about Elise was slowly syringed out, dripping steadily onto the therapist's pea-green carpet. I spoke as well, for the first time, about my terrible lie. Children lie sometimes, the therapist simply said. At times, my guilt went into remission, only to return with a cancerous vengeance. And then there were those two words, spinning in dark circles of despair, loaded with a dreadful history and a future that never was. *If only...*

The therapist knew Elise died all those years ago. She knew about my lie. She knew about the guilt that crushed me. She knew about the years of drinking, the drug-addled years where nothing seemed to block out the past, the nightmares where a water-logged child, tumescent, eyes eaten by fish, floated by. We went over the same ground for a long time but always stopped when it came to talking about how Elise died. Then two things happened.

I received documents from a solicitor. Aunt Beatrice, my grandmother's sister, the last remaining member of the Montrell family, had passed away. She had no children. When my mother passed away, my grandmother left the guesthouse to Beatrice, and Beatrice left it to me and my brother Brenton. I spoke to my therapist about how I wanted nothing to do with Gables Guesthouse. I'd have to speak to Brenton about what he wanted to do with it. I just wanted it sold. The therapist spoke about how going back there might be the solution to finally being able to talk about what happened. Perhaps you've been given an opportunity, she said. She leaned forward and looked at me with a steady gaze.

'If you don't deal with your past, it will deal with you,' she said.

Her words scrolled across my head for days. When I closed my eyes, I saw them written in big white letters on a black background. The next session, it all came out. I told Brenton that I was going back to Gables. What should we do with it? I asked him. Sell it, he told me. I knew Beatrice had let the business go under years before and the house had been vacant for a very long time. It would probably need a lot of work before selling it. Brenton didn't agree with the idea of me going back there. He told me I was mad. I knew he didn't mean it; to anybody else it was a simple phrase to which no literal meaning was attached. 'You're mad to go back there,' he said. But to me, that phrase cut deep. It was a mirror reflecting a bleak future.

Madness was in the family. These days they have names for it. It wasn't nerves anymore. But it all came down to the same thing. I put on my protective, matter-of-fact armour and told him that I had to see the state it was in and what work needed to be done before we sold it. Then I casually added that while I was there, I would visit Elise's grave. Leave the past alone, he said. I didn't tell him the therapist said it was a good idea. My cousin Camilla offered to come and help me and I said I'd consider it. I told her I would visit Elise's grave. She told me it was the right thing to do.

'It's no big deal anymore,' I said.

'Yes,' Camilla said. 'You're right.'

We were both lying.

I walked through the house that morning, the place where I grew up, running my hands along the walls. Getting the feel. I had been trying, willing myself to make it feel mine, although I had not been there long enough to become familiar again with the spaces and cracks, the smells, the patina of walls, floors, furniture, not long enough for something of myself to be marked on this place, to claw back the territory that once was mine. I found my grandmother's tortoise-shell hairbrush in a drawer in the bathroom.

In the house, the rituals of deception, the dark undercurrents of the tides of secrecy, were all practised here and passed on to me so that I mastered the art quite young. I understood the art of madness as well and the consequences of pretending that we were just like any other family.

The image of Billy's red toenails was burned into my memory, and although the colour had faded and time had softened the edges, the picture, now in sepia tones, still lingered almost three decades later. The image of Elise loomed up large; it grew bigger and bigger and then it exploded, fracturing into pieces that didn't fit back together. I saw Elise, twisting in her muddy grave. At night, my memories wandered over the island, as if I was high above it, looking down. I saw the turn-off tree, the place where, over twenty-eight years ago, I saw Walter Heather running through the rain, coming from the east. I heard the soft chant of Olivia.

'Saint Anthony, Saint Anthony, take a look around, something is lost and it needs to be found.'

She clutched a small medallion in her hand. St Elizabeth, Patron Saint for the Prevention of Death of Children.

They found her, finally. Brown and full, the river spilled its sides and gave up its secrets, carrying with it plastic picnic plates, old tyres, a doll's dress; the debris of daily life laid to waste on the surface. A week after the flood, it gave up Elise, but it did not give anyone any peace.

I remember the sun on the morning she vanished, an apocalyptic sun, a small tight grey ball that told us this was the end.

On that first day, when Olivia returned home from Gables after being sick, she made a steak and kidney pie. She always made the pastry from scratch: egg and flour. She placed the pie on the middle rack of the oven and picked up a packet of matches. She lit a match. The radio spat out a static report about a possible child abduction. She turned on the gas and said a quick prayer to St Jude, Patron Saint of Hopeless Causes. Olivia then blew out the match, took the pie out of the oven, and put her head in.

Chapter Two

Information was a curious commodity in Our House. We called our part of the house 'Our House' to distinguish it from the guesthouse, which was joined to our part, separated by a hallway. Inference and idiom were the way we understood the world. A stock set of phrases described the whole spectrum of human behaviour. One man's meat is another man's poison. Lie down with dogs and get up with fleas. Better the devil you know than the devil you don't. As a young child, I had known them all and must have understood their implied meaning, as I could predict with absolute accuracy when and which one would be coming up in any given situation. If I asked an uncomfortable question, there was always a firm colloquialism that cemented the situation. Empty vessels make the most noise. Youth is wasted on the young. The adoption of a position was everything to my grandmother. It was her safety net and there was no middle ground. Pearls of wisdom, the old sayings, my grandmother said. They left me none the wiser at all. Much later, I blamed idioms for staying in a bad marriage; the devil you knew was at least consistent and predictable.

The amount of information one received in the Montrell

household depended on who was in collusion with whom. Like a lop-sided triangle skewing from one side to the other, allegiances changed overnight, and in the morning new camps armed themselves for the day ahead, resplendent with an arsenal of colloquialisms with which to do battle. Combinations of family and occasionally staff united and fragmented and united again, Esther and I remaining neutral. Little pigs have big ears, my grandmother would say when I asked about what was happening. I listened well and over the years had built up a storehouse of information, thick with knowledge, its walls lined with scraps of dialogue, night-time whispers and dark plaster patches over body parts that were not fit for the ears of a child. A few weeks before Elise went missing, I overheard an uncomfortable exchange between my grandmother and my mother.

'You know who is arriving soon,' my grandmother said.

'I might go away then for a few weeks.'

'You will not go anywhere, Margaret. You will stay here and deal with it. Part of the bargain.'

My mother sighed deeply.

In contrast to my grandmother, my mother did not automatically take a position on anything, preferring to absorb and canvas all possibilities and let the things she disagreed with softly drift off and find their resting place. My grandmother would not let them find a resting place at all. Just when you thought an argument was over and quietly turning in its grave, my grandmother would exhume it, examine it for any morsel of truth, and at its inquest, proclaim it false and offensive.

Information regarding my father was scarce. I had asked about him a few times and was told he had left when I was three. I knew little about him except that he'd had both legs amputated after an accident.

'Didn't stop him using his third leg,' my grandmother had often said.

She was to nurse her tired old joke back into life at dinner parties and cocktail hours for years, injecting it with a fresh arch of the eyebrow, a knowing wink, a coy incline of the head. If presented with an opportunity to launch it on someone new, she'd wait until the right moment and pounce. Women with too much rouge and tightly fitting outfits would scream in delight at the temerity of the guesthouse matriarch to raise such a subject in public. Their husbands looked embarrassed, perhaps thinking of their own indiscretions. It never occurred to my grandmother that their laughter was at my mother's expense. My grandmother was scathing on the topic of husbands. Hers had never returned after a heavy drinking session one night and my own father had disappeared as well. Both my grandmother and my mother remained stoic. They still polished their wedding rings, which they never took off. My grandmother had declared she would not have a man in her life again, claiming they only brought trouble. I suspected, however, that it was more to do with her own physicality. Her obesity would have prevented it. She suffered from nephritis and the drugs that helped keep her kidney disease manageable were the same ones that caused her weight to balloon. I walked in on her in the bathroom once when I was seven and my first impulse was to climb all over her. I had never seen sagging breasts or wads of loose pink skin and a belly as big as a hula-hoop, its slack muscles no longer containing it. Her size made it impossible for her to move with ease and when she finally sat down at night, she didn't get up again until she retired in a haze of sleep, regrets, and aching bones.

When I first arrived, it struck me how dark the house was. What the house needed was light. It wasn't good having dark thoughts in a dark house. I walked through the house that morning, opening doors, opening curtains, letting the sun in. I opened doors tentatively, as though I was expecting some sort of new version of the truth about what happened all those years ago, some new twist or interpretation. Something that might assuage my guilt. Something that might persuade me that what the therapist said is true, that I have to stop blaming myself.

Our House had been tacked on to the guesthouse without any real thought. There were rooms joined on to rooms, rooms joined by halls, smaller rooms and anterooms coming off larger ones. On our side of the hall were the rooms belonging to me, to Esther, to my grandmother, my mother, my brother Brenton, and a spare room that my aunt Sunita used when she stayed with us.

The first door I opened, after opening the kitchen, was the door to Esther's room.

My grandmother's eldest sister was eighty-three in 1971 and locked in an infantile world of her own. Olivia came twice a day for Esther. She called Aunt Esther Essie. Esther didn't call Olivia anything. She couldn't. Demented, non-verbal, and confined to her chair after a fall from a horse that left her without the use of her legs, her days were spent being wheeled in and out of her small space, being fed, washed, and put to bed. On her lap, her drawing book sat. She scribbled all day with a pen and drew pictures with thick, blunt crayons. At times, she'd try to make me look at its contents and so I'd give them a cursory look and make the sort of comments that I'd make to a child. Yes, that's beautiful. You drew that all by yourself? How clever you are. Childlike and gentle, she watched the world go by, a non-participant in the theatre of the absurd that surrounded her.

Esther also wrote, but was reluctant to let anyone see what she was writing. My mother said it was rude to read other people's writing without asking and so we never read what Esther was writing about. Once, when my grandmother asked to see what she was writing, Esther flicked over to a new page and scribbled quickly. She passed her book over and my grandmother read the word 'sunny' twenty times. After that, no one ever asked to see what Esther was writing. Occasionally, Esther would let Olivia look at the pictures she had drawn.

Esther sat in her room for years in her layers of brown clothes. We fed her brown and white food, potato and gravy, cauliflower and gravy, sago puddings, everything a shade of brown and white. All her food had to be blended and spoon-fed to her, quite often resulting in the lumpy mash being dribbled out a few seconds later. Her dentures sat in a glass beside her bed, floating in their Polident ocean like mutant, leering piano keys. Her teary eyes rolled around the room like two dull marbles poached in gelatine. At times, she was perilously close to death, especially in winter, but she somehow always pulled through. Every morning, Olivia combed Esther's hair and fashioned it into a tight bun, but the hair still managed to escape and frizz all over her head. Brown clothes and silver white hair; Esther was a decrepit waffle-coned ice-cream waiting for meltdown.

My grandmother refused to put her sister in a nursing home.

'Montrells don't send each other away,' she said. 'We stick together.'

Esther lived in the brown room, an anteroom off my bedroom. There was no door in between. I called it the boring room, as this was the room where I fed my great aunt and waited with as much patience as an eleven-year-old could muster for her to finish her meals. It was in the brown room that I learned all the D words. Dementia. Dentures. Deluded. Diuretic.

On cleaning days, we would wheel Esther's chair behind the reception desk while Olivia changed her sheets and dusted her room. There Esther would sit for hours, oblivious to the comings and goings of the guests, to conversation, to the cook banging pots in the huge kitchen that served the guesthouse. I had often wondered what had happened to Esther, but my family did not deal in straight answers. There were vague references to an incident that had caused her to suffer a stroke and much later she developed dementia, but when I tried to find out anything about the past, the subject was quickly changed. The one charm of the past is that it is the past, my grandmother would say. She delivered this slice of wisdom with the authority of one who had made it up herself. Brenton told me it was from Oscar Wilde. At age nineteen, my brother knew more about the world and how it worked than my grandmother ever would. A voracious reader, he'd topped the state in English at school the year before.

Each evening, my grandmother sat down in the kitchen with Olivia. There, they would conduct a thorough health assessment of Esther. I heard about bowel movements, gum problems, incontinence pads, arthritis, the cost of new wheels for the chair, and the other minutiae of Esther's life. Because Olivia treated Esther with great care and respect, my grandmother was grateful. Before Olivia, a string of young nurses, only concerned with earning money, had come and gone. Olivia, for her part, was grateful to be far enough away from the mainland and her husband's disgrace as to escape unwanted attention directed toward her family. Occasionally, her husband came to Gables to see Olivia and to assist Walter Heather if there was a big job that needed doing. My grandmother paid him cash in hand. He kept to himself and we kept away from him.

Esther was Olivia's charge, but occasionally Brenton, volatile and unreliable, would surprise us all. Sometimes I would overhear his voice coming from the brown room and I would stop and stand perfectly still, holding my breath, because I did not want him to know I was there. If he thought I was spying, then he would twist my arm. Occasionally, he fed Esther if I was busy and when he did, he would talk to her so gently and with such patience that I often had to put my head around the corner just to be sure that it was Brenton. I watched him many times, sitting next to her on the green embroidered chair, the only thing in the room that wasn't brown, bending forward, spooning blended mixture into her mouth, studying her wrinkled face carefully.

'There, Esther. I'd spit it out too if I had to eat this muck. Look at it, totally disgusting shit. There you go, one more mouthful. I know something about you, Esther. You're a shrewd old girl and you can't fool me. You know what I'm saying, don't you? You understand me, don't you, Esther?'

Once I saw Brenton pick up the framed image of St Drogo, the Patron Saint of the Mute, that Olivia had placed on Esther's dressing table. He turned it around so that it faced the other way.

'You don't need him, Esther. You can fool him, but you can't fool me.'

Esther remained impassive, giving away nothing, seemingly unaware of anything around her. I'd tell my grandmother that Esther didn't like spinach or ice-cream that was still frozen.

'Esther wouldn't know what she liked,' my grandmother said.

I opened the door to my old room, off Esther's room, and I felt Boatman's presence. It sent shivers all over me. We always called each other by our surnames, copying the older boys in the village. Months before Elise disappeared, Boatman and I started the Heather Files, writing down every scrap of information we could about the maintenance man. His cottage, not far from the guesthouse on the side that slopes down to the river, was out of bounds for us. The cottage seemed at odds with its only inhabitant; a weatherboard, pale blue, with rose curtains and seaside daisies in the garden. Walter Heather was surly and smelled of pipe tobacco. I had never spoken to him directly; he acknowledged my presence with a curt nod of his head and always appeared to be in a hurry. Boatman longed for an excuse to have to ask him something, but there never seemed to be an opportunity.

'Walter Heather's creepy,' she said.

One night when Boatman stayed over, she was convinced the maintenance man was trying to get into our bedroom. The door handle turned very slowly, very softly. It stopped when it had turned all the way to the left. A small click and then nothing. The handle spun gently to the right. We both sat up in the dark, holding our breath until we thought it was safe. It's him, she told me, and the next day we filled in two pages of the Heather Files. It was unlikely that any of the guests had tried the door-knob. At ten every night, the connecting door between the guesthouse and Our House was locked so the guests could not come through.

'It's so exciting living in a guesthouse,' Boatman said.

Boatman loved staying over with us and I would have given anything to have stayed at her house, but my grandmother would never allow it. Boatman had five brothers, older than me, and a sister, Elise, three years old. The Boatmans' house had an air of sun, serenity, and lightness that I ached for. Their furniture didn't have scratches like ours and it wasn't made from dark, gloomy wood. Dan Boatman played classical music and conducted an imaginary orchestra with a splintered ruler he kept behind the bookcase. With seven children, there were regular arguments over the television, sporting equipment, and food. Boatman and I were in the same class at school and spent most afternoons together as well.

It was Boatman who told me things about what boys do; she'd spied on her brothers quite a few times.

'That's disgusting,' I said.

'That's boys,' she replied.

I stood and looked at the beds, the desk, the cupboards and then suddenly I couldn't look at any more furniture in my old room. I pushed open more doors in the hallway of Our House. Sunita's room was further down the hall. Sunita was my mother's brother's widow, who stayed with us every school holidays. This meant that her daughter Jamilla, three years older than me, shared my room every holiday, which wasn't ideal.

Sunita was a gourmet cook. Food was the only source of sensuality in her life. She found passion in the texture and tastes of the food she prepared in the kitchen. Her fingers were in the bowl, covered in cream and fruit pulp, liqueur and sugar. It was a source of fascination watching her give the final verdict to a new entrée or dessert. She'd look, smell, pause, and then, after tasting had taken place, we'd wait while she pondered. More salt, less sugar, too creamy, needs pepper, not balanced, untextured, soggy in the middle. By the end of the day, her sari was discoloured with drips, splotches, smears, and stains, dusted with flour, congealed with sauce, and splattered with oil.

My grandmother only barely disguised her dislike of Sunita, but Sunita, to her credit, rose above the disdain, acting as though she either didn't notice or didn't care. Despite her disapproval of Sunita, my grandmother would tell her guests about her ex-daughter-in-law's family background with an exalted air; that she was from a high caste Brahmin family whose sons were all doctors and daughters all academics. They'd had a British education. Montrells only associated with the best of foreign types, and she's a Brahams, my grandmother informed a guest one summer. It's Brahmin, my brother corrected. It's not Christian, that's what it is, my grandmother replied.

For as much as she knew about running a guesthouse, my grandmother's ignorance about most other matters was in inverse proportion.

Jamilla was disdainful where her heritage was concerned, not wanting to associate with anything Indian and always trailing several yards behind her mother when they walked down into the village. Haughty and beautiful, she kept to herself most of the time.

All this I thought about while I dragged the ancient vacuum

cleaner over the carpets, mats, and floorboards. Occasionally, I'd look out over the gardens. In my imagination, I saw the peacock roaming in the bushes, the shade house, Walter Heather's cottage, and further on, the river, lying still. A lump formed in my throat. I hauled the vacuum around the room. The dust rose, my nose and eyes stung. I started to cough and then I started to cry.

On the second morning of Elise's disappearance, I sat in the ante-room off the kitchen, trying to read but not being able to concentrate. The Partridge Family blared 'I Think I Love You' over the small transistor radio on top of the sideboard in the kitchen. Usually I'd sing along, but there was no joy in music that morning.

Our family seemed nothing like the Partridge Family, my favourite show. They sang together and laughed and drove around in a big family fun van. The Partridges didn't have a cousin who barely spoke to you. They didn't have a mother that smoked constantly and filled her highball glass far too often. They didn't have a best friend whose brother had hanged himself. There were no people from India or employees who had a Catholic remedy for whatever was wrong that day. Children didn't disappear in their world.

My grandmother walked into the kitchen and snapped off the radio, severing the chorus of a gospel song. I could hear my mother sniffling. I moved from the ante-room closer to the kitchen door and kept very still. Audrey Landers, the minister's wife, was in the kitchen.

'Pull yourself together, Margaret,' my grandmother said. 'You have to face it, she's gone. Elise is not coming back.'

'But Sarah, what about Sarah? How can she bear it? First Billy and now Elise.'

'The good Lord doesn't give us any more than we can bear. You need to be strong,' said Audrey.

'Sarah will hate me. How could I have let this happen?' my mother cried.

'Sarah will bear what Sarah has to bear. Have you thought about Siobhan? That she also might be blaming herself? Children are resilient, but still, there could be problems. And we don't want her turning to you know who. She's getting older now. There might be some interest.'

'That's all I need,' my mother said. 'I need a drink.'

'You drink too much,' my grandmother said. 'You need to go back to those meetings.'

I heard the clinking of ice-cubes as they fell into the highball glass, followed by the sound of liquid being poured.

'Bottoms up,' my mother said.

Somebody else had come into the kitchen. I heard crying and my grandmother asking whoever it was to sit down and have a drink.

'Siobhan, come in here,' my grandmother yelled out.

I went into the kitchen. Shocked to see Sarah Boatman, I tried to walk out again, but my grandmother wouldn't let me. I had just taken a seat when Dot Patterson barged into the room, talking about Olivia. She was hysterical. My grandmother took her by the arm and dragged her into the lounge room. I followed them in, and so did Brenton. There were many chores to do as Olivia had called in sick and so I tried to think about what needed to be done.

My grandmother could think of no fitting old sayings at all on that second day. I expected to hear that no news was good news, but for once she couldn't muster any colloquialism that fit the experience we were living. She roamed around the house, restless, filling the teapot, consuming the contents and filling it again. On that second morning, she told me to clean the sink in the kitchen. When I walked in, the radio was playing 'Ode to

Billy Joe'. My mother and I loved that song. I scrubbed stained pots as images of Elise and Billy Joe McCallister, drowned, floating, their eyes eaten out by river fish, filled my head. Nobody turned the music off. I felt sick. Didn't they understand? It was as though they couldn't hear it. Pass the biscuits, please. Get some more ice-cubes, please Siobhan. Mama said it was a shame about Billy Joe, anyhow. Can you empty this ashtray, Siobhan? I ran out of the kitchen and buried my head in my pillow. An oppressive pall hung over the house. Every time the phone rang, it made us jump. Our nerves were shattered.

After Sarah Boatman left, my mother walked around the house, pouring gin into her glass, chanting softly under her breath, reading from a piece of paper. Audrey stopped my mother in the hallway, an alarmed look on her face. She placed both hands on my mother's shoulders, looked straight into her eyes, and spoke.

'Margaret, why on earth are you chanting the Mercy Chaplet? You're not even Catholic.'

My mother looked down at the piece of paper.

'It's near the end,' she said.

'Come with me,' Audrey said. 'I can give you something to calm you down but you're not to drink with it.'

I asked Brenton what the Mercy Chaplet was. He didn't know, but by the afternoon he did. Saying the chaplet, said Brenton, grants you mercy at the hour of death. Priests recommend it to sinners as the last hope, he added.

'But our mother isn't going to die,' I said.

'Of course she isn't,' Brenton replied.

That night, I sobbed into my pillow. Jamilla told me to stop crying.

'It's my fault,' I said. 'Everything is my fault.'

'Yes, it is your fault,' Jamilla hissed.

Her disdain for me filled the room.

'And your mother's.'

'You don't understand. Mum might die. She was saying the Chaplet.'

'What are you talking about? I'm sick of your stupid shit. Go to sleep and grow up.'

I left childhood behind forever that year. Summer had started late, just as my grandmother said it would. Elise was missing. And then Bernadette Brennan came to Rachley Island and nothing was ever the same again.

Chapter Three

That summer, weeks before the tragedy, Brenton invented Wordsday, where Brenton's every utterance was delivered in frustratingly long sentences and highbrow language. At first, I found it amusing, but it quickly wore off. I thought I might learn some interesting new vocabulary, but Brenton spoke so quickly that I missed most of what he said. My mother looked bewildered. My grandmother said he needed a good dose of military training. He kept it up for two weeks before the sheer maintenance of its routine was too much even for him to bear. They rang his psychiatrist. Ignore it, he said. The psychiatrist had suggested to my mother that people not react to his outrageous comments, as it was part of his attention seeking. He therefore had the luxury of his idiosyncrasies and no one to stop him. On Christmas Day, he communicated all morning with quotes from the Bible interspersed with swear words. In the afternoon, he reverted to plain English. In the evenings, Brenton would often sit with me out on the guesthouse veranda. We'd watch the sun setting over the river.

'Why did Billy have nail polish on his toenails when he died?' I asked on one of those evenings.

Brenton flicked a fly away. The crickets in the trees chirruped loudly. My legs were sticky with Aerogard. Brenton's radio was not quite on the station properly; a scratchy version of 'Ain't no Sunshine' stuttered out.

'What suddenly made you bring that up?' Brenton asked.

I shrugged, wishing then that I hadn't asked. Billy and Brenton had been close.

Brenton frowned. 'Billy was just Billy,' he said. 'It doesn't mean anything, the nail polish,' he added. And after a while, 'Bob Patterson doesn't paint his toes.'

'What? I don't get it.'

'Bob Patterson doesn't fuck his wife. He's like Billy. Without the nail polish. Now do you get it?'

'Yes. How do you know that?'

'I just do.'

'Is it true about what Billy did with men in the old army barracks?'

Brenton sighed, then paused before he answered. 'Does it matter?'

Wednesdays were the busiest days at Gables as it was on Wednesdays that the big clean was done in the guesthouse. On those days, the air would sing with the smell of hard yellow soap, wax and furniture polish, a hot iron on crisp, white linen. Bleach and liquid smells wafted in and out of rooms; the dryer and the ancient washing machines would spin all day, creaking into life in the mornings and coughing and spluttering into the afternoons. The day the automatic washing machines arrived at Gables Guesthouse was like Christmas. My grandmother treated the machines with reverence for the first few weeks, as though they might break if used too often. For a while, she locked the laundry when it wasn't in use until the staff became utterly frustrated and informed her that if the guests were to steal anything, it wouldn't be washing machines but rather linen and somewhat more undetectable items.

My mother had taken to sitting in the back room, alone with her cigarettes and whatever was bothering her. She'd sit very still, the smoke snarling and circling for a moment until it finally rose to the ceiling where it was sliced up in the frantic propellers of the overhead fan. The smoke and the fan were the only movements in the room. My mother's impenetrable solitude stood out, frozen in its ability to connect with the outside world. She was a bas relief in a drab painting, dark colours broken up with ash grey. She walked through the house with an umbilical cord of smoke twisting and trailing behind her.

'Nerves,' my grandmother said when I asked.

And so, I turned my attention to the Heather Files, stowing them away in an old hatbox my grandmother had long ago discarded. Boatman and I would note down anything that was even slightly suspicious. I told my mother and my grandmother that I was keeping my sewing materials for school in the box to ensure nobody would be interested in ever looking inside it. We were on a mission, Boatman and I, girl detectives; better than Nancy Drew, smarter than the Famous Five and Secret Seven, better than any fictional investigative characters we could think of. We would outwit the adults around us with our powers of observation, astound them with deductions beyond our years, and then, the moment carefully chosen, we would spring, catching the culprit when he least expected it.

Now that the school holidays had come, Boatman and I had more free time. We did, however, have an assignment for Geography, as Miss Abercrombie would be teaching us again the following year. That summer holiday we sat on the veranda, our homework folders spread out over the table, the Heather File notebook tucked safely under *Australian Junior Geography*. We'd mostly work diligently, but if we heard the number two hit from the Partridge Family wafting from the kitchen, we'd put down our books and sing and scream until someone would tell us to tone it down. Brenton would sometimes sit with us, writing up reports for the *Rachley Reader,* the main town newspaper that paid him to write reports about news from the island. He liked me to read the reports he wrote for the *Reader.* Sometimes I found a spelling mistake and even suggested a better way of expressing the information.

'It's not real journalism,' he said.

Real journalism, he told us, wasn't about prize cows at shows, best cakes in competitions, crash tackles, missed conversions, collapsing scrums, and missing pets. One day, he'd go to Sydney or Melbourne and do the real thing. Boatman and I enjoyed listening to Brenton read out softball scores and tales of elation when pet owners were reunited with their wayward animals. Brenton was quick, irreverent, and sarcastic. As to why he had to see a psychiatrist, I never really understood. I supposed I was used to his behaviour, but I knew Boatman's brothers were not like Brenton.

'The five pm punt from Rachley Main to Rachley Island was cancelled on Friday due to a part in the engine overheating. Rachley Punt Co. said that a new part had been ordered and would arrive within the next four days.'

I nodded.

'Shit,' he said. 'There's trouble in the Middle East and children dying in Africa and I'm writing about fucking punt parts.'

My mother opened the door and came out onto the veranda. The strains of 'Harper Valley PTA' followed her. She looked at Brenton. Her brows knitted together. She looked at me and flicked cigarette ash onto the lawn.

'Watch what comes out of your mouth,' she said softly. She threw her cigarette butt onto the lawn and went back inside, leaving the wooden door open and the screen locked. Boatman laughed and scribbled an answer in her *Australian Junior Geography* book.

'Know what we need on this island? What we need here is a good old-fashioned murder,' Brenton declared. 'Although I wouldn't get to cover it, anyway. What'd you say about the new guest?'

I didn't say anything for a moment because Boatman and I were still smirking about a good old-fashioned murder. We sat for a while discussing who we would like bumped off. Miss Abercrombie, Boatman suggested, because then we wouldn't have to go to school. And Walter Heather because he's a creep, she added. Jamilla, I said, because she's a snob and I wouldn't have to share my room with her every holiday. Bob Patterson, because he's a hypocrite, Brenton told us.

We finished our homework, and my mother reappeared bearing homemade lemonade and Iced VoVo biscuits. She stood still in the doorway after she had opened the screen door and looked at the three of us, pursing her lips.

'Be careful what you wish for,' she said.

'Have you seen that woman, the new guest, somewhere before? She looks a bit like Barbara Eden from *I Dream of Jeannie*,' I said.

'Who? Oh, that new guest. Yeah, she does a bit. Or Marilyn,' Brenton said. 'Without the curves. Her name's Bernadette.'

Bernadette Brennan had walked into the reception area dressed like a candy drop. Pink dress and matching shoes, blonde hair and an accent that made you listen even if you tried not to. She arrived on a Wordsday, the first day of school holidays. The night before, a storm swept over the island. The rain petered out into small smatters that stopped and started and then finally stopped. School holidays were always busier for the guesthouse and so I sat at the reception desk. Brenton wheeled Esther in and positioned her behind the desk. Esther sat; her neck bent down so that her chin was buried in her chest. It looked awkward and uncomfortable. Occasionally she'd wake at the sound of the phone or the counter bell. The guesthouse was in chaos as one of the kitchen staff was ill and so they were short staffed at the busiest time of the year. There had been whispers in the hallway about buns in ovens and being nauseous in the morning. I couldn't understand the secrecy over baking and being sick unless someone had eaten a bun that had gone off.

Added to that, a pipe had burst in the guesthouse laundry and anxious staff were trying to fix it. Every now and then, they'd come into the reception area to ask if Walter Heather had returned from the hardware store. I made a mental note for the Heather Files. In the middle of the chaos, two officious-looking men in suits and with clipboards had arrived to do a hotel inspection. They walked with purpose, casting critical eyes over the reception area, filling the room with their own importance. One of the men strode up to the reception desk and asked to see the owner. Brenton sighed dramatically.

'With deep regret, I must inform you that my grandmother is hooked up to her life support system at this present moment,' he said.

Shock registered on the faces of both men. Their haughty demeanour was suddenly gone, replaced by faces crumbled into apology.

'Sorry,' they mumbled, looking at their clipboards, not quite knowing what to do next.

One of them scribbled hurriedly on the back of a business card.

'We'll come another time,' the taller one said, and they made a quick exit, this time with less authority.

Bernadette Brennan had come into the reception area just in time to hear the exchange between the two men and Brenton. It was the first time I'd seen her up close. Her hair was swept up into a French roll. The platinum blonde colour was at odds with her black eyebrows and dark, cavernous eyes. Under her pancake make-up, the smattering of freckles across her nose and under her eyes gave her an almost girlish demeanour. She wore short dresses and stiletto heels, which made sharp *clip-clip* sounds as she crossed the floor, and from the very moment she walked into the reception area in the guesthouse, tension hung in the air.

'Life support system?' she asked, and I was surprised at both the familiarity and concern in her voice. Her manner suggested she knew my grandmother well enough to know that this was not true.

Brenton raised his eyebrows, and then his face broke into a smile. Beckoning Bernadette and I to follow him, he led us to the right of the reception area, around the corner, and into the hall of Our House where my grandmother was on the phone, the long cord trailing down to the connection on the floor, the receiver pressed hard against her ear.

'Married a Chinese, she did,' I could hear my grandmother saying. 'None of your incense-burning kind, though. A Baptist, of course. Beatrice? Am I my brother's keeper? How should I know? Probably on the continent somewhere.'

Bernadette smirked. We followed Brenton back out to the reception desk, where she began to fill in a registration form. A crooked smile had spread across Esther's face and I supposed she was dreaming pleasant dreams in the land of dementia, far away from domestic strife.

Bernadette was still filling in forms when my grandmother appeared in the reception area. She looked at Bernadette and her eyes widened.

'This is our new guest, Bernadette Brennan,' Brenton said.

My grandmother nodded dumbly, saying nothing.

'May I extend to you my sincerest apologies for what I loosely call my family,' Brenton stated with a grand sweep of his hand. 'Some days they succumb to the same unfortunate plight as my great aunt Esther here.'

'Edwina Montrell, pleased to meet you,' my grandmother said, but she did not sound pleased at all.

'And I am pleased to be here,' the new guest said, sounding as though she genuinely was.

'I'll show you to your room.'

My grandmother never showed guests to their rooms. The stairs were getting too much for her and a staff member usually did the job of settling the guests in. Esther's hands fluttered up and down. My brother and I exchanged looks. He shrugged his shoulders.

Several hours later, my grandmother reminded Brenton and me of the rule about not fraternising with the guests. Occasionally, if a staffer was sick, I'd assist with some light duties in the guesthouse, but now my grandmother told me I was no longer required to do that. I'd still get the same amount of pocket money, I was told. She seemed to be able to read my mind, knowing that I would like to see what the glamorous Bernadette had in her room, knowing that girlish things attracted me: perfume, high heels, make-up, all things rarely seen in our part of the house.

For the next few days, something stirred in my memory but refused to come to the surface. It was to do with the new guest. I tried to let it go, concentrating on surveillance of Walter Heather, recording his movements from the moment he came out of his cottage in the morning if I happened to see him. For each movement that was extraordinary, Boatman and I would put forward possible explanations. Went to shed and stayed twenty minutes. Came out with something wrapped in canvas. Perhaps has something buried in there? Our imaginations took over and soon Walter Heather's status rose from mere maintenance man to international smuggler, double agent, and mass murderer.

'Did Mr Heather ever have a wife?' I asked my grandmother over dinner.

My mother stopped stabbing her steak and looked up. 'Why do you want to know that?' she asked.

'I just wondered.'

My grandmother scooped peaches and cream into a plastic bowl for Esther. 'Keep away from Mr Heather,' she said. 'Good fences make good neighbours.'

'Frost,' Brenton said to me.

'Bernadette is very beautiful,' I said.

'Irish trash,' my mother hissed under her breath. But I heard it and perhaps it was intentional that I did.

'She has beautiful hair,' I replied.

'From a bottle,' my grandmother retorted. 'Black roots. Take a closer look. No, don't take a closer look. Keep away from the guests. If I find her entertaining men in her room, I'll turf her out in no time.'

My head was filled with visions of Bernadette Brennan entertaining in her room, serving tea and playing records, laughing, passing around frosted teacakes and scones to men who sat in high-back chairs and smiled politely. I kept to the rules. Keeping away from the guests was not difficult; rarely were they interesting and at times they were very demanding, but each time I saw Bernadette I had the urge to talk to her.

I listened for the sounds of her footsteps and her voice everywhere I went. Bernadette Brennan was unlike anyone I had ever met. Her Irish accent curled and dripped and swept around the guesthouse, coming into Our House as well. It fell down the stairs and went up the chimneys. It clung to the walls and the floor; it seemed to fill up space, and like an inescapable fog, it drugged those who inhaled deeply, making them delirious and languid. Even the smell of her perfume seemed to leave a trace in every room. Her nails were French polished, white and pink, and when I looked at my own housework hands, with the short, broken nails and red calluses, I felt ashamed. My grandmother always said you could tell a lot about a woman from her nails

and shoes. Bernadette Brennan obviously didn't do much housework and her shoes were like the ones in the glossy magazines
in the reception area. I looked through the magazines and
discovered that the shoes had names. Brands. You couldn't buy
those shoes in any shop on Rachley Island.

During the next few days, my grandmother questioned
anyone who had cause to enter Bernadette Brennan's room. Her
room was number one on the second floor. I overheard the staff
member who cleaned the second floor telling of what she had
seen in Bernadette's room. Her room stank of cigarettes. She'd
left fancy underwear draped over a chair. She kept expensive
perfume in her top drawer. She hasn't done a river cruise since
arriving. One afternoon, I overheard my grandmother and the
cleaner speaking in hushed tones in the reception area.

'She's very messy.'

'What else?'

'She's got tablets that look like birth control pills. In the
second drawer.'

'You didn't touch anything? Did you move anything?'

'No.'

'What else?'

In time, I managed to find out bits and pieces about
Bernadette Brennan. Eavesdropping was an art I was quite practised in. Pretending to be engrossed in a book or homework or
cooking and preparing something for Esther, my ears were
tuned to adult conversation. I had learned not to look up or
respond in any way when voices were suddenly lowered. I
drilled myself to act as though I was not listening. I became so
skilled in this art that the noise of plates and cups dropping or
breaking had so little effect on me that my mother took me to
have my hearing checked and was surprised to find that there
was nothing wrong with it.

Trying to find out information about Bernadette was just as
exciting as the Heather Files. Some of the information I gleaned

from listening to the results of the covert surveillance of the cleaner, who reported back regularly to my grandmother. Every day, my grandmother would remark with disdain on anything, no matter how small, that displeased her about Bernadette Brennan's room. Boatman and I now had another fact-finding adventure. When Boatman came over, I'd tell her about the latest things I'd found out.

On Wednesday nights, when the house and the guesthouse were looking respectable after a day of cleaning, the old women from the Baptist Lodge retirement village, long-time friends of my grandmother, would come to dinner. I looked forward to Wednesday nights purely because of the food. My favourite was roast with potatoes and Yorkshire pudding, smoked salmon in crème sauce, and caramel tarts. Every week, the sisters came to dinner, and quite often the food was the same. The sisters praised my grandmother's cooking as though it was the first time they had tasted such dishes in their lives. Sunita often cooked, but my grandmother felt that Sunita's cooking would be too experimental for a Wednesday night.

The conversation was the same every week: aches and pains, pills and potions, town gossip, the weather, local council matters, marriage, babies, and illness. There was an area of exception that my grandmother afforded to the old women and was extended to no one else. They were allowed to smoke in the family dining room, something my mother was not permitted to do.

When I enquired why the elderly ladies were allowed to smoke in the dining room, my grandmother simply said that old people deserved some small concessions at their age. I didn't know what a concession was, but I figured it was something to do with getting special little things for being so old.

The week Bernadette Brennan arrived, the old women from the nursing home came to dinner as usual and it was when I mentioned we had a new guest who looked like a model that the feeling of having seen Bernadette somewhere before suddenly came washing over me like a dream remembered a few days after. Unclear, but there. I tried to hold on to it, but it was loose and fluid, refusing to attach itself to a place in my memory.

'I've seen her somewhere before,' I said. 'But I can't remember where.'

'You've never seen her anywhere,' my grandmother said.

'No, Siobhan, you haven't seen her before,' my mother added. 'She seems familiar because she looks like an actress or a model in one of those magazines.'

My mother picked up a cigarette from the packet on the table belonging to old Miss Ivy. She ignored the look from my grandmother and lit up. She held her cigarette smoke down and then attempted to blow a smoke ring. I almost laughed. Her neck stretched like a giraffe; she put her whole body into the effort.

My grandmother waved the smoke away.

'Margaret, you're not fifteen, you know. It's unladylike to blow smoke rings.'

I raised my eyes to meet my mother's, but she looked right through me, a distant expression on her face. She stubbed her cigarette out in the green lopsided ashtray that I had made her in art class. She twirled the butt of the cigarette between her thumb and forefinger.

'Sometimes,' my grandmother said, 'people look a lot like other people. Just the other day I saw a woman on the mainland who I thought was Beatrice, but of course it wasn't Beatrice because she's in the south of France.'

'Yes, she is,' my mother intoned. 'Beatrice is in the south of France.'

With that said, she began to laugh. I looked nervously at my grandmother, who asked my mother to pass the gravy. Old Miss Ivy fiddled with her serviette and old Mrs Woodford helped herself to more meat. Knives and spoons were suddenly busy, filling up the awkward silence threatening to engulf the room.

The detritus of the topic hung in the air. There were two choices: change the topic or plunge right in. I was feeling indignant. Brenton's eyes told me to be brave.

'But I have seen her,' I implored.

No one said anything. Jamilla coughed loudly into her serviette and said that I had imagined it. My mother banged down the caramel tarts in the middle of the table and then left the room. She went into the back room with her cigarettes and shut the door. I sat, refusing to eat, even refusing dessert. The phone rang, diverting everyone's attention away from what was turning out to be a controversial topic. My grandmother eased herself up from her seat and walked into the hall, and was soon engaged in a conversation with Beatrice on the other side of the world. Brenton left the table. I was left with the sisters, listening to a one-sided phone conversation between my grandmother and her sister. It gave me a chance to quickly push the peas off my plate back into the serving dish. It was also time to give Esther her dinner.

Blending a small piece of meat and a few potatoes, a bit of gravy and some salt, I racked my brain as to where I had seen Bernadette Brennan before, but nothing came. Usually I didn't mind feeding Esther, but that night I was not in the mood to do it, feeling annoyed because none of them believed me. Perhaps I was confusing her with models I had seen in magazines. Perhaps my mother was right.

Now that the school holidays had come, Boatman spent quite a bit of time at Gables. Sometimes she was allowed to stay the night. We set up a trolley bed under the window in my room. I was never allowed to stay at the Boatmans' because she had too many older brothers. Boatman thought it was a great thing to be able to enter other people's rooms and be privy to a slice of their personal lives. Once she came with me while I delivered dry cleaning to guests' rooms and soon realised that most people had the same things in their rooms as her family had at home. I was told never to enter Walter Heather's storeroom next to the laundry, but wasn't given a reason why. This fuelled Boatman's imagination in a big way and she was forever wondering just what he had in there. After we started the Heather Files, we'd wait until he went into the storeroom and then press our ears up against his door, but the only sounds we ever heard were the small radio and the shrill whistle from the electric kettle.

One evening when Boatman stayed over, she suggested that we try to get a glimpse inside Walter Heather's cottage. We could make up an excuse to knock on the door to borrow something, she told me. There was nothing we could borrow that couldn't be found somewhere else on the property, I told her. I was uneasy; his cottage was strictly out of bounds. A Private Property sign made sure the guests didn't wander into the neatly bordered garden that separated his space from the communal space of the guesthouse gardens. We reached a compromise; we'd spy on him through the windows.

After dinner and after my chores were done, we were left to occupy ourselves. We crept through the gardens until we were close to the cottage. A dim light told us that Walter Heather was home. We were close enough to hear the television in his lounge room. The windows were open, but the lace curtains were pulled across, so we stared into the room through a grill of white patterned material that stirred occasionally in the light breeze. He sat watching television. If either of us coughed or moved, he'd hear it.

After a few minutes, I motioned to Boatman that we should go and, just as I did, Walter Heather got out of his chair. He went to a drawer and pulled something out; we couldn't see clearly enough but it looked like a photograph. He put the object on the table. Now he was standing facing us. We watched him pull down his zip. His green Gables staff trousers dropped to the floor. His hand worked furiously, and we heard his laboured breathing. He heaved a sigh and held up his hand, sticky and glistening under the dull light. We stared with repulsion at the withered penis as he cleaned himself up. The breeze, which had become stronger, was now lifting the curtain; it billowed out, almost touching our faces. We both tensed as Walter Heather suddenly looked up at the window. We ducked down, our heads below the windowsill. I turned to Boatman and pulled a face. She grimaced and jerked her head in the direction of home, but neither of us moved. So afraid of making a noise, we crouched there for several minutes before we thought it was safe to move.

Sounds of running water and glasses clinking relieved us. Walter Heather began to sing. We heard the sounds of plates being stacked on a dish dryer and made our move. Crouching down, we almost crawled back onto the path that led up to the guesthouse.

Boatman wrote it up in the Heather Files. Use a code, I told her. We had many more nights doing surveillance on the cottage, but we never saw anything like we had seen that first time and after a while, I lost interest in Walter Heather. I was becoming more and more interested in Bernadette Brennan. She was staying longer than most guests.

I raised the topic with my mother again one night, but she assured me I had never seen Bernadette before. I decided to leave it and never ask again. On that same night, I had to feed Esther. She was half asleep when I entered her room. Her head had lolled to one side and her drawing book and black crayon had fallen out of her hand on to the floor. I picked it up and put it on her bedside table, then placed the tray on her lap. She woke slowly and stared at the food like it was beautiful jewellery, tilting her head from one side to the other as if she were considering buying an expensive diamond and couldn't make up her mind. She motioned for her drawing book, her hand slightly shaky, but I shook my head.

'It's dinnertime,' I told her.

I spooned the food into her mouth; she dribbled some of it back out and I scooped it off her chin and back into her mouth again. Deep grooves surrounded her thin lips and ran down her face. Her neck was like turkey skin, loose folds upon more folds, dry and sun-damaged.

'I have seen her before,' I said to no one in particular, certainly not to Esther, who couldn't even understand what she was eating.

Esther raised her head slightly to look at me. She sighed and closed her eyes slowly.

'I have, Esther, I've seen her somewhere before.'

Esther sighed again and put her hand on mine. Her crotchety palm closed over my fingers and, as if in agreement, she nodded slowly three times before her eyelids closed gradually.

She'd never taken my hand before, and as I lay in bed that night listening to the sounds that shut down the house for sleep, I wondered how demented Esther really was, whether at times she understood things. I wondered about buns in ovens and sickness, about what was so funny about Beatrice being in the south of France. I thought about frost and worked out that perhaps if there was a lot of frost, people wouldn't want to talk to each other over the fence. I wondered about Bob Patterson being like Billy and what that had to do with not painting his toenails. I thought about my mother and her self-imposed exile into the back room, stranded in her own wilderness of solitude and smoke.

Sometimes the adult world made little sense.

Chapter Four

Had Esther been in her right mind, she would have enjoyed the view from here.

In those days, Walter Heather washed the windows every spring, starting on the southern side of the house and working his way round. In spring, the glass shone, and the curtains were laundered periodically and even ironed. Esther could see the river from there as the land sloped right down to the bank, but I never once saw her turn toward the view. I assumed that she didn't appreciate the view, but perhaps I shouldn't. Who knew what went on in that head of hers?

Every spring, my grandmother would direct us to close all the curtains and keep them closed for the whole day. She didn't want staff seeing in to family rooms. I once opened the curtains to the sight of Walter Heather on a ladder. He was more surprised than I was and almost toppled backward. Boatman laughed as he struggled to maintain balance. He hung onto a window latch, regained his composure, and gave her a distasteful look. Olivia emerged from the Brown Room and hastily drew the curtains.

'You don't want people looking in and seeing you in your underwear,' she told me. 'Hasn't your mother told you that?'

'Underpants Man. Underpants Man,' Boatman whispered when Olivia had left the room. My mother had said nothing about drawing curtains. At that time, she wasn't saying much about anything, preferring the vacuous gloom of the back room.

The smells of mothballs and lavender always emanated from Esther's room. Now it smelled of dust and stale air, the smell of a room that had been locked up for years. I closed my eyes and tried to conjure the smells that were once here, but there was nothing left. Esther had no privacy in this room at all. I don't know whether the concept of privacy would have even registered with her. I had no privacy either, but that hardly mattered. When Brenton was fourteen, he had kicked in the door between Esther's and my room. He'd come second in English. He had always come first. The door had never been replaced. It didn't really bother me and in fact it made life more interesting as I overheard everything that my grandmother said to her sister.

I flapped the curtains and watched as the minutiae of dust particles danced in mid-morning slats of sun. I looked up and half expected to see the dinner tray perched on the small, brown side table and the blue plastic basin steaming with hot water and eucalyptus. The sun spilled warm yellow rays into the room, softening the austere furnishings. They fell on top of the bookshelf where long ago we kept Esther's drawing book and the picture of her dead fiancé. A thick layer of dust lay congealed in the light. The room was filthy, having slept for years in layers of grime. The threadbare carpet was blotched with age and food spills, fraying in parts, the dull floorboards underneath straining to make an appearance. Dead insects hung from thin webs that fell apart as I touched them. The windows were stuck fast, their sills thick with congealed dirt. There was a lot to be done. My head filled with lists: a bucket, mop, broom, sugar soap, stepladder, detergents, brushes and paint, scrubbing brushes. I brought up a machine to steam off wallpaper that my boss at work kindly lent me. The carpet needed to be ripped up; the floorboards underneath could be polished up by a trades-man. The rugs could be thrown out. As for the curtains, straight in the bin—or better still, cleaning rags.

It was in this room that my mother cut off her hair after breakfast one morning. The scissors had been left in Esther's room. Perhaps she wanted to look like Audrey Hepburn. She came out into the kitchen looking like a newly hatched chick, messy, fluffy, and uneven.

'It'll grow back,' she said.

Esther's face was sharp in my memory, her slow smile, her wrinkles fanning out across her craggy face like ripples in a pond. Her light snoring, her pencil scraping across the pages of her drawing book, are sounds housed away in my senses. I never imagined that one day I would be old like her. When I was a child, she seemed hundreds of years old, rather than decades.

Photographs from when I was a child were still on the night-stand. The frames were old, the wood dull, but they sat just as they did back then. One of the photographs showed the sisters when they were young. Esther, especially, was quite attractive. My grandmother was the shortest and thinnest, and even back then she didn't seem to stand up straight like Beatrice and Esther. Their eyes held keys to their personalities: Beatrice, dreamy and vague, not even looking into the camera, her eyes gazing off at some point in the distance; Esther, responsible and serious. My grandmother, determined and defensive, the upright citizen from a lineage of fierce Calvinism, stood with her arms crossed in every photograph. Her face had a haughty demeanour that gave clues to the tight kernels of pride that ran deep within her. Nobody could crack them. I picked up a picture frame lying face down and turned it over to be greeted by the image of St Drogo, Patron Saint of the Mute, that Olivia had given Esther all those years ago. Despite being under glass, the picture had faded over time and now looked like Esther had once looked herself, grey and brown.

Beatrice had left the room pretty much as it was, only adding a few decorative items of her own. The asymmetrical Mexican pots Beatrice bought from some avant-garde artist sat uncomfortably on top of the Victorian dresser, their glazed surfaces bucking against the tired, dusty oak wood. I thought about Beatrice and wished she was still here.

Beatrice was quite unlike anybody else. Fashion was an anomaly to her; colours that did not go together, mismatched outfits and shoes, rings on every finger and her trademark beads, right down to the waist, like a nineteen-twenties' flapper. She smoked long, slim cigarettes, was as thin as a stick, and travelled the world to look at art, the only subject she knew anything in detail about. Sharp nosed and with a long, angular face, Beatrice was not particularly attractive, but her features belied her nature, which was generous and outgoing. We called her Auntie Bee. She'd send me postcards from time to time with pictures of galleries and great art works. Those depicting Dali, cubist paintings, or anything modern went straight in the bin, as my grandmother had no time for what she termed as experimental nonsense.

I got to know Beatrice well when I was at university. As a child, I thought she was unusual. As an adult, I began to understand why she left home to see the world at nineteen.

Unlike my grandmother, Beatrice lived in a larger world, her orbit spinning in directions that afforded her a broader view of how things worked. She was not interested in the guesthouse or the comings and goings on Rachley Island or, for that matter, what anybody thought of her. Until she inherited the guesthouse, she had never called anywhere a permanent home. She had many lovers and sometimes had two or three concurrently, and belonged to poetry circles that scandalised decent society, shocking the rest of the family.

After Esther's first stroke, she returned home but was restless within a short space of time, taking off after a little more than a month. It was said of Beatrice that she showed complete disregard for Esther by not staying on the island to care for her sister. I recall the arguments during that time.

'Family image is important,' my grandmother had said.

'An image is just that,' Beatrice replied. 'An image is an artificial imitation of the external form of an object.'

'Don't give me your arty nonsense. I'm not running a sculpture course, for God's sake. I'm running a guesthouse. People like to see a family-run business with family values.'

My grandmother's hostility shone like sunburn. I know now that she was jealous of Beatrice and took great pains to remind people that a university education wasn't everything. My grandmother came back from hospitality conferences regaling us with stories of hotels that hired university students who had degrees in Ancient History and Philosophy but didn't know the first thing about how to do anything regarding running a guesthouse. They might have degrees, she told Beatrice, but they can't do a correct hospital corner on a bedsheet. Useless, she said.

My old bedroom was the way I had left it when I first moved away from the island. The beds Jamilla and I slept in still faced each other. The paint was peeling, the linoleum buckling in waves on the floor. Square patches on the walls indicated where posters and paintings had once hung. It was in this room that I cried about Elise while Jamilla sat silent, shaking her head from side to side. Opening the third drawer of the cupboards, I found my diary from 1971 stuffed in between some old pony club magazines.

Dear Diary,

Auntie Esther's really sick, and this morning, Dr Dalton had to come and visit. He listened to her chest and gave her some medicine. I want to ask him a question, but I'm too embarrassed. All the other girls have theirs, but not me. I can't ask anyone here, not even my mother. Dr Dalton must be quite famous because he has a reserve named after him, Dalton Reserve, where the boys play football. My grandmother sat on the end of Auntie Esther's bed and asked her to hang on.

I think my grandmother wants her to hang on for another seventeen years because then she'll get a letter from the Queen. I asked her why the Queen sends people a letter when they turn one hundred and she said that it was a great achievement and then Brenton said you achieve dementia, arthritis, incontinence, and false teeth and for a special treat you can have some dribbling thrown in as well.

Dr Dalton said that for a woman of her age and physical state, Esther had one of the most amazing constitutions he'd ever seen in his career, and then Brenton said that since Dr Dalton had never been off Rachley island, except for his university training, he hadn't seen many amazing things at all and so had no one else to compare Auntie Esther with. My grandmother said she despaired of the younger generation.

Yesterday I fell off my bike and said the 'F' word. My grandmother says that word is the worst word in the whole of the English language, but Brenton said there's a worse one. I waited for something awful to happen, like the house falling down or someone dying, but nothing happened. I hope that's not why Auntie Esther is sick. If anyone should get sick, then it should be me because I'm the one who broke the rule about swearing. I can't understand why saying Jesus Christ is blasphemy either. If you say his name, surely that means you believe in him, that's what I think. To me, it seems logical. Brenton taught me that word, logical. My grandmother said that Brenton is totally illogical.

When I brought Auntie Esther her dinner, she seemed upset about something, maybe not upset, but impatient. She kept pointing to her drawing book, and when I got it for her she pushed it at me but I don't know what she wanted me to do with it. I really wish she could talk so I could know what she wants. I opened it up and saw the pictures she'd drawn and some writing that didn't make sense. She didn't eat much, but I suppose that's because she's sick. Later she went off to sleep. When she sleeps, her mouth sometimes turns up at the corners and it's sort of cute, even if she is eighty-three. Something's wrong with my mum, but I don't know what it is. Dan Boatman took Boatman and me down to the river to fish. He said the old army barracks were haunted and we should go and see if we could find any ghosts. We didn't catch any fish, but I caught some plastic rubbish and a Barbie doll without a head.

I shut the diary and stuffed it back into the drawer. My eyes swept the room. I made lists of what I needed to start cleaning it up. More lists swirl in my head, checking off what I hope I'd packed: the high maintenance female stuff: wax and strips, hair colour, tinting brush, blow drier, facial masks, manicure set, and other items of necessity. There was a hairdresser in the village, but I didn't want to spend any more time down there than was absolutely necessary. I doubted the locals would have recognised me, but I knew what they'd say if I happened to run into them.

'No ring on your finger yet, girlie?'

They said it when I was eighteen, and it would do no good to tell them that in fact I'd had two rings since then and that these days I preferred to be ringless. Marriage was for life on Rachley Island and they would never have understood. On the island, women's lives had little value without a husband and children in tow. Beatrice was way ahead of her time. She got out before she was trapped. I could not imagine what my grandmother would say to me, after two divorces, if she were alive today. She would probably comment on my lack of staying power. You make your bed, you lie in it, she'd say.

In this room, I listened at night. I checked off the sounds. Esther's light snoring. My grandmother and the click of the calculator. Sunita's bangles clanging. The muted sounds of the small television. Brenton, loud and angry with the world. My mother, the silent presence.

Later, in the evening, the sky ripped open like a ripe water-melon. Pinks and oranges streaked across blue then disappeared. The rain poured down the windows where Walter Heather had once scrubbed so vigorously. I stood outside on the southern side of the house and took off my clothes, piece by piece. The rain fell heavier, and still I stood, letting the water run over me, feeling the need to be cleansed, scrubbed, purged of decades, generations of Montrell half-truths that sat under a veneer of respectability. Had anyone from the village seen me, I knew what they would have thought. Poor thing, gone the way of her mother.

Chapter Five

The sign was long gone. Remnants of the old, high fences were still there but other than that, the old army barracks remained, scouring the hillside like a huge, dead beetle, its skin shed, rotting in the morning sun. Looking back, children on Rachley Island had more freedom than any child today. We were largely unsupervised, riding our bikes all over the island, gone for hours, no questions asked unless we were late home and lunch or dinner was getting cold. I'd heard stories about what had happened to children on the mainland, children in other states, children who'd gone to the beach with their siblings and who'd never returned, taken by a man who was overly fond of them, worse than any Underpants Man. He didn't stand there crying like Olivia's husband. He took the children. He disappeared and so did they. Things like that didn't happen on our island.

Boatman and I had just turned eleven when we dared to disobey our parents and explore the eastern side of Rachley Island. We'd known there were disused barracks down there somewhere, but had never really been interested in them until Brenton told us about them being haunted. Armies and barracks were boy things. Brenton and some of the boys from the main-land used the old barracks as a drinking hole. Sunita had said that people practised witchcraft down there, but my mother told her that was rubbish. Boys and vandalism, she said. There had always been rumours: stories about séances with dead birds and pentagrams, drinking sessions out of control, and mutterings about Billy Boatman and another boy from the mainland always going down there. Brenton said that what Billy did with other people was no one's business except Billy's and no one should speak of the dead like that.

On the morning that Boatman and I decided to explore the barracks, Sunita and I had been getting Esther's breakfast ready. Janis Joplin's 'Me and Bobby McGee' rolled over the kitchen. Sunita was telling me about India, much to my grandmother's disapproval. She didn't like me learning about Hindu gods and holy men that walked around naked.

My grandmother had not the slightest interest in anything Indian and dismissed any information about Sunita's culture by flicking up her hand whenever Sunita told us about Hindu pujas, famous yogis, and the most expensive saris in the world. Even my mother would ask questions. Sunita would roll her eyes and sigh at my grandmother's comments as if she couldn't be bothered listening to her at all. This had the effect of making my grandmother even more irritated. Being argued with meant at least to some extent being listened to. Being dismissed amounted to total disrespect. Fascination with things Indian had me sitting with Sunita for hours, listening to her describe feats of holy men who take vows never to let their feet touch the ground or those who will never cut their hair. She showed us a picture of a holy man who had never cut his fingernails or toenails. I had expected to see nails stretching out as long as a ruler. The nails of the holy man were curved upward and wrapped around in circles. She told me about the man who rolled from one city to the next in his quest for enlightenment.

My grandmother asked pointedly whether that man had nothing better to do. Idle hands are the Devil's work, she said. Quite superstitious, Sunita had a feeling for just about everything from food to colours to certain days that were auspicious for reasons we could never understand, despite her lengthy explanations.

On the day Boatman and I went east, Boatman had just had an argument with her mother and so it seemed a logical form of revenge on her mother to do something expressly forbidden. Sarah Boatman had on many occasions warned her daughter about not going to the barracks. I asked Boatman if she had heard anything about Billy and the barracks, but she just shrugged, walking purposefully down the hill from Gables, muttering about strict mothers and stupid rules and older brothers who were allowed to do anything they wanted. I was itching to ask about Josh, what he was allowed to do that she wasn't. Any piece of information about her brother that came my way I held next to my heart. But I didn't ask that day.

We headed down the hill, leaving the village behind, and rode past farms and open countryside, up and down low hills, until we came to the flat fields of the east. Over a hill, then down a worn dirt road, the barracks lay before us, surrounded by a sagging cyclone wire fence. Boatman and I left our bikes propped up against the main gate, whispering and giggling as we climbed through the hole in the fence. Boatman put her finger up to her lips, motioning me to be quiet. The sun seemed too bright for the day, leaving us exposed under a canopy of blue sky. There was no one around for miles. The stillness seeped in under our skin, heavy and unnerving.

Cupping her hands up to her mouth, Boatman gave a loud *coo-ee* and of course nothing echoed back. She shouted out that all mainland boys were rats and that Rachley Island was the stupidest place in the whole world. Her shouting was so loud that I half expected people from the village to come out from behind trees with distressed faces to catch the person vilifying their beloved home.

With Boatman taking the lead, we walked quickly and quietly, right down to the other fence on the western side. We lay back against the wire, breathless and panting, amazed at our own daring. It took a few minutes for our beating hearts to be still, for our breath to return to regular patterns, but still we were quiet, mesmerised by the dull, grey surroundings, the total lack of colour and movement.

A wasteland in various shades of brown and grey confronted us. A lost city, so quiet and dead that it almost seemed like time had stood still for thousands of years. It smelled old and was old to the touch, from the weathered buildings, crumbling brick-work, and rotting wood right down to the waterless tap outside the main building. Rows of dull, beige buildings stretched out over the flat, grassless earth.

We got up and walked toward the barracks. Shattered glass, rusty hinges, and peeling paintwork met our eyes at every turn. In some buildings, the light fittings were still in place. A lone globe hung from a sidewall fitting in a building called A Block. Thin cobwebs like frail fishing nets crawled across ceilings. Window ledges streaked with years of dirt housed dead flies. On a grime-covered window with the glass still intact, someone had scrawled *Peter 4 Ever* in large, sloping letters. Paint peeled and curled in tiny semi-circles, laying bare, rotting brown wood underneath. Every crunch of a foot on glass or wood seemed to have a life of its own in the pervading stillness, echoing in our ears, forcing us to take careful steps. We walked as though in the middle of a minefield, holding hands, saying nothing, looking around suddenly if our footsteps seemed too loud, as if the noise would bring people out of the lifeless buildings. I remembered thinking about the air, how it had not changed or moved in years. I imagined we were breathing the same air the army must have breathed, sharing the same molecules. I sensed traces of the last movements of soldiers long gone. The air had hung in soporific stillness, in time and space, waiting for the day that Boatman and I would come to break the spell.

Neither of us spoke for half an hour. Boatman, always the more adventurous, led the way as if she had been in the place a thousand times before and knew exactly where she was going. She trod confidently up old stairs, stepping over broken glass, occasionally stopping to examine some piece of debris on the floor. An old shoe, a filthy blanket, part of a drawer. She found a table tennis net and pocketed it.

'You never know,' she said quietly, eyebrows raised. They were the first words in half an hour.

I told her not to shout. She said she wasn't shouting. We were in the kitchen, or what used to be one. To me, accustomed to a huge guesthouse kitchen and a busy kitchen in Our House, it wasn't a kitchen at all, bereft of heat and movement, smells of mass production, and conversation. I suddenly needed the strong sunlight, the heat on my back and neck. The place made me afraid. It was sad and unused; the shadows of the afternoon would soon make it dark and I thought of Sunita and her warning.

'Ablutions block,' I said when we were outside again, pointing to a low, brown structure to our left. I had learned the word the day before.

'Abloooootions!' Boatman shrieked, as if it were the funniest thing in the world.

She craned her head around the brick wall and then turned back to me, holding her nose with her fingers, laughing, and I laughed too. I was about to tell her that toilets that haven't been used for years don't smell, but then I realised she had been laughing about that very thing. We both knew about male toilets. She had five brothers, and I was used to a guesthouse. Conversations about toilets and bathrooms had us giggling in the middle of lessons at school. Boatman dragged me into the block, ignoring my protests. We walked down aisles, showers and toilets on each side. We turned corners only to find more receptacles. A maze of showers and toilets met our eyes at every turn. I didn't like it at all.

'Let's go,' I said, and I knew she felt it too. The decay, the stench where there was none, the unwelcome images that ballooned inside our heads. The concrete wall was filled with graffiti. Phone numbers and names. We stopped for a moment, surveying the wall to see if we recognised anything.

'Mainland numbers?' Boatman whispered. 'That one's an islander. Look at the prefix.'

She turned on a tap and kept turning, but the tap head spun round and round. The cracked porcelain of the basin was covered in grime. Silence again. A minute's silence for what used to be. For a moment, I saw a busy landscape. Green uniforms with bright buttons. Men and women walking at fast paces with a certainty of direction and intent. Faces pressed against windows. The clatter of cutlery. I imagined green Jeeps careering round corners on their way to other blocks, sergeants saluting, and flags raised high. At some point, years ago, someone would have made a decision, someone else would have received a phone call, letter, or telegram, and suddenly there would have been a flurry of activity, packing up, moving out, trucks roaring away—and then this, nothing. Around some concrete steps, small yellow flowers danced in the sunlight. They looked out of place; they should have been withered, but they were not. It didn't seem quite right.

'Let's go,' Boatman said.

If we hadn't turned the corner, we wouldn't have seen it. It was the curtains that attracted us. Lightweight, dirty strips hanging behind a broken window were the only soft concession to the destruction strewn about us. The curtains belonged to a room at the end of a building, the words D Block on the outside. It was a small room with a sloping ceiling, a bed with nothing on it except the wire base, a table, and a cracked vase. Huge silver cobwebs spanned the room, delicate bridges connecting the table to the bed, the bed to the wall, and the window to the ceiling. A thick coat of dust lay heavy on the floor. The room looked like a bedroom to me, but Boatman insisted it was somebody's office.

'Then why is there a bed in here?'

'They'd have a nap when they were overworked,' she said.

She stretched out on the bed, put her arms behind her head. I thought the wire base would snap beneath her, but it held up well.

'One day, I'm going to get off this stupid island. I'll get off it and I'll go to Cuba and Rio and I'll dance like the girls I saw at the movies. I'll do the Samba and eat chilli and stay up till eleven o'clock.'

It was the sort of thing that Boatman's mother Sarah said when she'd had quite a bit to drink. There was a lot of Sarah in Boatman.

'What are you going to do?'

'When?'

'One day. In the future. What are you going to do?' she asked.

'I don't know.'

That always seemed to be the problem. Boatman had plans, even at eleven.

I couldn't tell her that one day perhaps Josh Boatman might marry me and we'd build a house on the mainland. I hadn't thought beyond that and it didn't quite compare with Rio and the Samba. The girls in our class were now talking about what boys they liked. I didn't like any of the boys in our class. Boatman liked one of the boys at the high school, so I didn't think it was so crazy that I liked her brother.

We called the room the Hovel. I can't remember why. A week after we'd discovered it, we decided that this would be our secret place. Between the two of us, we raided the sheds at our respective houses and managed to siphon off blankets, a mat, some pillows and an old kerosene heater that Boatman's father used to take on fishing trips. We covered the walls in pink and green sheets. I considered moving my horse pictures into the Hovel, but changed my mind. We taped up the broken window with thick tape that we took from Walter Heather's storeroom.

The day before, we'd waited until Walter Heather had gone into the village, taking the truck. I knew he'd be a while, as he took the truck on days where he'd have to load things and that always took some time. Boatman and I waited until no one was watching, then slipped into the storeroom and began our search for anything that might not be missed by Walter Heather and that we could use in the Hovel. We pulled out drawers, looked in boxes, opened cupboards, scoured the workbench, and climbed the stepladder to reach the top shelves. Boatman pulled down old tins and glass bottles filled with nails, screws, and bits of wire. She opened the lid of an old biscuit tin and gasped.

'What is it?'

She handed me a pile of photographs. I'd never seen anything like that ever before. I'd seen diagrams of parts of the body and a film about birth. My mother had taken me to Mother and Daughter Night, where she said I'd find out everything I needed to know.

'Any questions?' my mother asked on the way home.

'Does the Queen do that to get a baby?' I asked. I could not imagine the Queen doing that. I couldn't imagine anyone doing what I saw them doing in the photographs in the tin.

'It's dirty stuff,' Boatman said.

I sat on the information about Walter Heather's stash of pornography for a week, then returned to the storeroom with Boatman and this time with Brenton as well. He sifted through the pile of photographs quickly, his eyes widening. He looked up once to see what was registering on my face, but I waited impassively for him to lead the way.

'Filthy old fuck,' he muttered. He placed them back into the tin. 'Wait,' he said. 'Let me look at them again.'

'What for? I thought you said they're filthy.'

'They are, but it's what they call "consenting adults". I'm looking for other stuff.'

'What other stuff?'

'Stuff with kids in them.'

Boatman's eyes widened. She sucked in her breath. 'That's a mortal sin,' she said. 'I bet it is.'

Brenton sifted through the photographs slowly. I craned my neck up to see, but he held them up further, at eye level. A few times, he snorted.

'All right, no kiddie stuff. Don't you go near him. If I find you talking to him, I'll twist your arm so hard you'll cry for a week, you understand? You too, Boatman.'

'Are you going to tell anybody they're in the tin?'

'Nope. That's his business. And then they'd know we were in here without permission. You just remember what I said.'

I couldn't understand why he seemed to be so angry with me. Walter Heather was the one in possession of what I knew to be dirty and disgusting material, and yet Brenton had looked at me like I was the guilty one. He must have realised I was hurt as he came to me that night asking if I could check his article for *The Reader*. I knew it didn't need checking.

'Headline stuff. Front page, definitely. Increase in tourism. Sorry I spoke to you like that. Just looking out for you, that's all.'

'Sure,' I said.

After the discovery of the biscuit tin, Boatman decided our surveillance had to be increased. One afternoon, we hid in the bushes on the southern side of the house and waited till Walter Heather went into the storeroom. A small, grimy window at the back was the only view afforded to us, high up. A stack of bricks and a log had already been put there, somebody else no doubt having the same desire to take a look. I expected to see something forbidden taking place. Boatman said for sure Walter Heather would be doing unspeakable things with the pictures in the tin like she'd seen her brothers do with magazines they'd bought on the mainland and like what we'd seen the night we spied on him in the cottage. Walter Heather was sitting in a wicker chair, slumped over, his head in his hands. He had his favourite green shirt on, the one with the missing buttons. I wondered if he washed it every week because he seemed to have nothing else. He sat for a very long time before he rose to pull out a drawer in the work desk. We saw a framed photograph of a young girl. He studied the photograph as if it was the first time he had ever seen it in his life, tracing his fingers over the face of the young girl, no more than nine. His fingers ran down over her face, her neck, and her chest, then stopped abruptly at her waistline, as if they were frozen there and could trace no further.

Tears ran down his face, and he reached for a handkerchief. He didn't have one. He wiped tears and slime dripping from his nose on the back of his sleeve. Boatman made a noise of disgust in the back of her throat. He put the photograph back into the drawer and slammed it shut. He sank into the wicker chair and reached for a spanner, turning his attention to a tap fitting. The tap fitting held his attention for a minute. Then he threw it across the room. Walter Heather slumped over and moaned. Animal-like sounds came out of his mouth. They became so loud that we looked around to see if anybody else could hear him. Boatman and I climbed carefully down from the pile of bricks and ran back into the bushes.

'Who was that girl?' she asked.

'I have no idea.'

'Maybe she died, that's why he's crying.'

'Maybe. Perhaps it's his granddaughter?'

'We should write it up right now in the files before we forget. Maybe the parents of the girl got divorced and one of them took her to live somewhere else.'

'I suppose it happens. Same as Jamilla.'

'What's wrong with her? She's so snobby,' Boatman said.

'She hates this place.'

'You didn't tell her about the Hovel, did you?'

I tried to adopt the haughty, dismissive tone that Jamilla often reserved for me, but my words just sounded angry and somewhat childish.

'I don't tell her anything. Just because she's my cousin doesn't mean I like her.'

Boatman made new curtains for the Hovel in sewing class at school and the left-over material, which was actually thick upholstery material, served as a tablecloth. She told Mrs Potts, the sewing teacher, that she was sewing the items for her mother's birthday. Mrs Potts addressed the class, saying that Kerrie-Anne was a marvellous example for other girls to follow, while I stuffed my face into my badly hemmed skirt and laughed quietly.

I took an old yellowing pillow from Esther's room, explaining to her that I wasn't stealing, just borrowing. She smiled like a child and then pointed at other objects around the room. I picked them up; she nodded and smiled again, and for a split second I had the impression that she knew I was decorating. A hand-knitted shawl, one that Esther had done herself before her stroke, was always hung, folded over, on the bedhead. She pointed to it; I took it down and put it in her hands. She held it out for me to take but I couldn't take it and I told her so. She looked disappointed.

Sunita had given me an Indian sari on her last visit, green and gold with tiny ruby coloured patterns. It made a good bedspread. The other item Sunita had given me almost didn't make it into my bedroom, let alone anywhere else. On one of her visits, she had given me a miniature model of a temple because I had expressed interest in the one she had on her dressing table.

My grandmother didn't want Sunita giving me heathen items and so the temple had to go in the bin. I found it back on my dressing table the next morning. When I sat at the breakfast table that morning, my mother gave me a wry smile. I took the temple to the Hovel, and it became the centrepiece on the table, not exactly blending in with the gingham tablecloth that I'd taken from the guesthouse storeroom.

There was no electricity in the Hovel, but Boatman had a portable cassette player with a radio. We needed an endless supply of batteries.

Over the next few weeks, the Hovel slowly began to look more like a bedroom. We brought books and pictures and we kept a brown and white mouse there as well. Boatman brought her sea monkeys too, but she must have done something wrong because they kept dying. I stole some plastic orchids from the guesthouse storeroom and put them in a glass jar on the windowsill of the Hovel. We raided the huge bins at the back of the guesthouse and sometimes found things we could use. Old mats with pulled threads, vases with cracks in them, prints in frames with splintering wood.

Brenton suspected something was up when he found me foraging in the storage shed. It housed larger items that were too big for Walter Heather's storeroom. There I found dust-covered rolls of wallpaper. The second-floor guestrooms had the same paper, a wan green colour with embossed climbing roses. Brenton told me to take them and if anything came up, he'd say they were for him. He didn't ask me what they were for and I didn't explain. Brenton could at times be the best ally.

Silent hours were spent in the Hovel on the weekends, our homework spread on the table, books and pens scattered on the bed. We'd found some old chairs in C Block, which we cleaned and covered with old pillowslips. Some days Boatman would bring the radio and show me all the new dance steps while I tried to follow her moves in my own awkward way. She had a new bright pink bra. I'd never seen any other colour but white. She let me try it on. It was the kind of thing we could do in the Hovel.

Boatman said that when we got a bit older, we could stay the night at the Hovel.

'Can't wait,' I said.

Soon the Hovel had food, an endless supply of tinned biscuits, fruit, and bottles of drink that I took from the guesthouse kitchen. I knew the cook wouldn't miss them, but I suffered bouts of guilt taking them. During the last few months, the cook's face had become more reddened than ever, her nose a giant, red triangle, the focal point of her face. Spider veins crisscrossed her cheeks and the reek of alcohol was strong at seven in the morning. By early evening, her speech was slurred and her small, pig-like eyes seemed to retreat into the flushed cheeks. I could never pronounce her name. I called her Cook, and she didn't seem to mind.

Sometimes I would come to the Hovel by myself, to read, to dream. I went to the Hovel to cry the day they came to take my mother away.

And as I ran my fingers over the splintered wood, I almost expected to feel something, some sort of sensation, a passionate fleeting moment of nostalgia or an anger of the unforgiving kind. Nothing. It happened here, all those years ago, and I felt nothing. Perhaps that's good. The scar on my temple was still there. All my life I've worn a fringe because of it. I used to want to have it removed. There were ways it could be done, with lasers and peels, but I'd come to see it as a mark of survival. In night-time dreams, I relived the rough hands and the crack as my head hit the bed.

The Hovel looked different now. The faded green and pink walls were the only physical evidence that Boatman and I were ever there. I often wondered about her, what she was doing. Perhaps she was in Rio, dancing the night away, eating chilli.

Maybe she reminisced about the Hovel in quiet moments, remembering the safe haven, a room with a sloping roof in a deserted army base. The Hovel was our home away from home. The surrounding buildings receded into the distance when we were there, ceasing to exist for us, ceasing to hold us in disquiet as they had on that very first day. We never entered any of the other buildings again. The Hovel became the centre of our universe.

It served us well that summer, hiding our secrets and future plans, offering two girls on the precipice of growing up a temporary respite from the adult world, which increasingly was becoming a place we wished to get away from. The Hovel held our girlish dreams. I could still hear Boatman's shrill laughter and see myself motioning for her to keep the noise down. She'd laugh again, even harder, and then I'd laugh as well.

'There's no one around for miles,' we'd say.

Little did we realise just how wrong we were.

Chapter Six

The first spears of heavy, hot sun stabbed the morning air, signalling the coming of summer, the promise of long, leisurely days and excursions to the river. At that time of the year, we climbed the mulberry trees and ate the fruit that stained mouths and fingertips a gentle purple. My mother dressed in cut-off trousers and oversized shirts, her ice-cubes clinking in a highball glass with gin as she watched *Matlock* on the small television in the kitchen. Mosquitoes droned above our heads, small insects hovered in dimly lit rooms, and in the guesthouse the overhead fans creaked into life, their frantic white arms whirring in the humidity. Bob Patterson wore shorts to council meetings, Brenton's pimples dried out, and the guests drank martinis on the balcony. Tropical fruits appeared on the breakfast menu and drying towels, one-piece and bikini costumes festooned the guests' balcony railings, sometimes dropping onto the gardenia bushes below.

'Looks like a bloody Chinese laundry,' my grandmother complained.

Walter Heather retrieved various colourful tops and bottoms

from the garden and put them into the lost and found box behind the front desk. Boatman asked me if he looked at them, felt their texture or secreted some of them away. She said she wouldn't be surprised if he took them out at night and rubbed them against himself. I bet he smells them, she said. I didn't want to think about what Walter Heather might do with girls' bikini bottoms, but I noted it down in the files.

Guests put their names down for Sunset River cruises and Rachley girls went down to the chemist to purchase coconut oil and Skol, browning and bronzing themselves for boys who took no notice. Boys went to chemists on the mainland, where they were anonymous, to buy condoms and surfing magazines and bleach for their hair, as though they lived near a beach and not on a river. The small community hummed with life; Fair Day was coming.

The annual Rachley Island Fair Day was the biggest event on the calendar, held the week before Christmas. It was a Saturday morning. *Countdown* was blasting out on the television in the front room. A crescendo of lead guitar riffs and wailing about love gone wrong belted out of the lounge room. My grand-mother turned the television off and I hoped she wasn't going to say I couldn't go. Instead, she suggested I get dressed and get ready. Josh Boatman would be there and I didn't want to miss the chance of perhaps talking to him on my own.

The punt made extra trips on Fair Day as people from the mainland came to the island for the day. Visitors from the guest-house went to Fair Day, hired boats on the river, and sampled jams and pastries, oblivious to island gossip about baby show-ers, petty rivalries to do with who made the best sponges, and which unmarried girl was rumoured to be in the family way.

My grandmother had several entries in the preserves and cake sections that year, and Sarah Boatman, who had been sewing for weeks leading up to Fair Day, had a tent all to herself. Miss Ivy and Mrs Woodford and several others from the Baptist Lodge retirement village had crotchet work and delicate lace for sale in the handicraft tent. My mother, who didn't care much for the fair and who lately didn't seem to want to go anywhere, stayed to run the guesthouse.

The staff were allowed the morning off after breakfast, as most of the guests would be at the fair for the day. The cook was in one of her moods because my grandmother had taken one of the guesthouse kitchen recipes to make a cake that she had entered. The days leading up to the fair had seen me work harder than ever. I cleaned with extra care, completed all homework, was more attentive to Esther than ever, and so I had leverage to bargain my way into a whole day at the fair. Boatman wanted to ride the dodgem cars, and although I expressed an interest in the dodgems as well, the truth was I wanted to ride the ponies as Josh Boatman would be there. He worked the ponies every year, leading the Shetlands in a slow circle marked out with chalk while the children clung to the saddle and sometimes to the pony's mane. I was too old for pony rides, but there were plenty of opportunities for me to offer to take one of the village children off their mother's hands for a while.

I saw Brenton as I wandered through the crowd. He gave me a vague nod and walked off, disappearing into a tent.

I looked for Josh over at the ponies and my heart sank when I saw he wasn't there.

Sarah Boatman sailed by in a swirl of material with bold tribal markings and a colourless liquid in a transparent cup. 'African theme,' she informed us. She dragged on her cigarette and exhaled vodka and smoke all over us. Her gait was slightly off centre. Elise was cocooned in her free arm, playing with a string of beads, her face covered in chocolate. I hoped she might mention Josh's whereabouts and began to feel hopeful again until she mentioned that Catherine and Josh wouldn't be home for dinner. In that instant, my buoyant mood vanished. So, he had a girlfriend. Elise held out her arms for me to pick her up, but I ignored her. Her face crumpled, and she whimpered.

Boatman rolled her eyes and seemed to want to get away quickly. When her mother was drinking, she usually tried to make a quick exit. We wandered down to the other end of the ground to where the rides were, Boatman kicking up dust with her shoes and crunching the five-dollar note into a ball.

'She's so embarrassing,' Boatman said. 'She won't wear normal clothes. She said she could never lose weight after Elise. I hate those caftans.'

'I know,' was all I could offer. I could empathise with my best friend on this topic. My own mother was becoming someone I didn't want to be seen with.

Walter Heather sat on a fence near the ponies, watching the children, an intent look on his face. My stomach lurched. It was the same look he'd had when he ran his fingers over the photograph of the girl when we'd spied on him in the storeroom. I didn't know what that look meant; I only knew that it made me feel uncomfortable.

Josh Boatman's girlfriend sat with him. Every now and then, they would turn and say something to each other, then lapse back into silence. I couldn't help staring at her; she was beautiful, a tall, slender brunette with shiny hair and the latest fashionable clothes. My own homemade dress, with fabric I had picked out myself, now seemed dowdy and horribly out of place. The fake pearls Olivia had given me looked yellow in the light. The romantic illusion that had been sustaining me for days was completely shattered. I threw my Coke can in the bin with such force that Boatman looked up at me. I looked over at Catherine again. I hated her. In that instant, I knew I was too young and could never compete.

I had always wanted Brenton and Josh to be friends. It might have been a way for me to get to know Josh. They had attended the same school and were in the same year, but had never become anything more than acquaintances. Billy was Brenton's closest friend. I formed the impression that Brenton actually disliked Josh, but then Brenton disliked most people, dismissing most of the population as idiots until proven otherwise. Brenton turned his nose up at sporting prowess and seemed to regard people like Josh, who excelled at sport, as boorish.

The sight of Bernadette Brennan in a light pink pantsuit, eating donuts, interrupted my thoughts. We exchanged greetings. Boatman went over to speak to Josh. The new guest and I sat together on a low fence, talking about nothing in particular. The locals waved as they passed by. Because I could think of nothing interesting to say, I filled in the space by commenting on who had just passed by, what they did, and where they worked. Bernadette seemed nervous, constantly looking around her, and I wondered if something was wrong or if somebody was following her. Perhaps she had agreed to meet a friend and was looking for them in the crowd. All the time I kept my eye on Josh, pretending that I wasn't looking at him at all.

'One day,' she said, putting her arm around me, 'you'll grow up and have a boyfriend, but now you are young and sometimes the people we like a lot are not really meant for us.'

I felt my face redden. She knew. I was taken aback. Not even Boatman suspected. Not even my own mother. Had I given myself away that easily? A hot, red flush of embarrassment crept up my neck and over my cheeks. She too stared at Josh Boatman, at the brown skin and piercing blue eyes, at the way he moved, bending over the children with an easy grace and just a hint of self-satisfaction.

'He's not for you,' she said, displeasure crossing her face. I wanted to ask her how she knew, but at that moment, the guesthouse cook emerged from the tent in front of the pony rides. She sat down heavily on a chair, very close to us, carefully easing her huge frame into it, trying to sit comfortably. She hoisted her uniform over her knees, revealing the large purple-red skeins running over her legs like French knitting. I'd never seen her legs bare before that day as they were usually encased in thick, unsightly support stockings. For a moment, I thought she might come over and talk to us, but she sat and closed her eyes, continuing with the paper fan, the wads of loose pink skin under her arms jiggling up and down.

'I must go,' Bernadette Brennan said suddenly.

I wanted desperately for her not to go. I wanted to know how she knew, and at that moment I felt like I could tell her anything, ask her anything, even those things I wanted to ask Dr Dalton and my mother, but didn't have the courage to raise.

Boatman had finished the conversation with her brother and suggested we'd have more fun by ourselves at the Hovel. I was inclined to agree. With the few dollars we had left between us, we were able to buy sponge cake and Coke, which we took with us. Boatman had her transistor with her; she sang loudly as we peddled and laughed. Every now and then, she'd turn around and sing, *Hare Rama, Hare Hare, Guru Rama, Guru Vishnu*. I didn't feel like singing.

Not even cake and Coke and the comfort of the Hovel could lift my spirits. We ate in silence, both locked in our own thoughts. I knew that Boatman would be thinking about Sarah and hoping that her mother wouldn't make a fool of herself before the day's end. I made a mental note to go through the storage shed and see if I could find an old fan because the summer was coming and the Hovel would be hot and then I realised that there was no electricity, anyway. I lay on the bed, daydreaming, and almost drifted off to sleep when Boatman poked me in the ribs. Startled, I began to speak, but she put her fingers to her lips, frowning, her eyes wide with apprehension and her fists clenched as if ready to protect herself.

'Sh!' she whispered. 'There's someone outside.'

We froze, listening, for what seemed minutes. The stillness was sharp; I could hear the rise and fall of Boatman's breath. Our heads were under the window, pressed up against the wall. I could see the pale hairs on Boatman's upper lip. I wanted to sneeze, but held my nose so tightly that it hurt. Boatman moved her leg slightly, only to send an empty Coke bottle rattling across the floor. My heart banged out a thudding rhythm; Boatman's eyes were wide with fear. A faint cracking noise came from outside. A cautious foot on a twig, perhaps, or a piece of glass. We stayed, motionless, waiting for a sign from the other. I still hadn't let go of my breath. Before I could stop her, Boatman picked up the empty Coke bottle on the floor, leapt off the bed, and screamed like a warrior woman as she opened the Hovel door.

The dog outside leapt back and growled. Boatman dropped the bottle and leant against the doorjamb, letting out a sigh of relief. My heart was thumping so badly I imagined it would burst. The stray dog sniffed around the door, raised its head, and ran off around a corner of another building. After some time had lapsed and we had both recovered, I started to laugh at what had just happened. I told Boatman that she should have borrowed her mother's tribal outfit. I imagined her with war paint in striped patterns all over her face and feathers in her hair.

By the time we returned, the fair was winding down. The carousel was being dismantled; the wooden ponies lay on their sides on the grass like wounded battle horses. Tents were being pulled down and cars were coming down the fairground drive to pick up family members. Bob Patterson was deep in conversation with the mayor over by the fence. I saw Dan Boatman pull into the car park.

My grandmother had won first prize in the baking section and was in high spirits.

Brenton had met a businessman from Perth who was into weight-loss formulas and had convinced Brenton that the new Souper Slim was the thing to sell. Consisting of only soup with special herbs, it was touted to reduce weight in weeks. The cook wanted to know exactly what the special herbs were, but the businessman said the recipe was a secret, and anyway, the herbs came from India and were unavailable in Australia. At the mention of India, my grandmother snorted. Brenton and the businessman discussed investment strategies, their eyes lit up with enthusiasm, paying no heed to my grandmother's warnings about herbs from places where people roll from one city to another.

Someone else had taken over the pony rides. Catherine was again talking to Walter Heather, Elise on her hip. I projected five or six years into the future, the same scene, Catherine, now Mrs Josh Boatman, holding her own child. I tried to dismiss it as quickly as it had come, but it lingered inside my head. Josh was nowhere to be seen. Sarah Boatman had been drinking champagne with her gambling ladies and Elise, she informed us, was with Josh and Catherine. Sarah's mascara was smeared in the heat. There were black lines under her eyes.

I spent some time talking to some of the girls from school and then wandered around to see if there was anything worth parting with my pocket money for. Another half an hour passed before my grandmother declared it was time to go home. Sarah sent Boatman off to find Catherine and Elise, but she came back saying she hadn't seen them. A few minutes after her return, Josh entered, looking worried, saying he couldn't find Elise or Catherine anywhere. He told us he had last seen them just before Catherine had taken Elise to the toilet. Despite having been drinking all afternoon, Sarah suddenly roused herself into action. Later, she cried and said she was a dreadful mother while my mother stroked her arm and consoled her, their cigarettes fuming as intensely as their regret.

Boatman didn't seem particularly worried about Catherine, but she was worried about Elise.

'She's only three,' she kept saying as we searched behind tents, under seats, in huge bins, and anywhere we thought a child might hide. Dan Boatman strode up to the crowd. Sarah walked up to her husband, as if in a dream.

'She's only three,' she said.

'And you're drunk,' he said. 'What sort of mother are you?'

Elise wasn't hiding, however. As more of the crowd fanned out, Elise came into view, clutching her teddy bear, looking lost.

Sarah ran toward her daughter and scooped her up in her arms. 'Where's Catherine?'

Elise pointed a tiny finger in the direction of the bushes on the eastern side of the fairground. Boatman and I looked at each other. Elise stayed with me while Boatman walked down to the bushes, and from where I was standing, I could see her bending over the ground, her hands in the earth. Perhaps she had found a lost necklace or a ring. Then she straightened and ran over to me, babbling something incomprehensible before she drew breath and raced inside the tent. I heard a shriek and Josh swore. He ran out of the tent and over to the bushes, Brenton following behind him. My grandmother held Sarah back. I asked Boatman what had happened, but she shook her head.

From where we stood, we could see three outlines crouched down on the ground. Then Josh came into view carrying Catherine, while Brenton and another man followed behind. They went inside the tent and set Catherine down on the ground. My grandmother told Boatman and me to go outside, but we lingered just near the doorway.

Catherine's head hung slack over Josh's arm. Her mouth was smeared with blood. Her shirt was torn and her hair held the remains of leaves and twigs. Josh laid her on the ground and took a tablecloth off one of the tables in the tent. Sarah clutched

Elise and sank into a picnic chair, howling like a baby. Olivia bent over the girl, issuing instructions.

'Give her room, she's a nurse,' Brenton bawled.

'Everyone out!' Olivia said. 'Brenton, get them out. You stay, please.'

Everyone was forced outside. Brenton pulled the flap of the tent across. A crowd had gathered outside the door, but Brenton let only Dr Dalton in. He had come to pick up his wife and had heard there'd been an accident. I peered through an opening in the canvas. Catherine was covered with a tablecloth. Dr Dalton bent over the girl on the ground. I could hear the doctor and Olivia whispering together. After some time, the doctor stood up and looked at Olivia.

'This is a police matter,' he said.

Brenton emerged from the tent. He had his fists balled, an angry look on his face. He walked over to where Josh Boatman was standing and pushed him down into a chair. He leaned over Josh and words were exchanged, but I couldn't hear anything they said to each other. Josh tried to get up, but Brenton, who was stronger than Josh, grabbed him by the arms and pinned him down in the chair. Brenton was firmly in charge of the conversation from the tone of his voice. Josh's mouth was set in a hard line. Brenton finally wrenched Josh up out of the chair and pushed him away. Josh walked a distance and then turned, glaring at Brenton. Bernadette Brennan was watching this exchange carefully.

Back at home, I asked what had happened. My mother said Catherine had fainted because of the heat. My grandmother told me Catherine was sick but would be all right. I noticed the way Jamilla looked at both of them when this information was delivered. She wasn't buying into it. Not satisfied, I went to Brenton. He was quiet for a while, thinking about how to navigate his way around the topic.

'Well, you know those pictures you found in the biscuit tin.

It's the same thing, like what those people were doing. You know what I mean, except one of them doesn't want to do it, so the other uses force. Understand?'

'I think so.'

Images ballooned in my head. Josh Boatman and Catherine doing what the people in the photographs were doing. Bits of bodies. Parts of bodies in other people's parts of bodies. I knew how babies were made, but this wasn't like that. It made me feel sick.

My mother was listening to country music that night. A maudlin tale of woe groped its way through the house, trying to find a sympathetic listener. She sat in the paisley armchair in her room, trying to master a smoke ring and laughing at her own efforts. I told her she smoked too much.

In bed, I covered my head with my pillow, while jumbled biscuit tin naked pictures inside my head fused with songs about people leaving each other. I couldn't sleep and thrashed and rolled in my bed that night. Jamilla told me she was tired and to stop keeping her awake. I told her about the biscuit tin pictures, and she suddenly sat up, her tiredness vanishing.

'If you're lying, you'll burn in hell, you know,' she said.

'I'm not lying.'

She wanted to know what exactly the people in the pictures were doing, so I told her. She sat there for a moment and then made a huffing noise in the back of her throat.

'Well,' she said. Her tone gave her away: she was jealous. I didn't stop to wonder about the source of her envy. I knew at that moment I had her attention and had seen something she had probably only heard about.

'Has Boatman seen them too?'

'No,' I lied. I couldn't have my triumphal experience diminished by it having been shared with someone else. I wanted Jamilla to believe I had been the only one, and in that moment, I felt a seismic shift in the power balance between my cousin and me.

'I'm going to sleep now,' I told her.

'I'm going to the Zoot concert,' Jamilla said. 'Bet you don't know who they are.'

I didn't reply.

'I hate this place,' she said.

Chapter Seven

atherine Parker never returned to Rachley Island after Fair Day. The story swept through our small community in a matter of hours, and along the way the details became so twisted, exaggerated, and so far from the truth that even now I have problems sequencing the whole day.

Boatman told me that her brother punched a hole in the lounge room wall of their house several hours after the police had taken Catherine away. He had tried to assault Walter Heather, who was the last person Catherine was seen with. The police could find no evidence of Walter Heather having violated the girl. No one had seen him anywhere near the vicinity of the bushes on the eastern side of the fairground. All of his movements were checked out and others were able to confirm his whereabouts throughout the day. Josh was ordered to stay away from Walter Heather.

Catherine Parker did not cooperate with the police, saying she could not remember what happened after she had taken Elise into the bushes. She said they had gone over to the bushland because the queues for the toilets were too long and after that everything was a blank. Refusing to answer questions, she said she just wanted to forget the whole thing and get back to her home, a remote property on the border of New South Wales and South Australia. She and Josh broke up, and while I should have been glad, I wasn't. I kept thinking about the biscuit tin pictures. In my imagination, I saw Catherine in those pictures.

No one, not even the police, was able to piece together the movements of Catherine and Elise. One of the villagers said she had seen Catherine and Elise walking toward the bushes but couldn't remember the exact time. She thought it was just before the wood-chopping competition. A few other locals said they had seen them throughout the day, but the times didn't match up with other people's sightings of them. Villagers argued with each other about times and who had seen what. They came up to the guesthouse, drank in the bar, and recounted their sessions with weary police. The police interviewed Bernadette Brennan out on the guesthouse veranda. They drank iced tea and spoke *sotto voce*. I strained to hear what they were talking about, but caught only a few words.

Weeks after the event, the story was still the most popular topic on the island, but, as stories do, it eventually lost its freshness and faded into the backdrop of daily life, a wilted pile of unanswered questions, speculation, and facts that were more like fiction.

Sarah started to drink more heavily than ever before after that day and there was talk that Dan Boatman had a woman on the mainland. Boatman told me that one night her father had raised his hand to Sarah's face, telling her she was not fit to be a mother. He didn't hit her, however; filled with shame, he broke down and cried.

Not long after, we had a phone call from the Boatmans. Sarah had contracted hepatitis. Dan could not take time off work, so Josh and Boatman were left to look after her, while the other younger children were packed off to the mainland to stay with Sarah's sister. Elise, it was decided, would come to us and be minded by my mother during the day and be picked up in the afternoons. Sarah was my mother's best friend. It was only proper that Elise should come to us. Sarah had on many occasions filled in when the cook or one of the kitchen staff had been sick. She would never accept money for the work she did, belonging to the old school of payment in kind.

Summer dragged on with relentless humidity, and soon the house was filled with laughter at Elise's antics. The days were long and hot, the guests were nowhere to be seen until late afternoon cocktails on the veranda, and I kept thinking about Josh Boatman. Above all, I had Bernadette Brennan to talk to. Despite the strict rule about not fraternising with the guests, I found ways to get around it and, in fact, had become furtive and deceitful. I didn't understand why she was staying so long, and when I asked about it one night at dinner, my mother told me she was taking time out.

'From what?'

There was silence.

'A romance gone wrong,' Brenton said quickly.

My mother, who had just raised a glass to her lips, suddenly spat liquid, almost choking as she laughed. Jamilla started to laugh as well. She looked at my mother and raised her eyebrows, as if they shared some secret information. I didn't believe what Brenton had said. Bernadette seemed very happy to me. I continued to see her when I could.

I carried my guilty burden around and tried to atone for my secret by being extra helpful to everybody. Everything about the new guest fascinated me. Besides Boatman, she seemed to be the only one who really talked to me and the only one who listened. In her room, she had a portable record player, a plastic, lightweight piece that looked almost like a toy. Sometimes I'd take my records up to her room and she'd teach me the latest dance steps. Modern pop music is fun, she told me, but it was essential to learn to waltz properly and do the more traditional steps. She could dance even in her stiletto heels, and beside her I felt big and clumsy, never quite getting the steps right. She never gave up on me, repeating the movements over and over until I managed at least the easier ones.

One afternoon, she showed me how to wrap up my hair in a French roll and fasten it with pins so discreetly placed they were invisible. She placed a tortoise-shell hair-clip at the bottom of the roll. It made me look older; it made me feel beautiful. And from that day, I began to see her as somebody who really cared about me, about the way I looked, about what I was doing at school, about all sorts of things. When the bell rang for dinner, I took the clip out, but she thrust it back into my hand and closed my fingers over it with her own.

'It's yours,' she said. 'Your mother must be very proud of you.'

I had no answer. In fact, I didn't really know what my mother thought of me. While my grandmother was moored tightly in routine, my mother was drifting aimlessly, vague and disengaged from everything around her. My grandmother was a barnacle; she clung to a secure post of smoothly run operations, while my mother made waves that smashed up against that post and threatened to wash everything away.

I ran down two flights of stairs, my hand sliding down the polished wood of the banister in the guesthouse, the other hand clutching the hair-clip. There was a jam jar in which I kept ribbons and trinkets and nail polish. I placed the clip there. I still have that clip.

A few nights later, I overheard my mother and grandmother discussing Bernadette.

'When's she going?'

'Margaret, she goes when she always goes, when school goes back.'

'Can't come soon enough. Every bloody year.'

'It's not that bad, Margaret. But one day you will have to tell Siobhan about her. The child will find out one way or another.'

I couldn't ask my mother or grandmother about that conversation. I would have been in trouble for eavesdropping. I told Boatman about the conversation. I also told her about my grandmother threatening to turf Bernadette out if she was entertaining men in her room.

Boatman was far worldlier than me. She said 'entertaining' was another word for going to bed with men for money. 'A high-class hooker.' She said she'd heard her brothers talking about women who do that sort of work.

I now understood why I was told to keep away from Bernadette. They were trying to protect me from the knowledge that there was a prostitute in the guesthouse. The only other person I could discuss this with was Brenton. When I told him about the conversation I'd overheard between our mother and grandmother and then Boatman's explanation, he laughed until tears formed.

'No, Siobhan, not true. She's a guest like any other. She obviously likes this place. It's relaxing. It's picturesque. No cooking or cleaning. What more could she want?'

I felt better after the conversation with Brenton.

When I told Bernadette that my mother was looking after Elise as Sarah was ill, I was surprised at her response. I thought she might have said something about an act of kindness toward the Boatmans, or what fun Elise would have staying with us, but instead she looked worried. Then she bent down, her head almost touching mine, and put her face up close so that I could see the lines where the pancake make-up hadn't quite blended in. She looked me in the eye.

'Promise me you will help your mother look after Elise,' she said.

'All right,' I said.

'Don't let her out of your sight.'

I asked her why I had to be there if my mother was there, but she said something about the more people the better, especially if someone wasn't well. I thought she meant Sarah Boatman wasn't well.

And when the time came, the time that marked my passing into womanhood, it seemed only natural that I should go to my new friend and not my mother. I had often worried that something was wrong with me because all the other girls had their periods, although I did overhear Beatrice talking about the daughter of a friend who started at sixteen. Dr Dalton often visited the house to have a look at Esther, but I could never speak to him alone. I would rehearse the conversation that I wanted to have with him in my head, knowing that I could never, ever ask him a question like that without an adult present. I even made up an imaginary headache that lasted for days so that my mother would take me to the surgery.

Dr Dalton's surgery smelled of stale cigarette smoke and cheap air-freshener. The faded orange carpet was threadbare in places and splotched with stains, and the Venetian blinds were coated in dust. On the third day of my imaginary headache, I sat in the surgery while the doctor peered down my throat. A dying fly buzzed on the windowsill. The surgical instruments lay sneering in their cold autoclaves. Dr Dalton then sent me out of the room to have a private word with my mother. I hovered outside the door and heard enough to understand that the doctor told my mother I was craving attention. My mother took me straight from the doctor's rooms, on to the punt, and then on to the mainland shopping centre where we walked from shop to shop. She made me try on tops and skirts and sandals. She bought ice-creams and then we went to a movie. I was still none the wiser regarding my problem. I couldn't ask, and in the end, I didn't have to. Bernadette Brennan seemed to be able to read my mind.

'Didn't your mother prepare you for this?'

Her face creased in a frown. I couldn't tell her that my mother had not spoken to me about it. Like most things, it was information that one was just expected to know. Information that was picked up through friends or by listening to my relatives as they lowered their voices when speaking of matters concerning parts of the body that were rarely mentioned in public.

They say she has trouble in that department.

According to Harriet, she has troubles down there.

I remember Beatrice referring to that part of the female anatomy as the place where the sun never shines and my grandmother wincing. Beatrice is coarse, she told us.

When the day finally came, I had so much pain I couldn't walk, so Bernadette went for me, walking the fifteen minutes there and back to the village chemist. On her return, she handed me a package in a brown paper bag, gave me careful instructions and a gentle push into her bathroom, shutting the door.

'There,' she said. 'It is a happy day, after all. Welcome to the world of being a woman.'

'Why do people call them friends? They're so painful, they're not friendly at all,' I shouted through the door.

But I felt in that instant as though I were part of some dark and delicious secret society, as though she and I were part of the same thing. In the following days, I went around carrying a certain happiness and a certain haughtiness as well. My status in the world had been elevated and, more importantly, I was just like the other girls. I had surpassed even Boatman in that department, and she grilled me thoroughly on every aspect of the new phase. I went through my cupboards and drawers, throwing out clothes, shoes, and ornaments. My world had suddenly changed.

'They're childish,' I told my mother when she asked why I was throwing things out. I told her about my first period.

'Mm,' she responded, snorting small streams of smoke from

her nostrils. Strangely, she asked me no questions about what I had done or whether I had bought the correct things at the chemist or even if someone had taken me to a chemist.

I looked at my horse posters on the wall and began to tear some of them down. In the end, I couldn't part with two favourite posters so I left them there, but I never quite felt the attachment to them I once had. They were part of an era in which I no longer lived. Pictures of pop stars went out too. Bernadette Brennan didn't have pictures of pop stars in her room. She had bottles of perfume and tubes of lipstick, powder compacts, nail polish, and high heels. She also had the same strange objects that I had once seen on the top shelf of the pantry in Our House: a small rubber cap and a white stick. I know this because I looked in her drawer. It was strict guest-house policy not to look in either cupboards or drawers when cleaning, when running errands to guests' rooms or entering them when returning dry cleaning, but I know my grandmother had broken her own rules a number of times.

Sometimes when I asked Bernadette questions, she would hesitate before answering, as if my questions had taken her off guard or as if she had had no experience with children. She never answered by saying that a fool and his money are easily parted, or lie down with dogs get up with fleas.

'Well,' she would say, and there would be a few seconds of silence before her answer came, and even then, I believed that those few seconds gave her enough time to think quickly and make something up on the spot. She was not used to the questions of a young girl, and I knew later that she was careful as she chartered a course that had no map to guide her.

I stopped discussing Bernadette Brennan in front of Boatman. She was my best friend, and I didn't want her to think that the new guest had usurped her in my affections.

Boatman was struggling herself. Since the Catherine incident, her mother had been drinking more than usual and then hepatitis had struck. This had consequences at the guesthouse, as Sarah couldn't fill in for the cook's best assistant, who was taking quite a few days off sick, always in the mornings.

Sarah, like Sunita, excelled at cooking. She didn't cook like anyone else I knew. She cooked 'new food' as it became known: savouries packed tightly in tiny pastry cases, luncheon meats rolled up filled with finely chopped vegetables in sauce and secured with toothpicks, Bombe Alaska that was actually lit and burned on the table in front of us. We were amazed. On my mother's birthday the year before, she had cooked Chinese duck —red, glazed and spicy—and oleaginous pork buns in individual paper wrappers. We'd never tasted anything like it.

Sarah Boatman didn't walk like other people either; she floated, drink in one hand, cigarette in the other, swathed in diaphanous green and gold layers that she made herself. Insisting she didn't sew, she 'ran things up'. Perhaps it was the eyebrows, huge and highly arched above her often bloodshot eyes, that gave her a permanently startled look. Her personality, vivacious and unruffled, was the total antithesis to my mother's circumspection and reflective nature. It was an improbable friendship, but a friendship nonetheless. My grandmother even approved of Sarah, despite the fact that she drank and was a Catholic.

'Her heart's in the right place,' she said.

Elise crept into our affections that summer, almost without us being aware.

There was, at the beginning, an underlying tightening of the boundaries that limited how much emotional room we could give a three-year-old child. An automatic resistance lay in all of us, never voiced but hovering below the surface. We were not going to get too close to her. Before too much time had passed, however, a rivalry for her affections had sprung up, taking us all by surprise.

Brenton, especially, doted on her. He could be reckless, but he was a responsible adult with Elise. Never voicing my fears and puzzled by the fact that nobody else seemed to be worried, I watched him closely with Elise but saw nothing but kindness, the same strange charity he afforded to Esther.

She learned Brenton-speak as fast as he could dream it up.

'Doog gninrom,' she said over and over again, and laughed like it was the funniest thing in the world.

'Don't teach the child rubbish,' my grandmother would implore.

'It's not rubbish. You have to think quickly to flip words backward,' Brenton said.

'Brenton got me a guinea pig. Esther's got dribbles,' Elise piped up.

While on a sojourn on the mainland, Brenton had bought a brown and white guinea pig. He insisted it was for Elise, but in reality, we knew he had wanted one for some time. Brenton set up a cage for the guinea pig in the shade house. He showed Elise how to feed it and look after it and the small, furry animal captivated her. She named it Martin. Elise's other passion was drawing. She drew bubble ladies with huge misshapen oblong heads and bodies, filling them in with tiny circles. She must have drawn thousands of them that summer.

Sometimes Boatman and I would take her for a walk to the village. We'd buy ice-cream and sherbets every Saturday. Elise couldn't walk that far; she'd walk for some of the way and then Boatman and I would take turns carrying her the rest of the way. One Saturday, Boatman started to ask me questions about Bernadette Brennan. A bit of a tomboy, Boatman was not really interested in feminine things, but that day she asked me where Bernadette bought her clothes and shoes and if I knew how to do a hairstyle like Bernadette's. I decided to let Boatman in.

Some afternoons, Boatman and I would take Elise down to the front of the garden. We'd sit in front of a large hedge where we could be out of sight. Bernadette joined us there and we'd talk. She was easy to talk to. We'd ask her questions about boys and dating and other things that we felt we couldn't ask anybody else. She always had answers. Of her personal life, we knew very little. She came from Ireland, was Catholic, and had never married, but she liked the things we liked and that was enough. Boatman and Bernadette had a lengthy conversation one afternoon about First Holy Communion and First Confession and other things that were common to them both; they spoke in terms unfamiliar to me. Later, Bernadette told me she was glad I had a friend like Boatman who came from a good family. Bernadette thought Sunita's anklets were pretty and so did I. I told her that my grandmother said Sunita wasn't going to heaven and that the miniature statue of Ganesh was an idolatrous object.

'Your grandmother *would* say that,' she replied, and it struck me, even at the age I was, that she seemed to know where my grandmother's sensibilities lay. Boatman and I told Bernadette about the Hovel.

'The east of the island is quite isolated,' Bernadette said. 'Be careful.'

And later Boatman asked how Bernadette Brennan could know that. I had no reply.

That summer, the house was filled with the smells of curry and coconut milk as Sunita was teaching my mother to cook Indian food. At night, I would listen for the swish of Sunita's sari and the sounds of her bangles as she walked down the length of the hall. Down in the village, people stared at her in her traditional clothes. They looked at the red dot on her forehead with curiosity. Elise loved the red dot and would try to pull it off Sunita's forehead. One morning, Sunita attached a red dot that Elise could pull off, and when she did pull it off, everyone clapped. Elise thought it was very funny. Jamilla, sullen as ever, trailed behind her mother on our walks down into the village—as if walking a few feet away could put genetic and cultural distance between the two—but I felt I was with someone quite exotic. I tried to engage Jamilla in conversation about things Indian since I had to share a room with her, but she made it quite clear that she was uninterested in discussing anything remotely connected with the sub-continent. I don't think Jamilla knew much about her father, my uncle Robert, and I never heard her discuss him.

I had overheard conversations between my grandmother and mother about him investing in hopeless schemes, ill-researched and bound to fail. There had never been any money and Sunita had worked to support the three of them and pay off his gambling debts in the early days of their marriage. After Robert's death, Sunita threw herself into work and stated she would never remarry. After many years alone, she declared herself detached from romantic sensibilities. She had her books, her daughter, friends, and her faith, and that was all she needed. She threw herself into her studies and into her Hindu beliefs, and as far as I know, she was never involved with anyone ever again.

My grandmother played down Robert's faults. Robert liked a bit of a flutter, that's all, she said of her son. As for Sunita's many degrees, my grandmother dismissed them just as she had dismissed Beatrice's knowledge of art. If it helped run a guest-house, then I'd get one too, was her standard reply.

Around the time that Elise came to stay, I witnessed an incident that I couldn't explain. One afternoon, while I was taking some rubbish out to the bins, I saw my mother at the side of the house. She held a small mirror up to her face and was applying lipstick in careful coats. After she had finished, she smoothed down her skirt and tucked back a strand of hair that had fallen over her face. I wondered where she was going. She opened the top button on her blouse and adjusted a string of onyx beads. She took a furtive look around and took her mirror out again. At the sound of a vehicle coming up the gravel drive, she quickly put the mirror in her pocket.

A minute later, the Shelley's soft drink truck rounded the bend in the drive. My mother waved, and I saw her hand flutter toward her throat as if the sight of the truck had caught her without words. A man alighted, a reed-thin man with an Akubra hat and a loping gait. He had a casual assurance about him. He came toward her and said something I couldn't make out. My mother laughed, a nervous, girlish, high-pitched laugh. I'd never heard that sort of laugh; I didn't recognise its timbre. They stood there talking and soon my mother was frowning and so was the Shelley's soft drink man. I crept closer, hiding behind the Casuarina tree, holding my breath. On closer inspection, his face revealed a man bewildered by life, a man with more questions than answers.

My mother and the Shelley's soft drink man were standing so close their noses were almost touching, but the laugh was gone and now she was hissing, low and furious. As she continued, her voice rose louder and louder until I could hear everything she was saying.

'You think I'm too independent? Is that what it is? You think I'd stay with you when you can't kick that habit? If you don't stop gambling everything away, there'll be nothing for me to stay *with*.'

The Shelley's soft drink man went to touch her arm, but she caught his hand and held it for a moment before letting it go. He stood, his head down, his long arms hanging by his side, looking like a pantomime puppet whose strings had broken. Then she wiped the lipstick off with the back of her hand and left him standing at the side of the house. I heard the screen door bang and knew she had gone out onto the veranda with her cigarettes. Brenton came out from the side door, gave the man a perfunctory greeting, and helped him unload boxes of drink. A few minutes later, the truck rumbled down the hill and I was left wondering why my mother cared so much about the amount of money the Shelley's soft drink man was gambling away and why it mattered so much to her.

When I was cutting up vegetables one morning, I dropped the knife I was using on the floor. I wasn't quick enough; Elise, hovering near me with her toys, got there before I did. She picked it up by the blade and cut her finger. I wrapped her finger up in a hand towel and tried to calm her down. Nothing seemed to stop the crying.

'Elise,' I said. 'Listen. Guess what? You heard of blood brothers? No? Well, here's how it works. I'll cut my finger and then we'll hold our fingers together and we'll get each other's blood.'

Elise stopped crying. Her eyes widened as I made a small nick in my index finger. We held them together. Boatman came into the kitchen, catching me off guard. I told her what we were doing, quietly, as I didn't want anyone else to know.

'Blood sisters,' she said. She took the knife and made a small cut on her little finger. We held our fingers together, the three of us. Elise was now laughing.

'No telling,' Boatman said. 'It's our secret. Blood sisters forever, no matter what happens.'

Nobody noticed the three of us had Bandaids on our fingers.

All this I'd tell Bernadette Brennan. She seemed quite fascinated by the daily family squabbles, the running of the guesthouse, Brenton's jokes and his Wordsday antics, Esther's illness, the Boatmans, the cook's assistant's morning illness, Sarah's drinking problem, and the strange encounter I witnessed between my mother and the Shelley's soft drink man. I understood much later how she had tried to protect my feelings by telling me that my mother had a special friend who was a man. My girlish conversation never seemed to bore her, and I was glad I had someone that I could trust. She asked a lot of questions and seemed very interested in my answers. She told me to steer clear of John Newmark, but I already knew I had to do that. I told her I thought Walter Heather was a creep, but held back what Boatman and I had witnessed. I confided in her about wanting to know more about my father. They change the subject, I told her. All of them. They don't want to talk about him.

Bernadette Brennan raised her eyebrows.

'Tell you what,' she said, 'pick a time when there's just your mother and you. Just Margaret and Siobhan, no one else. You'll know when that perfect moment arrives. You'll feel it. Ask her then.'

I held on to that advice. The perfect moment. I would wait for it.

As I became closer to Bernadette Brennan, I became more remote from my own mother. Added to that, my own mother was becoming more and more remote from reality, and for the first time in my life, I began to fear for what the future might hold.

Chapter Eight

Beatrice was embroiled in an affair with a gallery curator when she took over the guesthouse left to her in my grandmother's will in 1988. She really didn't have time to do anything with a business. Despite being able to tell anyone who cared to listen about art history and obscure painters, she knew nothing of business and had no head for practicalities, the total antithesis of my grandmother. She was more interested in deciding what artwork should grace the lobby and dining room in the guesthouse and what sculptures would look good in the gardens. If my grandmother had been alive, she would have told Beatrice that the sort of people who came to Rachley Island wouldn't know an impressionist or a cubist if they fell over one. Tourists are interested in sunset cruises and the location of the nearest chemist, she would have said. They need maps, menus, lists of cocktails, laundry information, that sort of thing.

Beatrice wanted to ditch the name Gables; too Gothic and old, she said. We need something modern and edgy. Zables, she said. Sounds like a nightclub. It's got energy, she said. She had much resistance from the locals, and in the end she left the name as it was.

Due to her lack of knowledge in the business area, Beatrice employed a manager, a conman who at one time she imagined herself in love with. His name was Federico. He came from Italy originally and had no experience running a guesthouse, but he answered an advertisement Beatrice had placed in a Sydney newspaper and managed to convince her of his accomplishments in running hotels on the continent.

Beatrice and I met up every six months after my mother passed away.

For a woman so widely travelled, Beatrice was surprisingly naïve. Her judgement of character was never done with depth or circumspection. She didn't even ask to see references or any sort of documentation. Rather, she developed a 'feel' for people, she was fond of telling us. She promptly dumped the gallery curator and Federico installed himself at Gables, preferring the term 'director' to 'manager' and embarking on a spending spree that even Beatrice questioned.

'Beatrice bellisima!' Federico would say, and she would flirt and laugh like a young girl. Beatrice was hardly what one would call an attractive woman, interesting definitely, but nothing close to bellisima. I met Federico only once when he and Beatrice came to Sydney for business. He kissed my hand and made a comment in badly pronounced French. I told Beatrice he was a phoney, but she just laughed and told me not to be so serious. We went to dinner down in the Rocks area and while Beatrice was at the bar, he made several overtures to me that I found embarrassing. Toward the end of dinner, Beatrice and he had a slight altercation over his expensive purchase of a statue for the gardens. By this time, I had decided that I really didn't like Federico at all and had nothing to lose by remarking that in my opinion, reproduction statues of Romulus and Remus had little relevance to most people in New South Wales. Further, I added, tourists from Europe want to see something Australian.

'Pah! Something Australian. Listen to you. Two hundred years of history and what have you got to show? In Europe, we are thousands of years old, not hundreds. Where is your great art, literature, and architecture?'

Beatrice was attempting to explain about Indigenous history, but by now Federico was quite drunk and trying to charm a waitress.

'He really is a darling when you get to know him,' Beatrice said later.

Federico went through most of Beatrice's money and let the place fall into a state of ruin. He managed to escape the country and the last I heard was that the police had tracked him down in Spain, where he was running an unregistered hostel for backpackers. I hold Federico partly responsible for the closure of Gables Guesthouse in 1992.

As I stood in my grandmother's old room, I could feel her presence. The double bed was gone; a square of dark wood took up space where the bed once stood and the lighter wood of the rest of the floor was covered in dust. I drew back the curtains, and they fell apart in my hands, fluttering onto the floor in ragged pieces. Her bedroom, like Esther's, had a view of the river. The bay window was so dirty that the view wasn't much at all today. She'd always had the curtains closed, no matter what season it was. The wallpaper had been changed since I was last there, but it wasn't much better than it used to be, so it would have to go.

In this room at the age of eight, I rummaged through my grandmother's drawers one day and found her old corsets, stockings, and girdles—'stays' they were called—stiff-boned garments that looked as formidable as my grandmother herself. Elise loved this room; she was always trying to get into it to brush her hair with the tortoise-shell hairbrush my grandmother had on the dressing table. It was too heavy for Elise to hold, so I would brush her hair with it while she held on to my hand as I brushed, as though she were doing it herself. We called it the special hairbrush and I told her we could only use it once a day.

My grandmother's dressing table was still there. Today, it would be considered an antique—carved, dark, dignified wood. On opening the drawers in the dressing table, I found boxes and boxes of pins, clips, rubber bands, string, cotton reels, and envelopes. A true child of the Depression years, my grandmother never threw anything out. The kitchen drawers were full to the brim when I was a girl.

'You just never know. Waste not, want not,' she'd say. 'That's a handy little box, so don't throw it out. Give it here. You're not throwing that out, are you? That's a handy little pin. Give it here.'

The contents of my grandmother's drawers had kept me fascinated for hours. As children, Jamilla and I had rummaged through them, holding up cheap and gaudy objects as though they were precious jewels: beads and baubles, coloured and plain, bits of ribbon in different lengths, mothballs in old lady crocheted pouches, bobby pins and bangles. And things not so cheap: shiny jet earrings, an ivory cigarette holder, a tortoise-shell hair-clip, Marquisite brooches and clip-on earrings made from hard coloured plastic or stones with tiny glass shapes embedded in them, the sort of small treasures that antique shops in the Blue Mountains display under finger-stained glass counters.

My grandmother was the stalwart of the Rachley Island Presbyterian Church and everything associated with it: president of its Ladies Committee, organiser of the cleaning and flower rosters, treasurer of the Collection for the Missions, matriarch of fetes and all things charitable. My mother had once said that she long suspected my grandmother's commitment to the Lord ran about as deep as the Rachley River in the drier months, but she was glad for the release valve that it provided for the rest of us. My grandmother's calendar was crammed from January to December. Almost every little white square that marked off a day was filled with her spindly writing. Miss Ivy and Mrs Woodford to dinner on Wednesday. Sewing circle on Thursday. Missionary talk on Friday night. Working bee on Saturday. Flowers Sunday. Make jam for the fete on the second. And all this on top of running the guesthouse. Whether there was anything genuinely spiritual about her was difficult to tell, and if her own familiar adage 'Charity begins at home' was any yardstick by which to measure it, then it was a dismal failure.

'That old bird has a better social life than me,' Brenton was often heard to complain.

Had she not been forced to leave school at fourteen and go to work, she might have gone into medicine. For her, it held a fascination and she certainly had the memory that it required. She was capable of giving you an up-to-the-last minute report on every medical condition suffered by just about anyone on Rachley Island. If ever a fire was to consume all medical records at Dalton's surgery, my grandmother could have supplied a complete oral history in a day, down to what people were taking and how many milligrams. She relished in new brands of pills and potions, although complaining they never did her any good, anyway. Once, when she thought no one was looking, I caught her in the pantry examining Sunita's shelf of herbal remedies, sniffing the contents and peering at the labels. She often threatened to throw the lot out, but I suspected she never did in case she had to use them if conventional medicine failed.

My grandmother did not drink; I suspect because she had a husband who was a drunk. She lived on tea. One cup and you knew things were basically under control. Two cups in a row was an indication the world was an irritating and baffling place to live in. Three cups meant some terrible evil was at large that would rock the very foundations of society and threaten the stability of all good law-abiding, God-fearing citizens. If my grandmother could have exchanged places for a day with Dr Dalton, all patients would have come away bearing prescriptions for tea, no matter what the ailment.

She held the Queen and Duke next to her heart as the most impeccable role models one could wish to find. She didn't approve of Princess Margaret, however. Black sheep of the family, she called her. She delighted in any news about the British royals, speaking about them as though they lived next door. In my grandmother's world, the pinnacle of achievement was to reach one hundred so one could receive a telegram from the Queen. If ever there was coverage of the royals on television, she would hush us all up.

'Turn that up, please. I want to hear about the Queen Mother's hip operation' or 'Did they say when the Duke of Edinburgh is out of hospital?' as if she were going to visit him the following day.

When my grandmother came to visit me at university and heard me declaring that royalty was rubbish and heard my friends speaking of neo-colonialism and fascist regimes and the like, I did not get a particularly good reception. Corrupted by university, she told people.

She treated Brenton and me with a manner that implied we were a nuisance and yet there were times when she would suddenly come up and put an arm around me, telling me that I was a good girl, times when she excused Brenton's behaviour, saying he couldn't help it.

'That's Jack Tyler's fault,' she said. 'It's not Montrell genes.

Your mother made a bad choice. I know he was your father, but it's no good looking at the world through rose-coloured glasses.'

My mother never took me anywhere, but my grandmother did. She took me to the Blue Mountains once. I had heard about the mountains, how cool and beautiful Katoomba was, how the mists come sweeping over the Megalong Valley and swirl up into the lookout. I wanted to lean over the railing and let the mist cover my face, breathe it in, be lost in it. We went in summer, however, and I looked out at the Three Sisters, feeling the incredible disappointment of one who has conjured up a childhood attachment to something magical and important only to finally feel disappointed. The Three Sisters stared out in their sombre, ochre brown, looking hot and rugged.

If it weren't for my grandmother, I would never have seen any other part of New South Wales. We went up to the New England area on the mail train, which hurtled through the blackness for hours. The country towns passed by in fast forward and after a while, there was nothing to distinguish one from the other. Looking out my window as the train pulled into another station in the middle of nowhere at two in the morning, I saw the fog lying heavily on the platform, heard voices shouting, the forlorn bellow of whistles being blown, baggage being shifted on and off, the sounds of bells ringing and the rattle of the old-fashioned carriages.

My grandmother took me to church every Sunday. Occasionally, my mother would go as well, but most times it was just my grandmother and me. I remember the heat and the congregation flapping their Order of Services in their faces when the fans weren't working, the organ that sounded like it was wheezing with asthma, the drone of the minister's voice. I always had the feeling that she attended to be seen there. Before church every Sunday, she would make up the dough for the bread, the Yorkshire pudding, and the cake that we would have for dessert. She also baked special soft bread that Esther could chew. I watched her kneading and pounding the dough on the board as if she were suffocating the life out of it, as if moulding it and then destroying it gave her a control that was lacking in another area. She would cover them and leave them until we returned. I used to look at her hands as I sat next to her in the pew. Her hands still bore the marks of baking, remnants of dried flour in the crevices between nail and skin and more still congealed on the tarnished wedding bands. The diamonds were dull from neglect and there were scratches on the metal. The rings looked too tight or her hands too big, as if the fingers were being strangled, little mounds of flesh appearing at the sides of the bands. I asked her if the rings hurt her fingers and she told me that she couldn't remove them as her fingers had put on weight over the years. She said she'd get the rings cut off one day. Elise would try to pull the rings off my grandmother's fingers; she thought it was a game and they really might just come off.

My diary entries were not very favourable about Sundays:

1971

The minister brought in a teapot today. At first, I thought he liked tea so much that he couldn't even get through a service without a cup. It sat on the edge of the communion rail like a fat camel sitting down with its legs tucked under it. I knew it was a good teapot because it's like the one in the guesthouse kitchen that only gets used when someone important is coming. Silver service, it's called. The minister said that when everyone is first born they're like the teapot, all shiny and new. But, he said, that's not where the story ends. He lifted the lid and made the children look inside. Look, he said. That's what you are like on the inside. Born with the stain of original sin. Black and tarnished. Only Jesus can take the stain away, he told us.

He's omniscient. That means he can see everything because he's every-where at the same time. My mother says that when babies are born, they're completely new and not dirty. We learnt about that in Science when we did reproduction and we saw a real film of childbirth. It didn't look very nice, especially when poo came out just before the baby did. Boatman says she's never having a baby after she saw that.

I told Boatman about Jesus being impotent. She told me that she already knew and so we had to be careful what we did as Jesus could see everything we did.

Church is supposed to make you feel good, but I always feel sad because the songs are all about blood and nails through hands and spears through sides and burdens and yokes and lambs and crucifixions on green hills. Even the organ sounds reluctant, like it couldn't be bothered to make the effort and would rather be somewhere else churning out quick and bright circus music under a big top. It sounds like it has asthma and it wheezes. Sometimes Brenton goes, but he never sings and he always stares at his fingernails. Sunita doesn't go to church because she's Hindu, which my grandmother says is heathen.

And there's one more thing about Sundays. It's roast lamb day and that means peas. At Boatman's house, her mum actually asks if she wants peas or carrots or whatever and sometimes they just stick the dish in the middle of the table and everybody just helps themselves and they don't get the lecture about the starving children in Africa. But we have ours dished out for us. It's really hard to get through a meal when they're on my plate, but I've got a few methods like putting them on my fork and when no one is looking, lowering them down onto my lap into a waiting tissue. I can't do it all at once though; they have to be siphoned off in small amounts every now and then. Another method is to stuff them into my mouth and then ask to be excused to go to the toilet where I can spit them out. Sometimes this is hard too because my grandmother tells me not to speak with my mouth full. She gives me that look, the same one she gives Brenton when he says 'Jesus Christ Almighty' when something goes wrong. Boatman told me her father says that all the time.

When I was really little, I wondered how the whole Africa thing worked. Was there a special service, like the milkman and the bread delivery, that collected the uneaten peas? And how did they keep the peas warm all the way to Africa? Did they take the peas away on the same plate or did my grandmother put them in a plastic container like the ones from the Chen's take away? Did the starving children all run out onto the tarmac when the pea plane arrived? Did my grandmother ring up and say, 'Yes, hello, yes, that's right, Gables Guesthouse, two lots of peas to Africa? Siobhan and Jamilla. Yes, well, I wouldn't have picked those names either, ungrateful girls, but what do you expect these days with people naming their children after flowers and crystals and Indian desserts. Yes, half-past eight is fine.'

I still don't eat peas.

Occasionally, I was banished to the pantry and had to stay there for an hour if I didn't finish my peas. The pantry had many advantages as a place of punishment. There was food and all the old newspapers, which were quite helpful for school. I knew all about the first royal visit in 1954 and Lang Hancock discovering iron ore in Western Australia. I remember reading things that didn't make sense at the time, like the spies doing terrible things in 1956 and the British exploding a bomb in a place called Maralinga. I didn't really understand that because my grandmother said bombs were dangerous, but she also said that the British were the finest examples of everything from bone china to moral character, so it didn't really add up.

The old magazines were still on the floor after all these years, slumbering in their musty dark cell, faded, stiff and rippled with time. I couldn't understand why Beatrice hadn't thrown them out, but I'm glad she hadn't. They were stacked according to years, the oldest being 1952 with pictures of the coronation.

Unbelievably, there were still bottles from Sunita's collection of Indian medicine on the fourth shelf; jars and bottles with labels written in a curling script that used to contain strange-smelling bitter herbs, roots, lotions, and potions. The jars were stiff to open, the bottle tops only twisted off when I ran them under hot water. Inside, crusty powders without any smell at all lay rock-hard with age. I tried to break them up with a fork, but they were impenetrable. There was no liquid substance left in any of the bottles. The corks had rotted, leaving fragments at the bottom. When I poured hot water into the powders, I expected a smell, a small scent of the old days, but there was no smell at all wafting from the containers.

Sunita often procured medicine from India for Esther. I remember my grandmother saying she wouldn't touch it with a ten-foot pole and my mother wondering how on earth Sunita got them through Customs in the first place.

I leafed through piles of paper, postcards, and old shopping lists. Most of the writing on the postcards was faded. The postcards were scenes of the English countryside, thatched cottages, and fox hunts. There was one addressed to Esther with the name McNaughton on the bottom. He had been the love of Esther's life.

McNaughton had come to the island to buy property and build a hotel. I had only vague childhood memories of him so perhaps they were not accurate, but I remembered him as a tall, thin man with black receding hair who was not handsome but who nevertheless had a certain charm. McNaughton was proficient in sign language, having had a brother born non-verbal, so he and Esther developed a bond. They would sit for hours, their hands flying in the air, according to Beatrice. She also told me that sometimes my grandmother would become suspicious and think that they were talking and laughing about her. McNaughton and Esther had become engaged and planned to marry and settle on Rachley Island and run a hotel. McNaughton had a background in economics. He'd done his homework; he knew that there were more and more visitors both holidaying and passing through. The island had potential, he believed, to become a major holiday destination. He said that in the next twenty years, the Japanese would be looking for holiday destinations in Australia. He spoke about the expanding Asian economies, a burgeoning middle class in the developing world. He had plans to open an establishment on the northern side of the island, not just a hotel, he said. A resort. Knowing his plans might unsettle my grandmother, he went to great lengths to reassure her that there was room for both the guest-house and a resort on the island.

'Different clientele,' he said. 'Different socio-economic brackets. There's room for us all.'

McNaughton was found dead at the bottom of the cliffs on the northern side of the island, and because of the strange nature of his death, people kept away from the cliffs for some time. There were rumours, Beatrice said.

'Ghastly business,' my grandmother used to say when McNaughton's name was mentioned.

I remembered hushed conversations in winter rooms behind closed doors and the sound of Esther's hysterical sobbing every year on the anniversary of McNaughton's death. Reg Dalton was often in Our House attending to her, his black doctor's bag open on the floor.

'What happened to Mr McNaughton?' I asked my mother once, years later.

I never found out any details. They closed ranks, protecting me, perhaps protecting each other. Certain looks passed between them, but what I remembered were Esther's eyes, wild with fright, and the way she looked at my grandmother, her brows knitted together as if she were privy to some piece of information denied to the rest of us.

Brenton told me the details when I was in my second year at university. My mother had told him the story. By then, my grandmother and her sisters were long dead and my mother had been ill for several years. He told me that my grandmother was totally exonerated from any connection with what happened. She was simply the last person to see him alive, having taken a walk with him along the cliff tops to survey the landscape and make decisions about where to locate the resort. My grandmother had said they discussed builders and budgets. He told her much about Japan where he had been several times, and they discussed wedding presents: what Esther would like, what they needed to start their new lives together. My grandmother said she left him there on the cliffs with his plans and his camera, as she had to return home. Beatrice was arriving for the wedding and my grandmother wanted to go down to the punt and meet her.

McNaughton's body was found at the bottom of the cliffs that evening. His sister said at the investigation that he had no reason to take his own life; he was about to marry and start up a business. An inquest into his death decided that in all probability, he had fallen. There were no witnesses to his death and so no one really knew what had happened. Sometimes when I looked at Esther, I wondered what would have become of her life if it had all worked out the way she had planned. Beatrice took the material that Esther had bought for her bridal gown and made curtains out of it for her own house, saying the sight of all that material in Our House would just cause Esther more distress. My mother thought that was a terrible thing to do.

'Waste not, want not,' my grandmother reminded us all. 'A curtain's a curtain.'

Beatrice couldn't sew, and we never did get to see the finished product.

A small silver-framed photograph of Esther and her fiancé sat on her bedside table for the rest of her life. After McNaughton's death, my mother and grandmother tried to remove it but Esther became agitated and so they left it where it was. It stayed there until the day she died, next to Saint Drogo. Perhaps the reason she never looked out at the view from her bedroom window is because the cliffs are in that direction. She preferred the view on the other side. She deteriorated mentally after her fiancé's death, never really recovering. McNaughton's ashes were scattered in the river and then Esther turned her back on the river for the rest of her life.

Somewhere down in the murky depths of the river lay the grey ghosts, the spirits of the betrayed and the betrayers, with secrets that will never be known. I wondered what Elise's ghost would say. I wondered if she could ever forgive me.

Chapter Nine

It began with the tea strainer. My mother had started to strain the tea several times over in a paroxysm of energy, anger, and suspicion, braiding the three strands together until the ritual was complete.

'You can't trust anyone these days,' she said, tipping the tea out of the pot, putting it through a sieve, and letting it drip into a Tupperware container. She paused and sighed and tipped the contents of the container back into the teapot. Her coral-coloured lips were drawn in a thin line, disproving. She handled the teapot as though it were infested with a deadly virus. She started again, tipping, sieving, dripping, pouring. She wore a bright yellow blouse. It clashed with her lipstick. It clashed with the green and silver jewelled sandals that Sunita had bought her at a Delhi market. She seemed determined to clash with everything.

'Traitors,' she muttered.

'Who's a traitor?' I asked, but my brother silenced me with a look.

'You don't know what goes on inside their heads,' she declared, banging the pot down on the table.

'Whose head?' I asked.

'Don't indulge her,' my brother said. 'It only lends legitimacy to whatever's going on in her brain.'

My mother had decided that the kitchen staff were trying to poison her. The odd thing was that she had always had a good relationship with the kitchen staff, especially with the cook. When my grandmother was out for the night, my mother, Sarah, and the cook would often play cards and drink brandy. Brenton told me that Sarah and the cook between them could drink any sailor under the table. It was on one of these nights that I overheard my mother talking about my father. She mentioned something about his accident when the cook, puffed red with alcohol, screeched: 'It didn't stop him using his third leg, though!'

I hear them all laugh uproariously, my mother's laugh, soprano high and tremulous, competing with the rumbling bass of the cook. Not once had she laughed when my grandmother administered the joke. It was usually ignored. But that night, her arms around the cook, her face flushed with drink, she laughed until she had tears coming down her cheeks. I understood something that night. My mother felt battered by my grandmother. She couldn't compete.

I asked my grandmother if my mother was all right. She said it was just nerves. I didn't understand this, equating nerves with nervousness. I could see nothing she should be afraid of or nervous about. I wondered if she was worrying about how much money the Shelley's soft drink man was gambling away. She spent more and more time in the back room, secured in her chrysalis of paranoia, her chain-smoking now resulting in a phlegmy, turbid cough that made her spit from the window. A tight tourniquet of anger was twisting inside her. We felt its torsion and dreaded its release. At the age of eleven, even then, I felt anxious about her caring for Elise when she didn't seem able to look after herself. I hovered around them both, my mother and Elise, making sure that neither was very far out of my line of sight. Only after Elise had gone home in the afternoons did I escape to the Hovel with Boatman. She was finding it difficult to escape herself, being needed at home more often with Sarah so ill.

Then there was the morning Bernadette Brennan misplaced her room key. The reception desk was momentarily unattended and so Bernadette had walked through the connecting door around into the hall of Our House to ask if she could have another. I heard my mother shouting and ran to see who or what she was shouting at. She was shouting at the guest while Brenton tried to hush her up. He was forced to put his hand over her mouth, whereupon she bit him, drawing blood. Later, I heard Bernadette Brennan crying as I crept along the corridor in the guesthouse.

I felt disturbed; two people I liked very much were upset with each other over a key, which Walter Heather could replace quite easily. Brenton couldn't write for a few days due to the injury to his hand. He dictated the news for *The Reader* while I scribbled as fast as I could. My mother, after she had calmed down and apologised to Brenton, wanted to take him to the doctor, but my grandmother intervened.

'How's he going to explain human teeth marks on his skin? Reg Dalton'll believe the whole family's gone mad.'

My grandmother was adamant that no one was going anywhere near the family doctor. She handed the problem over to Olivia, who dealt with it quickly. After she had swabbed and bandaged my brother's hand, she turned to my grandmother.

'It hasn't escaped my attention, you know,' Olivia said. 'Something is troubling her. I'll send up a prayer to St Bartholomew.'

'She doesn't need a patron saint, she just needs to rest,' my grandmother snapped. 'It's a busy time. She's run off her feet. Running a guesthouse isn't a piece of cake.'

'Then I shall send up a prayer to St Amand as well,' Olivia offered.

My grandmother raised her eyebrows.

Patron Saint of Hotel Keepers and Bar Staff, Olivia told her.

'You'll keep this incident to yourself, I trust, Olivia. This is a respectable family and with a good business name in the community. I can't afford anything less than your complete discretion. I know how much you value your job here.'

'Of course,' Olivia said.

Brenton examined his wound, declaring it a respectable bite from a respectable family member. Olivia smiled.

'Thanks for telling me about St Amand,' said my grandmother.

'You might need him some day,' Olivia said.

A short time after this, Marjory Horton from the village came to visit, bringing a cake and photographs of her daughter's wedding. Without reason and in front of everyone, my mother took the cake apart with her hands, scrunching it up and examining her fingers every few seconds. She put the crumbling pieces on a serviette and inspected them carefully. My grandmother told her to go and lie down while she called Reg Dalton. There were hushed voices in the corridor, the visitors leaving quickly and Sunita giving me a hug, telling me that my mother was tired and that it would be all right in the morning. My grandmother, who did not make a habit of airing dirty linen in public, as she was fond of saying, relayed nothing from Reg Dalton and so I was left in the dark. The hallway became a tunnel of whispers. My grandmother and Olivia, their heads bent together, were speaking softly. Later, it was Olivia and Sunita keeping their voices low. When I came into view, they stopped abruptly, changing the topic to a loud conversation about food orders. Olivia commented on my new sundress, but I wasn't interested in compliments. I wanted to know what the doctor had said. Much later that night, Sunita and Brenton stood together, whispering in the hallway. I heard the words paranoid, nervous breakdown, the right drugs.

When morning came, my mother seemed to be all right, just as Sunita had predicted. I took her breakfast into her room and sat on the end of her bed. She seemed in a talkative mood. Was Marjory mad about the cake? Did everyone look at the photographs of her daughter's wedding? I answered as best I could and then my mother started to laugh. I asked her what was so funny and she said Marjory deserved everything she got. The perfect Hortons, she said. I started to laugh as well. We laughed so hard that my mother had tears running down her cheeks. When we had exhausted ourselves over the Hortons, my mother put her head forward and touched the top of my head with hers. We stayed like that for a few seconds. I felt like the rest of the world was shut out. It was only us; a perfect moment.

'Mum...' I started, but just then my grandmother came into the room. I would wait for another moment. There had to be one. I just had to be patient.

Despite my mother's odd behaviour, the daily routine went on without interruption. Josh Boatman dropped Elise off in the mornings and picked her up in the afternoons. I always managed to miss seeing Josh. The next day I'd wait again to see him, but I'd always be called to do something or had to feed Esther and so he eluded me.

Boatman and I went to the Hovel as often as we could. I told her about my mother's strange behaviour and she said that sometimes when Sarah had had too much to drink, she did weird things too. But no one had actually ever bitten anybody else, she told me. She said that Sarah once took a hammer and smashed all the glasses, cups, and plates in the kitchen. She screamed at her husband, telling him she didn't want any more children and if he felt the need, then he'd have to stick it in something else. After she had calmed down, he asked her if she wanted a cup of tea. At her affirmative reply, he sent Boatman down to the village to buy a set of teacups. I felt somewhat consoled on hearing that. So, other families did strange stuff as well.

However, things improved only for a while. Walter Heather found Prudence, the female peacock that roamed the gardens, dead one morning. The bird's body was lying close to the shed. My mother, who loved the peacock, was convinced that Bernadette Brennan had killed it. We asked her why Bernadette Brennan would kill a peacock. She could give us no reason, and after that she slumped into a depressive state, shutting herself in her Cimmerian cave in the back room. My grandmother sent for Walter Heather, who knew a bit about birds, to explain to my mother about the signs of old age in a bird, but she would not let him in. When I entered her room with a tray for her, she'd hold my hand and tell me she was tired. Nothing I said seemed to elevate her mood. I told her I'd buy a new peacock. She said she didn't want a new one. She wanted Prudence. Brenton made phone calls trying to locate a place to buy peacocks. He even rang Taronga Zoo.

'Bernadette needs to go. She's been here too long,' my mother said.

My grandmother said Bernadette was a paying guest and could stay as long as she liked.

Sunita was the first person to take me aside and talk to me about my mother. I had known something was wrong with my mother, even before the tea strainer incident, not in obvious ways but in subtle ways detected only by those who knew her best. The retreat into the back room, the peacock incident, the paranoia concerning food—all these were extreme signs of her illness. Anyone who lived with her would have noticed that months before those events took place she seemed to be shutting off, her emotions tamped down, her responses vague. Sunita remained positive when she took me aside; she spoke of medication, special places where people like my mother could go to get better, doctors called psychiatrists, which I already knew about because Brenton had a psychiatrist, and all sorts of therapies, which I didn't understand. I noticed also that she too was more attentive to Elise's whereabouts and what she was doing. We'll look after her together, all of us, she said.

Dear Diary,

I don't like having to share my room with Jamilla. There's not much privacy in here anyway with Esther's room off mine. It's not fair. Brenton has his own room. I suppose we have to share because we're girls. And we're eleven. Jamilla is very tidy but she's not very friendly. I asked her last night about India when we were both lying in our beds. I thought I was being friendly.

'What would I know about India?' she said. Boatman would never think of doing that. Last time she stayed over, we talked till half-past eleven and then my grandmother told us to go to sleep. Boatman says it's not fair that my grandmother can stay up late and we can't when we're not even tired. I said that old people don't need as much sleep as we do.

Yesterday I was sent to the pantry because I laughed at something disgusting that Brenton said. It's not fair. He was the one who said it, so he should get into trouble. I only laughed but got sent to the pantry. Marjorie Horton came over to show us her daughter's wedding photos. Brenton was singing, 'Quick fuck, bad luck, stomach swells, wedding bells.' He sang it under his breath, but we all heard. Marjory said the dress had scalloping and the veil had diamantes and then Mum started pulling the cake apart into little bits and looking at her fingers and saying weird stuff. Then Marjory said she'd better go and then the doctor came but he didn't say what was wrong. Jamilla said my mum has paranoia, but Sunita told her off and said that's not necessarily true. It wasn't too bad in the pantry. The cook had made fudge cake so I had some of that. Olivia gave the cook a tiny picture of St Monica, which the cook thought was very kind until she discovered that Monica is the patron saint of alco-

holics. I saw it in the bin with the leftover Pineapple Surprise that got burnt in the oven.

Two days ago, I went down to the village. I used a credit card at the Minimart and the man serving behind the counter worked out the connection.

'Ah, the Montrell girl. Margaret's daughter. I knew your mother and your grandmother. A fine woman your mother was. I was sorry to hear what happened.'

I didn't answer, not knowing whether the comment was made out of the simple social graces that one shows to a stranger or as an opening to talk about the past. Either way, I resented it. No one, especially a person I didn't know, was going to dredge up the old history, only to express his own opinion. But afterward, I was slightly regretful that I didn't engage him in conversation because I might have learned something, not something new because there was nothing new to learn, but just something that may have added to the retrospective, some slant on a personality or point of minute detail that only an outsider might have seen. I even thought of trying to find some of the families and businesses we used to deal with in case they remembered my mother. Next time I went back, I would engage him in conversation.

I went through the local paper and saw names I remembered well and businesses that were still operating. Bracken's Hardware. Gleat's Butchers, where they're pleased to meat you. The Wong's Chinese takeaway had become a huge restaurant called the Imperial China run by the Li family. They were open late at night and on Sundays. The advertisement took up half a page and the pictures of dumplings in small steamers made me hungry. Who would have thought that Yum Cha would come to Rachley Island? The Boatman house was no longer on the hill near the village shops. It had been bought by developers and knocked down to make way for a gym and day spa. The day spa was called River View, which was quite misleading as the view looked out on the village. I decided not to find anyone. The tradesman I rang about the roof said he had worked on the Gables Guesthouse over twenty-seven years ago, doing work on the eaves, so I thought I might ask him some questions, depending on how I felt.

A new company had been running river cruises for the last few years. Bookings were essential, so the tourist industry must have been thriving. There were moonlight honeymoon cruises, singles nights with three-course dinners and wine, family cruises, dinner and dance cruises, and the latest—eco-cruises— which highlighted the island's flora and fauna. There were resorts, B and B's, camping grounds, large hotels, boutique hotels. So much had changed.

The layout of the village was pretty much the same, but the buildings had changed hands. The community and council saw the value in preserving the old Victorian architecture. The pub was still there, but now had hanging baskets filled with brightly coloured flowers and a green and gold facade. The only shoe shop had gone and so had Merton's Manchester, along with the cake shop and the beauty salon. A new post office was located at the end of the main street next to the Dalton's old surgery, which had become a florist. The supermarket was pretty much the same. Big enough to serve you, small enough to know you, the sign still said. I didn't see one person from my old days and I really didn't want to.

I walked up and down the hill, as I had done thousands of times with my mother, feeling on the one hand like a stranger in a new town and on the other like a traveller who has at last come home. The turn-off tree looked smaller than I remembered, withered and shrunken, like an old lady, gnarled and bent. I was disappointed when I saw it again. In my memory, it had been a large tree, but then, I was a small girl. The dirt track was overgrown with weeds, obviously not having been used for some time. Beatrice would always complain the walk to the shops was too long. I used to imagine her being carried in a sedan chair, an arm lazily extended in order to point out the direction, a cigarette fuming between heavily ringed fingers.

On my return to the house, I noticed for the first time the original signage of the Gables Guesthouse, covered in dirt and hanging at an angle off the wrought iron gate. I felt a sharp twinge of sadness; I remember the day Walter Heather put it up, brand new, drilling holes and wiring it into the gates, not quite straight. The sign writer hadn't emphasised the stroke on the letter G, so from a distance, the name read Cables.

Camilla rang and said she might come up for a few days. I told her she could come, the company would do me good, and seeing she is a clean freak, four hands would be better than two as far as cleaning the house was concerned. She said she was talking to a therapist about stuff, her identity and childhood. I didn't ask questions. Two heads better than one, I told her.

Back at Gables, I put the shopping in the pantry. A combination of dust and sad memories swept over me as I wiped the shelves of the pantry, picking up old bottles and reading faded labels. Mouse and rat droppings littered the floor. I tried to reach the very top shelf, extending my arm as far forward as it would go with the cleaning rag. There used to be a stepladder in the kitchen, but I couldn't find it, so I stacked the piles of newspapers on top of each other and tried again. The shelves were quite deep and as I reached as far back as I could, my fingers touched paper. I grasped at it, pulling it toward me, and then the newspaper pile gave way underneath and the whole shelf crashed down. I jumped backward just in time to avoid being injured.

After recovering from the shock, I examined the objects on the floor. A cake tin, a bottlebrush, an old calendar, and a book. As I picked up the book, it fell open on a page with a drawing I recognised, one of the guesthouse, sketched in a child-like hand.

I held Esther's old book, the pages stiff and yellow with age, some of them slightly crinkled at the top as if they had curdled. I wondered if Beatrice had known it was still there. The picture of the guesthouse was proportionally incorrect, the veranda too large, the French windows too small, but my interest wasn't in the accuracy of the drawing. Something else caught my eye. In the left-hand corner, a roughly pencilled small girl stood with her guinea pig clutched against her chest while a larger girl sat watching. A woman in a sari with an enormous red dot on her forehead held the hand of a dark girl, her mouth turned down. The red tikka on Sunita's forehead took up most of her forehead, the sort of proportions a very young child might have drawn. At first, I smiled when I saw the tikka, but then my attention turned to the expression on one of the girl's faces, the older girl watching the small child. The older girl in the blue shorts and white T-shirt was me. I put the book in a drawer in the kitchen cupboard and decided not to look at it again.

Chapter Ten

That drawing unleashed the memories from that time. My mother was starting to fray. The threads of rational thought, normal behaviour, and balanced responses were slowly being pulled away. Not just fraying at the edges, fraying from the inside, from the seam, the pattern becoming less recognisable as the days went on. She was stick thin, hardly eating and at times barely cognisant. She lit up all over the house, stubbing out her cigarettes on the floor, in saucers, in Wedgewood china, and anywhere else she liked. There were burn marks on the rugs. My grandmother now admonished the eternal cigarette in my mother's hand.

It started as an entreaty, grew into kind but firm advice, eventually blossoming into a grenade of anger tossed full into my mother's bunker of vagueness. Margaret, please don't smoke at the reception desk. Margaret, don't smoke in the kitchen. Margaret, don't smoke in Esther's room, Olivia gets asthma. Bloody Hell, Margaret, this is not the House of Dunhill. It's a guesthouse. The whole place stinks. That's Royal Doulton, for God's sake!

Yesterday afternoon, I made the first foray into the guest-house, thinking back to the times when the cook and my mother dropped ash into soup, piles of mince, casseroles, and anything they were making at the time. I don't think there were occupational health and safety rules or inspections at the time. She and the cook would stand at the long kitchen counter, ciga-rettes dangling from their lips while they fashioned minced up meat into balls with parsley and egg, dropping them into large silver containers, the ash falling like grey snowflakes onto the food.

The guesthouse kitchen hadn't been used in years. Camp-like and cold, once a place of thriving mass food production, the guesthouse kitchen smelled of mould, dust, and abandonment. Much of the kitchen equipment was still there. Two soiled white kitchen aprons hung on a hook, along with a key on a dirty piece of thin rope. The meat grinder lay on the floor, on its side, like a wounded silver soldier. A huge silver urn stood on the bench-top. Large saucepans of different sizes were piled on top of one another in a cupboard under the bench. The cupboard doors were missing, the wooden crossbeams intact. The saucepans stared out like battery hens. Someone had taped the refrigerator handle onto the door in a pathetic attempt to make it to stay on. Three microwave ovens, their doors open, their carousels miss-ing, stood on an opposite bench, electric cords trailing onto the floor. Someone had taped over a power point.

Thin layers of grime, congealed with age, covered the surfaces. Grease splotches marked the walls; the floor was sticky with dust and oil. I opened the sliding partition where the cook and the other kitchen staff would push the food through to the serving bench in the dining room. Brenton sometimes served the guests in a waiter's uniform if we were short-staffed, black pants and white shirt with Gables monogrammed on the pocket. Through the small serving window, I looked out on the dining room, now empty. The front bar was gone, the back one remained.

Whenever Sarah Boatman was helping out in the guesthouse kitchen, she would bring the radio in, something the cook would never do. Sarah and I would sing and dance around while chopping, slicing, and making lunches and dinners. Sarah drank wine while she cooked and smoked in the kitchen, much to my grandmother's horror, but the results of her labours were spectacular. She cooked beautiful food. Sometimes my mother would join us, but she would never sing and dance, preferring to watch from the sidelines. Occasionally, she would smoke as well at Sarah's encouragement, but would hide in the pantry if she heard my grandmother coming into the kitchen.

The night we did the Indian banquet was one of the happiest times I can remember. The kitchen staff had been listening with interest to Sunita telling them about the ten-course meals in the upmarket hotels in Delhi and Bombay. Suddenly declaring she was bored with standard English fare, the cook approached Sunita with an idea. My grandmother turned up her nose at the whole concept and went on about cost and profit margins, but when presented with a menu, a budget, and figures that showed a projected healthy return, should the required guests book for it, she reluctantly agreed. Anything that would make money for Gables suited her just fine. I don't think she liked the idea of Sunita being in charge of the project, so she feigned disinterest and left Sunita and the staff to manage it themselves. We advertised in the local paper and bookings were essential. Jamilla scowled at the mention of the banquet, refusing to be involved.

'Nobody wants to eat that sort of stuff,' she said with scorn.

Jamilla made a habit of trying her hardest to be Anglo-Celtic in everything she did. Thick, spiced tea smells coated the kitchen when Sunita made Indian tea. It was stronger than perfume.

'Normal tea for me, thank you,' Jamilla would say. 'English tea. French toast, thank you.'

My grandmother was surprised when the phone calls started and the guests and many of the locals put their names down. Right up until the final night she said it would never work, but she was in for a shock. We had more bookings than seats that night. It proved so popular that my grandmother dropped her pride and asked Sunita if she'd do another one and Sunita replied vaguely that she'd consider it. I believe the success of the banquet and the fact that my grandmother had to wait a few days for her answer became Sunita's revenge on my grandmother, although Sunita never showed the slightest hint of smugness.

On the afternoon of the banquet night, the cook asked Sunita to play Indian music in the kitchen while Sunita showed the staff how to cook curry and make roti, naan bread, and dhal. Olivia came into the kitchen and asked if she could have a small plate of whatever we were cooking for Esther.

'Esther won't eat that,' said my grandmother, who had followed Olivia into the guesthouse kitchen. 'You're wasting food.'

'It doesn't matter whether she eats it or not, it's the process of involving her,' Olivia stated firmly.

'Newfangled psychobabble nonsense,' my grandmother said and when she had exited the room, we heard her mimicking Olivia. 'The process of involving her,' we heard, delivered in a sarcastic, high-pitched tone.

The mayor and his wife were there on the night, Bob and Dot Patterson, families from the church, and most of the guests had opted for the banquet as well. Sunita dressed all of us and herself in saris of red and yellow and placed a tikka in the middle of our foreheads. My grandmother was not impressed with the exposed midriffs, but Sunita explained that the atmosphere, décor, and dress had to be authentic. Sunita wore her best heavy gold jewellery and smelled of vanilla and cardamom. She dressed Elise up in a shalwar kameez and put a tiny dot in the middle of her forehead. Sitar music danced in the background. The usual white, starched linen was kept off the tables in favour of red and gold tablecloths that Sunita had sewn up two days before. The next day, down in the village, the banquet was all people talked about and my grandmother was complimented on the whole affair.

'Well, I've been wanting to do it for a long time,' she said. 'Variety is the spice of life, isn't it?'

Now the kitchen, silent and joyless, was home only to a few cockroaches. The jokes, the sweat, the laughter, the smell of baking bread, gone. The clatter of cutlery, the thrash and hum of the industrial dishwashers, gone. The warmth, camaraderie, music, tastes and textures, all dried up.

Leaving the kitchen for the reception area, I noted some changes. In the main area at the front, Beatrice had installed new lounges, side tables with lamps, and two more phones. At the side of the reception desk, the stand with the Staff Only sign lay on its side. During the day, the sign stood at the front of the doors that led from Our House into the reception area. The doors stayed open during the day and were locked by my grandmother every night.

The smell of musty old curtains hit me as I wandered around the room, but apart from that, the rest of the place was in pretty good condition. It desperately needed airing, that's all. The room had been painted a light rose colour, which was in keeping with the rest of the guesthouse. As I stood staring across at the place where I had spent so much time, behind the desk, just for a fleeting moment I imagined I saw Brenton wheeling Esther in and I could hear Reg Dalton's voice reminding us that Esther needed variety and stimulation just like everyone else. He and

Olivia belonged to a new school of progressive thinking when it came to Esther. Change her position every few hours, he'd tell us. Move her chair somewhere new. Don't feed her the same thing all the time. Olivia always remembered to move Esther. When times were especially busy, particularly in school holiday periods, we occasionally forgot about Esther until one of us would suddenly remember that she'd been on the front veranda all morning or that she'd been left in the hallway.

As I drew the heavy curtains back to let the light in, I was startled to see a man coming up the front path. My first thought went to a postal or delivery service before my head caught up with the knowledge that there hadn't been mail or deliveries for a very long time. At first, it looked like he might turn off to the right and go back down the hill as he hesitated when he reached the top of the driveway, squinting into the sun; however, he came right up to the door and stood there for a while, his hand up against the wrought iron pole of the balustrade. I drew the curtains right back and looked at him. He was staring at the now peeling paintwork as if it would suddenly yield some secret piece of information, and then he was staring straight at me. Of average height and weight, he had dark hair and intelligent but sad eyes. He waved and shouted a greeting.

'I don't want to buy anything,' I shouted, knowing I sounded irritable.

'Not selling,' he shouted back. 'Can you open the door?'

He peered in through the mesh of the security door.

'Hello,' he said. 'I'm looking for accommodation.'

'This isn't a guesthouse anymore. It's been closed for years.'

He looked disappointed. 'Oh, I saw the sign Gables Guesthouse when I was walking up the hill.'

'It *was* the Gables Guesthouse. It's been closed for years.'

He hesitated, then said, 'I suppose I should introduce myself. My name is Matthew McCardle.'

I told him there was some accommodation in the village.

'Yes,' he said. 'I'm looking for the best room rate.'

He looked relieved when the screen door was finally opened. I stepped out onto the veranda and closed the door behind me. From where we stood, near the front steps, we were in the line of sight of the houses of Dot and Audrey, or whoever lived there now, should something go wrong.

'I'm Siobhan Montrell. My family actually owns this place but as I've said, it's been closed for some time.'

Matthew looked up at the arches on the veranda. He ran his hand over the balustrade. 'What a shame. It must have been a beautiful place in its heyday.'

'It was,' I said.

'No one lives here? At all?'

'No, not anymore. It's going to be sold in the near future.'

'It's completely unused?'

'That's right.'

'What about you? Where are you staying? Here?'

'Round about. I've got friends here.'

I wasn't about to tell a complete stranger that I was here by myself. I excused myself by telling him I had a lot to do. He said goodbye, and I watched him walk down the drive until he was out of sight.

I turned my attention to the lobby. There was nothing on the shelves under the reception desk except dead flies and cockroaches and a lot of dust. The phone system had been taken out, and the drawers were full of old paper, pens, clips, and telephone bills. For a split second, I looked down at the floor as I used to do I all those years ago, but there was no cat under my feet, no old woman in a wheelchair behind me.

The lobby was a bright, cheerful room in its heyday. French windows and doors opened up onto a veranda that ran around two sides of the guesthouse. The sun streamed down and guests would sit out there drinking tea, coffee, or martinis and taking in the view of the river, the manicured lawns, and the shade house. Elise played out there in the sun, surrounded by her toys. Esther sometimes used to sit in her chair on the veranda while her room was being cleaned. Plush chairs adorned the lobby for those waiting to be shown their rooms or those waiting for others to come down to dinner. The staircase that led to the first and second floors looked smaller than I remembered, but I was a girl when I last climbed those stairs, so everything may have seemed larger. I remember my grandmother having trouble with the stairs. Brenton used to slide down the banisters when no one was looking. He fell and cut his head doing that.

At Christmas time, the lobby was filled with the church choir, who came up to sing for the guests. The staff served Christmas cake and eggnog laden with alcohol, and Boatman and I decorated the tree and put the manger scene underneath. When Elise and I dismantled the tree and the manger scene, long after Christmas, she wanted to put a plastic wombat in the manger, but my grandmother said there were no wombats in Bethlehem so she couldn't. I asked what difference it would make as we were going to pack it away in the next few minutes, anyway. Brenton then said that if Jesus had been born in Australia there would have been wombats and kangaroos and my grandmother yelled at him, stating that he wasn't born in Australia so it was a stupid argument. Elise, startled by the argument, began to cry. Brenton placed the wombat in the nativity scene and made a wombat sort of noise and Elise laughed. He then picked up one of the three wise men from the manger scene, only to find it was broken.

'Couldn't have been that wise. He's lost his head,' he said. My grandmother said we'd go to hell if we made fun of the holy season. Brenton found the head in the bottom of the manger scene under the fake straw and told my grandmother that the wise man had been restored to the manger with his head, frankincense, and dignity intact. We spent the next half an hour hiding his head so that Elise could find it again

When I was a small child, perhaps four or five, one of the guests left me a little surprise under the tree in the lobby, a charm to put on a bracelet or necklace, a tiny ballerina in gold and zircon. The charm is still on my bracelet today.

The formal dining room was the next place I inspected after I had finished looking around the lobby. On special occasions, the dining room shone with newly polished wood and silver cleaned so thoroughly you could see your reflection in it. The best linen tablecloths and serviettes were pulled from the dark, camphor-smelling cupboard to be starched and ironed. The silver service teapot came out as well. Doilies were washed and ornaments dusted. The blue china with the impossible handles was placed on the table. There were lemon butter tarts and cinnamon cakes and savouries like the ones Sarah Boatman made. There was mashed potato with parsley rolled up in Devon slices and held together with a toothpick, a coloured cocktail onion on the top. We cooked pastry cases with creamy mixtures inside and set up the tables with delicate fluted champagne glasses. Guests had their names printed on small, white cards and every table bore a flower arrangement in the middle.

Three days went by. I took long walks, sat by the river in the sun, read, and washed anything I could find anywhere in the house that looked as though it needed it.

It was time to explore the guesthouse. I made my way up to the first floor. The rooms were basically the same, small and austere, with the standard accommodation of a guesthouse. A Gideons bible on the bedside table. A plastic tissue holder. A phone. The beds had been removed, and so had the cupboards and side tables. I supposed Beatrice must have sold them or perhaps donated them to a charity. A few of the rooms had a wardrobe and a lounge chair in them, but mostly they contained nothing but cobwebs and dull curtains.

I made my way along the hallway of the second floor, pushing open every door to the guest rooms. There was no furniture left in any of them. Some of the doors were warped, so it took some effort to get them to open. I hesitated before I pushed hard at the door of what used to be Bernadette Brennan's room. It was number one. The door was difficult to open. I put my whole weight against it and pushed again. It gave way so quickly I almost fell into the room. And then I stared.

Nothing had been touched. The room had been left as it was. The wallpaper was peeling off in large sections, revealing patches of dried yellow glue underneath. The carpet was threadbare. On the left-hand side of the room, framed in dark wood, was the biblical passage John 3:16 in elegant calligraphy. Off-white doilies adorned the dressing table with a few small decorative objects placed on top: china cats and baskets covered in dust. It was the only room still intact. Everything was as it used to be. A sudden rush came over me; goose bumps, a lump in my throat. I remember sitting on this bed, feeling confused, eating squashy leftover cake while Bernadette Brennan tried to explain things about the adult world that were beyond my understanding. In this room, she urged me to watch over Elise.

The bed was still there, but there was no bed linen. Dead cockroaches and flies were piled up on each other. A thick mustiness hung in the air from the room having been locked up for so long. I searched through the heavy bunch of keys and located the window keys. The window pushed open easily. The view was the same as it was back then: the red roofs of Dot Patterson and Audrey Lander's houses. I opened the cupboard to see men's shirts and trousers and ties hanging in the cupboard. Three jackets, two pairs of pants, and two pairs of jeans. I heard my grandmother's voice in my head. *If I find her entertaining men in her room...* The clothes must have belonged to a guest or perhaps a lover of Beatrice. Federico perhaps. I sat down on the bed and let the memories surface.

She gave me the tortoise-shell hair-clip in this room. She told me what to do when I had my first period. She showed me how to wrap up my hair in a French roll. We put on music and danced the latest steps. She was so full of life. She showed me how to have fun. She had poise and grace and seemed to rise above difficulties, not that I knew what her difficulties were back then. I wanted to be grown up, just like her. She didn't moon around in her room, sulking on account of some man who wasn't interested in her, and I did try to be dismissive of Josh Boatman, like she would have been. I didn't mention him in front of Bernadette Brennan after Fair Day, and I hoped she had forgotten about our conversation. I didn't ask anyone about him in case I gave myself away. While I let the past wash over me, something else was bothering me. Something to do with the clothes in the cupboard. I got up and inspected them again and then I knew what it was. At my touch, I half expected dust to fall off them, but they felt new and soft. They looked too modern. They didn't smell. I gave up trying to work out who they belonged to. I sat back down on the bed and thought about the Hovel, the other place that provided relief from a family slowly imploding.

I often went to the Hovel to practise my dance steps and to have some respite from the tensions that hovered over my home life. Boatman would meet me there when she could get away. My mother would swing between being well and being ill, and nobody seemed to know why. She took tablets that sometimes made her sleep during the day and when she wasn't smoking or sleeping, she was talking about things that didn't make a lot of sense and at times she would do very strange things. It was me who was looking after Elise more often.

Jamilla informed me one morning that I had begun to talk in

my sleep. I was horrified and accused her of making it up. She then told me that I had talked about a person called Josh and I almost fainted. On some nights, I had even woken her up, she informed me.

'Esther and I can hear everything you say,' she said smugly.

I didn't care if Esther had heard me talking in my sleep because Esther couldn't understand a thing I said in my waking hours, let alone in my sleep. Jamilla, however, was another matter completely. The thought of her telling anyone about Josh Boatman was too awful to think about. Over the next few days, I tried to be as friendly to Jamilla as possible. She knew she had me where she wanted me and didn't fall for my sudden affection for her. When I praised her mother's cooking, she just looked at me and said that Indian food made her sick. I tried taking her into my confidence and asked her advice about reading Esther's writing, as Esther was always motioning to me to look in her drawing book.

'Reading other people's letters is rude, especially Esther's, as she isn't in her right mind,' she stated with authority.

'Do you think Esther understands what we say sometimes?'

Jamilla snorted.

'Olivia says we should never treat Esther like an idiot or like a child.'

'You're the idiot,' Jamilla said.

I had to do something about talking in my sleep, but I didn't know what to do. My grandmother wasn't very helpful. She simply said that if I had nothing to hide, then it wasn't a problem. My mother tiredly said that everybody talks in their sleep at some point, and so I asked Bernadette Brennan. She told me not to worry. It's your mind taking time off, having a party, relieving you of stress, she said.

The time came when I knew that I really had to do something about talking in my sleep. Jamilla rolled over one morning and looked at me with curiosity. She said nothing; she just stared as though I had suddenly become interesting overnight.

'What?' I said.

She stayed silent and raised her eyebrows.

'What is it?' I asked, now with irritation.

'What's a hovel?' she asked.

Chapter Eleven

I sat up quite late trying to write about Elise, convincing myself that the next glass of wine would free me from inhibitions, open a floodgate of description, vivid memories, and emotions. It didn't quite work that way. Scraping the sediment from the bottom of the murky depths of memory was hard work. Decades ago, I was terrified when I couldn't conjure up her image after her death. These days, I see her face so clearly it was as if I saw her yesterday. I see the detail, the colour of her hair as it caught the sunlight, her blue eyes and long lashes. I have no pictures of Elise. I do not need them.

The alcohol didn't help. After a few sketchy notes, the electricity cut out. I reached for the nearest thing to hold on to and knocked the wine glass over. It broke and then I just sat there, swearing in the dark. I knew there was a back-up generator but didn't know where it was. Using the light from my mobile phone, I searched the kitchen for candles and matches. My torch was in the car under the front seat with empty thick-shake containers. The dark didn't frighten me, but tripping over and breaking a leg or an ankle did. I knew where the candles and matches used to be kept and hoped that Beatrice hadn't thrown them out or moved them. Beatrice was a smoker, so there were bound to be matches or lighters and if there weren't, I could use the gadget that lights the gas rings on the stove if it was still there and still worked.

An image flashed through my head of Beatrice hovering over a cooking pot, cigarette in one hand and a stirring spoon in the other, loud jazz music flooding through the house. Beatrice always drank champagne as she cooked, floating around the kitchen in her multi-layered outfits, singing in her throaty, husky voice, tipping alcohol into whatever she was cooking. Adds to the taste, she always said.

'Beatrice, you're a saint,' I said aloud when my hands found the thin candles and two boxes of matches in the third drawer. The first box of matches was empty, but the second was full. However, the matches had been there for years in the damp and mould and it took half the box before a small orange flame hissed into life. I lit two candles and pulled back the curtains to let in more light, but it was a moonless night—just my luck. I needed something to stand the candles in as wax was already dripping onto my hands. Two cups came in handy while I looked for some candleholders and just as I opened the door of the cupboard where the cups used to be kept, I heard a door slam. I stood perfectly still, holding my breath. Then I heard it again. The noise came from upstairs in the guesthouse, from the rooms to the right of the hallway.

I froze on the spot, the cups in my hands, my heart pounding. The sound of my own breathing seemed to fill the room, loud and fast. I waited, listening, but I could hear nothing more. For a split second, I considered blowing out the candles, but then decided against it. Whoever or whatever was upstairs was not able to see through the floor down to the kitchen, and two candles were hardly going to light up the whole house. I thought about Camilla, wishing she were there. Still, it was no good thinking about Camilla now. She was hundreds of miles away. I thought about how much wine I had drunk and regretted it, now needing a clear head. Picking up the mobile, I dialled triple zero, as I didn't know the number for the local police. As the ringing tone buzzed in my ear, the room was suddenly ablaze with light, catching me off guard. The phone fell onto the floor and I could hear a voice on the other end. I ended the call. With the return of the electricity, something shifted; the light had normalised everything, and I now thought I had imagined the sounds. Still, I should try to find the generator just in case it went again.

Still listening and perfectly still, I waited and then heard the wind and a light splatter of rain on the tin roof. I felt stupid. Half-drunk in the dark, I had imagined it was a door. The house creaked and shuddered against the wind. I cleaned the spilled wine in my room, corked the bottle, and left the light on for the rest of the night.

When I woke in the morning, a vague headache danced within my skull. Half asleep, I could not distinguish between the sound of the wind thrashing against the side of the house and the sound of my own breathing through my blocked nose. From under half-closed eyelids, I could see the wine bottle in the corner of the room, the label splashed with the dark red-purple of its contents. I don't remember knocking it over, but I don't remember drinking the whole bottle either.

The guesthouse didn't seem to have been disturbed. All the rooms were exactly as they were when I last saw them; nothing was missing, so there hadn't been an intruder. It was simply the wind. I looked into room one and something compelled me to look in the cupboard once more—and then I wished I hadn't. I felt sick and confused. I could have sworn there were three jackets. Now there were two. It was only yesterday that I ran my fingers over the material of three jackets. This was the sort of thing I feared, that I may not have a grasp on reality at times, that I may go the same way as my mother. Anger took over at that point. I ran through the rooms, flinging the cupboard doors open. Nothing. Perhaps I had imagined it. Or dreamt it. I hadn't been drinking. Certainly not during the day. That was one of the contracts I made with the therapist. I wouldn't drink during the day. I couldn't promise her I wouldn't drink at night. She thanked me for my honesty.

Assessing my own sanity made me think back to all those trips I made to see my mother after they put her in the Joseph M Lynell psychiatric hospital on the mainland. We visited her every two weeks, making the trip across the river to the mainland and catching the bus out to the hospital. Sometimes we would also visit my grandmother's distant relatives who lived not far from the hospital. We stayed for lunches with smoked ham, devilled eggs, cherry tomatoes in cut glass bowls and lettuce cut up so finely it looked like green string. They had ice-cream and Coke. We served those things in the guesthouse but never had them in the family home. Cautiously, they would enquire about my mother, knowing it to be a delicate subject but also realising that not asking about her would likely offend my grandmother deeply.

'And how is Margaret?' they would half whisper, just as we were leaving.

'Margaret is doing nicely,' was my grandmother's standard reply.

The relatives had dubious looks on their faces. My grandmother waved her hand dismissively. Denial made her world run smoothly. Any ugly bumps of perverse human behaviour that suddenly raised their heads were pricked sharply, deflated and covered, so they left no gaping wounds, not even small scratches. Certain things just weren't happening.

Margaret had not been doing nicely for a long time. Months before things went wrong, she was increasingly locked in her own world, wandering over a landscape of paranoia, obsessed about certain small things that were to me just part of the daily routine. People were listening, she kept telling us, but she could never tell us who those people were or why they were listening.

My grandmother was no longer comfortable for my mother to man the reception desk on her own. When someone needed to be relieved, it was left to Brenton, Jamilla, Sunita, and sometimes me. Elise was now with me most of the time until she went home in the afternoons. Boatman was with us on most days.

My mother had taken up the habit of cooking her own meals, saying that she didn't trust anyone and that you never knew what was in something unless you made it yourself. There were a few times I came across my mother and the cook laughing about the third leg joke and I could never understand why it was so amusing. If I entered a room when this was happening, they would spring apart, put on their workday faces, and talk about mundane things.

One morning, my grandmother entered the pantry to find all of Sunita's herbs from India completely wet and laid out on a shelf. My mother explained that herbs had to be washed because they were from a foreign land and she didn't want us falling ill. Sunita wasn't angry at all. She looked concerned, telling my mother that the herbs had already been washed and were fit for use. Sunita explained that she'd imported them with all the correct government regulations. My mother shook her head. Brenton told my mother that her behaviour could be construed as racist. She waved him away.

She started cleaning things that had just been cleaned and if a guest ever came into Our House, she would spray disinfectant around the room because you never knew where people had been and what germs they were bringing in.

She didn't spray when family had been in the room but she sprayed one afternoon with a vengeance when Bernadette Brennan came to the reception desk to ask whether there was a dry cleaner in the village. A pest control company arrived one morning, much to my grandmother's surprise. My mother had ordered the spraying of the rooms without telling anyone else. Informing my grandmother that a cancellation fee was in order since they had come from the mainland, the men proceeded to fumigate. Guests were unceremoniously thrown out of their rooms with a few minutes' warning and were not allowed back in for four hours. My grandmother fielded comments from angry guests, promising them a discount on their bill at the end of their holidays. My mother hovered over the men, directing them where to spray next. They asked her not to interfere. They knew their job.

The next morning, I manned the reception desk with Brenton until he left to pick up a delivery. My mother came in, bringing me lemonade and a coconut ice slice. She seemed rational. We sat together, reading the local paper and looking for the stories written by Brenton. She put the hands-free headpiece on her head and adjusted the microphone.

'Remember not to get involved with the guests,' she suddenly said.

'I never get involved with the guests,' I said.

'That's good,' she said. She smiled at me. I smiled back.

There were no guests around. They were all on the veranda. The phone lines were silent. A perfect moment.

'Mum,' I said, 'I want to…'

The switchboard lit up.

'Good morning. Gables Guesthouse,' she said.

Gone. The perfect moment always seemed to escape me. Once again, I would wait.

Reg Dalton was not much help at the time. He prescribed tranquilisers that knocked my mother out and so she rarely took them. After some time, the doctor was added to the list of people she mistrusted and she refused to see him, going instead to a doctor on the mainland. The family doctor was in collusion with *them*, she said. We could never quite work out who *they* were and my mother wouldn't tell us. Much to my grandmother's chagrin, my mother changed her mind about Sunita's herbs and now asked for them to be cooked up several times a day. They stunk out the kitchen and after some time my grandmother insisted that if they had to be made up at all, then they had to be cooked in the guesthouse kitchen and not in the kitchen of Our House. The cook agreed to let my mother boil the mixture in the guesthouse kitchen. The sudden turnaround regarding the herbs was extended to other areas as well. She threw out her favourite dress, declaring she no longer liked that colour. Nothing she did was making sense.

Olivia and Sunita were united in getting help for my mother. At night, I listened to them talking in the hallway in hushed tones. They spoke of doctors and clinics and psychiatrists while I lay in fear, wondering what was happening, wondering if it was possible that whatever it was could be passed on to me, whether the illness was in my blood, in my cells, in me, somewhere. I heard them mention the name of the psychiatrist who saw Brenton. I shuddered. Mother and brother. I saw my name on an imaginary list in the psychiatrist's office. I saw white pills. I tasted fear; projecting into the future I saw lost jobs, broken marriages, days in darkened rooms, friends shaking their heads. I saw straitjackets and white uniforms and visitors carrying flowers and Honey Jumbles.

My mother had been going to the mainland every Tuesday for months. It was her day for seeing her mainland doctor, but what she really bought was something money couldn't buy, a whole day to herself without the battering dialogue of my grandmother, Brenton's sarcasm, demands from the guests, and the general lack of privacy. Sunita didn't think it wise that my mother went alone on her Tuesday visits and the rest of us agreed. We feared her being lost, floating away into a crowd and never re-emerging. Or making a scene somewhere and ending up on the front page of a newspaper.

'I'll go with you, Mum,' I said.

My mother declared that if she was to have a chaperone, then she wouldn't go at all. And so, with our grandmother's permission, Brenton and I decided to follow her. Sunita would take care of Elise for a few hours while I was away. In some ways, I wish we hadn't executed this plan at all. Brenton and I boarded the first punt in the morning and waited till our mother came over on the next. I wore a hat drawn over my head. Brenton had borrowed Eddie Hopper's motorbike and two helmets. We waited some distance from where the punt docked, and as it drew nearer, we saw our mother hanging over the railing, flicking ash into the water. Once the punt had reached the mainland, she boarded a bus. Brenton jammed a helmet on my head and we sped after the bus.

She didn't get off at Rachley Main, but at a town another fifteen minutes away.

We watched as she alighted. She turned a corner and went to a pharmacy. We followed her as she turned back to the main street. She seemed to know the town well. She crossed the main road and stood outside a budget hotel called McCarmes. I felt like I was watching someone else, a person I did not know. She waited for a long time and we almost gave up when a man came down the street. I recognised him straight away, the thin body, the loping walk. No hat this time. The Shelley's soft drink man walked up to my mother and stopped. He took out something from a large bag. It was a green handbag. My mother reached up and kissed him. She put her thin arms around his waist, but he removed them and gently pushed her into a café. They took their seats by the window while we sat on a bus stop seat across the road.

'A secret lover. Huh.'

'Shut up,' I said, hurt welling up inside. I didn't like the idea of my mother kissing the Shelley's soft drink man.

'That wasn't a peck on the cheek and you know it.'

I watched carefully for signs. I thought he might take her hand across the table and hold it to his lips, but he didn't. I waited for him to give her a rose. He gave her a menu. She didn't lift her head and laugh or smile or fiddle with her hair the way women in the movies did when they sat at tables with a love interest. I hated the Shelley's soft drink man. I wanted to cry, but didn't want my brother to see that.

How long had my mother been doing this? I thought back to the day I saw her coating her lips and smoothing down her skirt. I waited until they had finished their lunch. Coffee or tea followed and suddenly the door of the café swung open and they stood on the street, my mother clutching the green handbag. The man whispered in my mother's ear and she laughed. He put his arm around her waist. They walked on a few steps and he pulled her gently into the McCarmes Hotel. The glass front of the hotel afforded us a view. I watched while the man spoke to a girl on the desk and then I saw my mother's pale legs climbing a staircase inside until her brown pumps disappeared.

We waited for more than three hours, Brenton reading *Crime and Punishment* and me sitting in silence, fighting back tears. I didn't want my mother doing the things with the Shelley's soft drink man that I had seen in Walter Heather's photographs. Finally, she emerged, carrying the green handbag. The man was not with her. She made her way down the street and turned into a department store. There was no spring in her step; her face gave nothing away. We followed her while she bought panty-hose and lipstick and then made our way back to the bus stop.

'You're not to tell,' Brenton said as he again jammed my helmet into place and did up the straps. 'She's entitled to some happiness.'

I tried to convince myself that my mother had found the love of her life. Deep down I knew it wasn't true, otherwise she would have brought him home to meet us. If it were really something serious, we would know. I took Brenton's advice; I tried to be happy for her and almost convinced myself that there was a great romance blossoming under our noses, so intense and consuming that it had to be kept secret for a while. The images I have today are different; I see her thin, sinuous body wrapped around a stranger, her cigarettes on the splintered wooden table, cheap Scotch in cracked pink crockery. The carpet in the cheap hotel is threadbare and the mattress is splotched with stains from rendezvous between desperate strangers. There's no room service. He wouldn't be calling for champagne and smoked salmon. I felt angry at the time. My mother had swapped her dignity for a green handbag.

On arrival at Gables, we had a captive audience. Was she all right? Where did she go? Did she do anything to embarrass the family?

'No, nothing. She bought a green handbag,' I said.

My grandmother and Sunita exchanged meaningful looks, but they didn't question me further. Brenton went back to the reception desk and Sunita crushed small brown nut-like objects in a mortar and pestle while I played with Elise on the kitchen floor, building Lego houses, and wondered about my mother and her lover lying in the McCarmes Hotel. I wanted to be left alone, to sort through what I had witnessed that day, to see if any of it resembled the person I called my mother. I couldn't concentrate on anything. I tried to watch television and then re-read the Heather files. I wanted to tell Bernadette Brennan, but I also wanted to keep my word to my brother. I had told no one until the day I was bringing in the washing and saw one of the delivery trucks pull up on the eastern side of the guesthouse where the storerooms were. Trucks pulled up frequently, backing onto the strip of grass near the storeroom so as to unload. The drivers were always the same, waving to me as they passed. I didn't know their names, referring to them by the goods they delivered. The beer man is here. The ice-cream man is waiting. The Arnott's man is at the door. The furniture man needs his money. And one afternoon the Shelley's soft drink man got out of his truck, slightly stooped, his hat drawn down over his head. My mother met him at the door and gave him a cheque. She stood, one leg curled around the other, blushing. They spoke in lowered voices, their heads close together. He took the cigarette out of her hand and put it in his mouth. She giggled like a schoolgirl. I felt slightly sick. Walter Heather came out to count the stock; my mother and the Shelley's soft drink man sprang apart. She talked loudly and suddenly about soft drink prices, and he nodded in reply. Lemonade on special. Yes. Top prices for your best customers. See you next time. He kept the cigarette in his fingers as he walked back to his truck. He smiled at me as he reversed the truck and turned down the drive. I hated the Shelley's soft drink man more than ever. In my imagination, I saw him being hit crossing the road, poisoned by a snake bite, bashed by a drunken mob.

'She won't marry the Shelley's soft drink man, will she?' I asked Brenton.

My brother just shrugged.

Righteous indignation on behalf of my father Jack, even though I never knew him, blossomed up inside me. I began to think about him for the first time in my life. I had seen photographs of him before and after his accident, photographs of Bob Patterson, his brother and other men, their arms around each other, in their football colours, beers all round. His face never changed; he didn't indulge in self-pity because he had lost his legs. His smile remained the same. He had been in a car accident many years ago with Bob Patterson's brother Jimmy and a man from Sydney. They had driven to Sydney for a cricket match and on the way back, they had collided with a truck somewhere near Coffs Harbour. Bob

Patterson's brother was killed in the accident and the other man lay in a coma for months until he died. Jack Montrell escaped with his life but lost his legs. He had been the driver. Bob Patterson and my father were never on friendly terms after that. There was talk of not doing the right thing by your mates. Bob blamed Jack for the death of his brother and he never let Jack forget it.

The past loomed large in my head as I sat in a Wi-Fi café in the village. I waded through names on the island. No Newmans. No Johnstons. No Pattersons, Hoppers, Hortons, or Boatmans. There were still Landers and Brackvilles and others I remembered. I ran into Matthew down in the village. He suggested coffee, and I agreed. My instincts told me he was all right. Matthew was friendly and intelligent. Not bad looking either, but I wasn't even going to think about anything like that. He'd come all the way from England.

Brought up by foster parents, he lived in England, studied chemistry at university and worked for pharmaceutical companies for many years until he had a gnawing to find his biological parents. Like me, he'd been married and divorced, and unlike me, had a son from the first marriage who lives with his first wife. We spent an hour discussing all sorts of things, comparing rent and food prices between London and Sydney, restaurants, careers, failed marriages, books and films. I didn't tell him that much about myself, but nor did I feel uncomfortable with him either. Matthew seemed in no hurry to leave, and I finally said that I had to go back to Gables and do some work. He said he'd walk back with me and so we walked the fifteen minutes up to the guesthouse. I showed him the turn-off tree on the way.

'Where does your friend live, the one you're staying with?' he asked.

I motioned vaguely in the direction of the houses near the top of the hill.

'Over there,' I said.

After I got back to Gables, I sat in Brenton's old room for a while. It had the best view of the river of all the bedrooms and a part view of the gardens.

When I was a girl, latticework overgrown with ivy formed arches and trellises. Roses, daffodils, and gardenias grew everywhere. Down near the corner, the cook's herb garden, covered with shade cloth, provided a quiet, green solace. Sunita had introduced a cornucopia of new plants: coriander and curry leaves, a kafir lime bush, and other plants with unpronounceable names that she'd brought from India. She kept the seeds in a gold earring box and treated them with more reverence than jewellery. My grandmother had complained that Sunita must have known someone in Customs to get the herbs in. I recall my grandmother talking about the strict laws in Australia and how she wouldn't be held responsible if the police came swooping down on Gables Guesthouse to raid the illegal herb garden. She said she'd have no option but to turn Sunita in.

I remember Brenton saying that the Rachley police had better things to do than raid people's private herb gardens, and anyway, the Rachley police wouldn't know an illegally imported herb if they fell over one.

When I rang Brenton that morning, he seemed irritated.

'You're not writing some bloody awful family history, are you?' Brenton shouted down the phone. 'Because if you are, I don't want any part in it.'

'No. I'm not writing a family history. Yes, I agree. If I wrote one it would be bloody awful, but I'm not.'

'Well, what are you doing there then?'

'Cleaning. Throwing stuff out. Going through all the rooms. Buying stuff in the village. The turn-off tree's still there. I found my old diaries. I thought I might write something, though not a family history, but perhaps how I see things now.'

'I don't know why you'd want to do that. If you've written about me, please do me a favour and either burn it or keep it somewhere others can't see it.'

'Does it matter to you that much, the past?'

'That's my point. It doesn't matter at all. It's got nothing to do with my life now. So, I want nothing to do with it.'

'Then it does matter to you. If you feel so strongly about it, even now, then it matters.'

He sighed and there was silence for a moment.

'I don't like the idea of you staying in that huge place by yourself. Is Camilla coming?'

'Not sure.'

'Do you want me to come up to help you? She left the house to both of us but I feel like you're doing all the work.'

'No,' I told him. 'I need to do this alone.'

'What about the legal stuff?'

'Still fixing all of that up, but I'll tell you about that later. Gotta go.'

I felt bad, hanging up like that, but when Brenton got irritated, there wasn't much use in continuing a conversation. After that, I couldn't write about him at all. There was nothing worth watching on television, so I sat with a glass of red and memories from the year I was eleven.

Dear Diary,

This house is going totally crazy. My grandmother has been going on about the herbs that Sunita planted in the garden. She actually called Sunita a smuggler. Brenton laughed his head off when she said that and wanted to know the name of the man at Customs because he'd like to bring in a few things of his own. He didn't say what though. My grand-

mother said if the police arrived for a raid, she'd have no compunction, whatever that means, about turning Sunita in, even if she is an ex-daughter-in-law. I asked my grandmother about talking in my sleep and she just raved on about some relative who talked in their sleep and said that if you've got nothing to hide then it isn't a problem. Brenton said that talking in your sleep is the first sign of madness. Jamilla called him an idiot and said it's not talking in your sleep that's the first sign of madness, it's talking to yourself. My grandmother said Jamilla was correct. Brenton found it quite difficult to accept that he was wrong.

Later on that day he got her back. Jamilla asked him if he had remembered to say happy birthday to Esther. He handed her an answer on a piece of paper. Eye did, did eye? it said. Of course, Jamilla laughed and said for a person who prided himself on language skills, Brenton's spelling was pathetic. Then he smirked and told her that not only did she have no sense of humour but also she was ignorant of palindromes. He told her to go and look it up. I had to explain to her about palindromes reading backward as they do forward and then she called him a smart arse. I'm going to ask Sunita if there's an Indian herb or medicine that can make me stop talking in my sleep. I've tried other things but they don't work. Last night I put a hanky over my mouth so Jamilla wouldn't hear me so clearly but after a while I couldn't breathe properly so off it came. Then I put a lolly in my mouth and left it there, hoping that it might dissolve slowly and prevent speech. Then I had a dream that I was crunching on a lolly, which is what I was really doing so that didn't work either. I gave the lollies to Elise.

My mother is going really downhill. She sleeps half the day and when she isn't sleeping she's saying things that don't make sense. She asked me if I was going away and then she said Dr Dalton was trying to poison her.

I got top marks for my project on Ireland. The teacher said Boatman's writing was too messy and that's because she left it till the last minute and she was rushing. Yesterday we went to the Hovel and ate ourselves stupid with chocolate and sherbets. Jamilla's been putting on Beauty Fade Face Cream every night. She should just go and stick her head in a bucket *of bleach. I don't know why she doesn't like being half-Indian. If she smiled, she'd look pretty, but sometimes there's not a lot to smile about in this house. Jamilla said this morning that my mother is crazy and so I said her mother is a smuggler. Bernadette Brennan said that fading cream is useless if you're half-Indian. Natural is best, she said, but then she told me that she used to have black hair and she laughed. I couldn't imagine her with dark hair.*

My mother had dark hair until the morning she dyed it an unsuccessful blonde. It came out looking like a tie-dyed skirt, bits of dark swishing through the glaring lightness in uneven splotches. She stood out near the delivery truck area in a very short skirt and tight blouse, the first lot of buttons undone, smoking, her apron stained. She looked like a waitress from an American roadhouse. I watched her moves, her speech, the way she tilted her head and spoke to delivery men with the low-pitched intimacy reserved for lovers.

'Jesus,' my brother muttered when he saw her.

'Don't take the Lord's name in vain. Audrey Landers says you'll go to hell.'

'Audrey Landers can go to hell herself,' Brenton retorted. He narrowed his eyes, squinting.

'How long has she been standing there dressed like that?'

I couldn't watch anymore.

I read my diary for a while and then switched to a trashy crime novel. The blurb on the back cover didn't inspire me that much. *The police had a new lead in the hunt for Matt's killer, but Samantha had other ideas. Why would no one listen?*

After a few chapters of Samantha's antics with her boozy friends in London nightclubs, a wave of tiredness swept over me. I put my hand out to switch off the bedroom light and then, once again, I heard it. A door closing. The sound was coming from upstairs. Unmistakably, that's what it was. It wasn't the wind. The night outside was still and quiet. What I should have done was ring the police, but again, the thought was there: What if it's me? Wait five minutes. No sound. Ten. No sound. Fifteen. Nothing. Twenty minutes went by in silence. After half an hour, I crawled back under the covers. Silence. Now I was fully awake. I picked up the novel again and started where I had left off. After ten minutes, I realised I had been reading the same page over and over again. Not one word had registered. My whole body was tense. I put the book down and kept the light on all night, thinking about two possibilities, neither of them pleasing.

One. I am slowly and gradually losing my mind.

Two. I am here in this house and I am not alone.

Chapter Twelve

I found out how he got in.

I assumed it was a he, or maybe a them. On the right side of the guesthouse, where the delivery trucks used to pull up, was a small recess behind the laundry. A large window at ground level allowed people to see into the cellar below. Bars once covered the window, but they had since been removed. The window, which was really more of a trapdoor, was the same sort that pubs have so that crates and barrels can be unloaded at street level, straight from the truck into the cellar.

Someone had kicked it in. I'd discovered it that morning while doing the rounds and immediately rang the police. Constables Michael Bow and Jenny Cameron took over an hour to arrive from the mainland—I hated to think what would happen in an emergency. I couldn't imagine there'd be that much crime on Rachley Island, and when I pointed that out to them, they said I'd be surprised at what went on. Constable Cameron squeezed through the trapdoor and lowered herself into the cellar, had a look around, and came back up to report that there were no visible signs of anybody having been there.

'Anything missing or anything unusual? It doesn't matter how small.'

I told them about the clothes in room one but I didn't tell them that on one day there were three jackets and then there were two. They would have thought I was unhinged. This was what I dreaded, that it might be the start of something.

'When was the last time you saw the trapdoor locked?'

I was waiting for that question; I didn't have an answer because I'd never looked at it.

Constable Bow bent down to examine the trapdoor. He ran his fingers over the wood. 'It's been recently broken,' he said. 'Do you have keys for the whole place?'

'Yes. Just a minute and I'll get them.'

'Is there any way of getting from the cellar into other parts of the building?'

At the top of the cellar steps was a door that led into a cupboard built under the staircase going up to the second floor. That cupboard had a door as well, facing the reception area. Boatman, Jamilla, and I played many games of hide-and-seek in the cupboard under the stairs, and Brenton and the island boys had once spent a night down in the cellar, sampling every bottle of alcohol there was. He was sick for two days, but earned himself a reputation with the island boys.

My grandmother had stood over him that morning, making him clean up all the smashed glass and vomit. He pleaded for mercy, saying he had a raging headache and still felt like vomiting. He told us he'd clean it later and that he just wanted to sleep, but she was adamant. At one point, he pushed past her and started up the stairs but was met by my mother, who threatened to punch the living daylights out of him if he didn't stay down there and clean up the mess. The loss of the alcohol was paid for out of his wages. It took months before he was paid again. My grandmother had to buy quite a few bottles from the pub at pub prices before the next delivery arrived from the mainland and she never let him forget it.

Thankfully, Beatrice had labelled all the master keys, so I went around and secured the rooms downstairs. I didn't lock the rooms upstairs as it would be impossible for a thief to get up there without access from the ground floor. The police had been very patient and polite, but I was left with the impression that they didn't see a real problem, partly because the door could have been smashed some time ago and partly because Gables is on a hill and more affected by the wind than the village would be. The other reason, I suspected, is that they probably saw a woman on her own in a huge house believing she heard noises. And there was a chance that this had been true. Before they left, they gave me a number to ring that bypassed the switchboard, straight to Constable Michael Bow, and said to ring immediately if anything at all bothered me.

The problem was that everything was bothering me. The handyman, who I found in the local paper, charged a fortune to fix the cellar trapdoor. Thankfully, he didn't recognise me. He might have assumed I was the new buyer of the property. He prattled on about crime getting worse and worse on the mainland. He said mainlanders often came over purely to rob tourists and that someone was murdered over on the other side of Rachley Main last year, so by the time he left, I was feeling quite uncomfortable.

'It's mainlanders you gotta watch,' he said. 'Haven't had a real crime on the island for decades, not since the days of the Boatmans and the Montrells. Families were friends too. Way before your time.'

Had the incident the night before not happened, I might have asked him some questions, but the mention of a real crime followed by those two family names made me feel sick. I was starting to think that coming back to the island was a mistake.

I needed a breather after that. Lunch at the pub and some

conversation with anyone felt like a good idea. The walk down the hill improved my spirits; it was hot, but the air felt fresh, as though it had been washed and hung out to dry. I thought about the thousands of times I had walked and ridden my bike up and down the hill as a girl in the sun, rain, and wind and in storms as well. I passed the turn-off tree and remembered all the times I'd sheltered under its leaves. By the time I reached the village, I'd worked up a sweat, even though it was downhill all the way. I walked through the main street, feeling at home and yet not at home at the same time. On the side of the town hall, graffiti in bright red paint screamed *Rachley Rebels 4 Ever. Tracy is a slut. Ring this number for a good time.*

The pub wasn't crowded. It didn't even bother me that I recognised a few old locals. I didn't recognise them by their appearance; it had been decades since I'd seen them. It was their voices I picked up on and when I heard others calling them by name, their faces from years ago were clear in my memory. They were surprised when I told them I was staying at Gables and doing up the place. I added that friends were staying with me and helping. Not one of them asked about my mother or Brenton and no one mentioned the Boatmans, and for this I was grateful. Some people are circumspect when they need to be. I thought I recognised a distant relative of Sarah Boatman eating lunch at a table near the door, an uncle who was slightly eccentric. The barman knew him by name and the locals waved and bought him drinks. He was present at Elise's funeral and, like many others, looked on my family with disdain. He didn't recognise me and I didn't expect him to after so many years, but I kept my back to him nevertheless. A part of me was curious. I would have liked to know what happened to Sarah and Boatman, but another part told me to leave it.

Meat and potatoes were always on the menu at Rachley Village Inn. They'd made a few concessions to modernity: curry, focaccia, and penne with pesto. I couldn't imagine anyone on the island eating curry, but since tourism had become the mainstay of the economy, they obviously had to expand their culinary horizons.

I'd come in the middle of renovations. A badly written sign informed customers of the circumstances. The female toilet was closed for the next two hours so everyone had to use the men's, and that's how I ran into Matthew again; I was entering, he exiting. We gave each other one of those looks that pass between people when one is leaving the toilet, the other entering, the half-embarrassed recognition of the physical workings and basic needs of the body being the only bond between strangers.

'See you upstairs,' he said, and I nodded.

He was drinking by himself at the bar when I made my way back up the narrow stairs. We talked about what I was doing at Gables and I told him that I would be cleaning out the cupboards in the guesthouse over the next two days. He offered to help, but I said I could do it on my own. I didn't mention my night-time troubles, the police or the break-in at the risk of doing the helpless female thing. He hadn't eaten. I suggested we have lunch, but he said he wasn't that hungry. We moved from the bar to a table. I ordered a bottle of wine and a lamb kofta. In my head, the therapist's face loomed large. Drinking during the day. Breaking my contract with myself. Not before five-thirty. Two glasses and then put the bottle back in the fridge.

Exceptional circumstances, I told myself. I found Matthew easy to talk to. He told me about growing up in England and how he had always wanted to visit Australia one day. Conversation flowed easily, but at the same time, a tiny knot of apprehension was growing inside. I felt a certain attraction to him, but it was the type of attraction that bothered me. I wanted to be strong and self-contained, and yet right at that moment I was feeling anything but that. He ended up eating half my lunch. We went through a bottle of wine. He apologised for not being able to pay for half of it but his wallet had been stolen and he was waiting for money to be deposited in his account from England. I knew I was drinking more quickly than I should have been, but I wanted to de-stress after the night before and to drive out the doubt I had about him. Not so much about him, but about me and him, whether it would be a good idea. I'd been down that road too many times after too much wine. He didn't make any moves or say anything that had even given me an inkling that something more might come of our meeting.

'What will we drink to?' he asked.

I shrugged and smiled.

'The future,' he said with confidence and I hoped he meant the future in general and wasn't intimating something to do with us as a couple.

'The past,' I said, trying to sound as confident as he did, gulping wine. He smiled and clinked his glass against mine.

'Have you uncovered anything interesting with all this renovation?'

'Well, I'm not sure that you would find it interesting. Just family stuff. My silly diaries and rubbish that my Aunt Esther wrote in a big drawing book when I was a girl. She was non-verbal and demented and couldn't walk, but she could still write and draw. I looked after her quite a bit when I was a girl. It's strange, you know, she couldn't speak, wasn't sane and yet there was a bond between us, between niece and aunt. The community nurse used to come twice a week to bathe her, and my mother and grandmother took turns on the other days. It was my job to feed her at night. She was always trying to get me to look at her book and I never did—well, I looked at some of the pictures but not the writing. I was taught not to read private things, even Esther's private things.'

I didn't know if the contents of Esther's book were rubbish because I hadn't really looked at them yet. I found myself talking to him about Esther and I surprised myself at how much I remembered about her. I could still picture her thin arms and her hands, covered in brown age spots. I tentatively talked about Elise; not about what had happened, but how I used to look after her and take her down into the village with Sunita and Bernadette Brennan to buy ice-cream. As Matthew and I were sitting drinking, John Dowell came into the pub. He was the first person I ever went out with after the trouble. He asked me to marry him when I was eighteen. Like the Boatman's relative, he didn't recognise me either.

'I turned him down.'

'His loss,' said Matthew.

'I doubt it. If I'd married him, we would have been divorced a few years later for sure. He's still on the island, still working in his father's business. Married an island girl. Never been off this island, I'm sure.'

'Is that so bad?' Matthew asked.

'Maybe not for some people, no, but I couldn't have lived a life like that. I needed to get off this wretched island, to get away from things.'

'To get away from what?'

'Things. Just things,' I replied.

I returned to Gables mid-afternoon and tried to write but couldn't settle. I sat where my mother used to sit, in the corner of the back veranda, tapping my pen on a blank pad. Too much wine in the middle of the day. I walked down the slope on the eastern side to the riverbank. Through patches of trees along the bank, I could see the reflection of the sun on the river in long, yellow streaks. The river cruise boat glided on the water like a huge swan, and I could hear soft music and laughter. Sixties' songs floated up and then they faded as the boat went upstream, and suddenly I had tears streaming down my face, tears for the past, for Elise, for my mother, for everything that had happened. I walked further upstream, to the place where my mother had tried to beat the river into submission with a dirty length of cable. The past swallowed me up. No more alcohol in the middle of the day, I told myself, but it wasn't just that. I wanted to have my childhood all over again, but differently. Exhaustion set in after that, and a headache as well. There was nothing on television but I sat and watched it, anyway; re-runs of sitcoms I'd seen hundreds of times before, the news, more news, a movie, the late news. I turned to my old diary and skimmed over an entry.

Dear Diary,

I am in big trouble and it's not fair. I blame my grandmother for it but I can't tell her that, of course. She always says nasty things about India. Bloody India, she says. She says it when Sunita isn't there, but not in front of her. I'm so used to hearing about bloody India that perhaps I thought in my mind that that's what it's really called. Bernadette Brennan said that it was an association thing, but I don't really know what that means even though I told her that I understood coz (Miss Abercrombie said don't get into the habit of writing coz but 'because' is too long) I don't want Bernadette Brennan to think I'm dumb. Then she explained. She said I have come to associate the word India with the word 'bloody' so much that it seems as natural as saying black tar, yellow sand, hot chilli. When Miss Abercrombie asked on Quick Quiz Day (when we're allowed to call out instead of hands up) which country had a salt march, I called out 'Bloody India'. The boys up the back all laughed and so did some of the girls, especially Boatman. She couldn't stop laughing. And then (Miss Abercrombie said you shouldn't start a sentence with 'And' but I don't care) she asked Boatman what was so funny. Anyway, we both got detention and had to scrape the chewing gum off from under the desks with our nails and they broke. And then she rang both our mothers. Boatman's mum laughed and Miss Abercrombie got a bit mad. My mum didn't get mad at me. But I think she thought it was funny.

I drank about six cups of water before I went to bed to ward off the inevitable hangover the next morning. Waking three hours later, busting to go to the toilet and feeling a bit seedy, I looked at the clock. Eleven pm. A throbbing head made it difficult to get back to sleep and so I was up again searching for tablets. Back in bed, I had just pulled the covers over me when I stopped still, listening. There was no mistaking it, the sound of furniture being moved. Upstairs, it was coming from upstairs. The sound stopped. I held my breath. There was silence and I dared to breathe out again and just as I did, I heard it again, a door being shut. Someone was in the house. I was on the phone immediately. This is real, not my imagination, I kept saying to myself. My hands were shaking as I held the mobile phone with two hands and my voice was husky with fear. I kept saying: 'The Gables, the Gables' and they kept asking where it was. I couldn't think of the address.

'The Gables, on the hill, on the island. Not the mainland. The island,' I shouted. 'The old guesthouse, you can't miss it. It's the only thing on the hill.'

It seemed like hours before the police arrived. They came up the back way, with their lights off, parked about a hundred metres from the house. They told me they didn't want an intruder—if there was one—seeing the police cars and lights because then the intruder would run. I led them through the house and we stopped in the hallway. They would have a better chance of hearing anything from the hallway as it was closer to the guesthouse than my bedroom. They asked me questions, too many questions, and I just wanted them to go upstairs and do something and get the whole thing over and done with. I was whispering, but they spoke at normal volume. Then we stood, the three of us, listening, and I breathed a sigh of relief. A door slammed; they heard it too and nodded at each other. They told me to stay where I was but I couldn't bear to be alone and so, with me trailing quite some distance behind, they went up the hall and through the door into the lobby area, climbing the stairs carefully. As they went through the house, they asked me not to switch on the lights. I couldn't remember where all the switches were, anyway. They both had torches. Circles of torchlight moved around the floor, the walls, doors, and onto the ceilings. Finally arriving on the second floor, they asked me to wait at the end of the corridor and not venture any further. They walked to the end of the corridor and stopped in front of room one, the only door that was closed. For a split second I felt sick, thinking of ghosts and spirits inhabiting the room, tossing and turning on beds with no linen. I imagined Bernadette Brennan, old and wizened, barely recognisable, her voice croaking and crackling with old age, her back bent over, her beauty wrinkled and faded. My heart was beating so loudly my chest hurt.

I expected them to go crashing through the door like they do on television, but instead one of them knocked, informed whoever was in there that the police were on the other side of the door and asked them to come out. There was silence. The procedure was repeated, and after no response, the police turned the door handle. It was locked and so they did what I thought they'd do. I heard a man's voice shouting as they crashed through the door, a voice that sounded almost familiar, a hurt and tired voice. Waiting nervously outside, I could hear a conversation but couldn't make out what each person was saying. The bigger of the two policemen poked his head around the door and asked me to come in.

'Do you know this man?' he asked.

'What the hell do you think you're doing in here?' I shouted, not out of anger but out of absolute shock. A frightened and miserable face stared up at me.

Matthew McCardle, huddled on the bed, looked at me blankly.

'I can explain,' he said.

Chapter Thirteen

It's surprising what a four-year-old can remember. Perhaps it's not so much what they can remember, but more that certain incidents and events stick out because they were pleasurable or beautiful or associated with colour. He had brightly coloured shirts—I remember that. Life of the party, they said of him. A ladies' man. Never took anything seriously. His name was Jack Tyler, and he left when I was four. The details are sketchy. Then I just came right out and said it.

'My father played around on my mother and was an undiagnosed something or other. Quite mad. Oh, and no legs either. An accident. He left my mother when I was a kid. I didn't know him and I was very young so I'm not messed up about it.'

Matthew nodded. He said he had an aunt on his mother's side who had spent most of her life institutionalised. I know he revealed that to lessen the shame he assumed I felt. I was touched. It was a small connection, and I was grateful for it. My grandmother occasionally referred to my father, but never by name, I told Matthew. *Him,* is what she called him, and she sneered at the fact that he wasn't an islander. Later I came to believe that I couldn't trust anybody, no matter where they were from. My mother rarely spoke about my father, although I over-heard her say that he was totally mad and if she had realised, she never would have married him. I never met my grandparents on my father's side. There had been some sort of rift between them and my parents, which culminated in my grandparents moving away and losing contact not long after my mother and Jack were married. Beatrice had mentioned that my mother was proposed to by another man before she met my father, but again, there wasn't much information. The other man was from the island but wanted to live in England as he had business ventures there. I only know a few details and there's no one left to ask.

In the few photos taken of my mother and Jack, he was always smiling and often had a glass in his hand. She, however, always had a frown. Beatrice told me long after the trouble that they were not a happy couple. She began to tell me all sorts of things, believing that after what happened in 1971, I was suddenly mature enough to hear anything. I'm sure I suspected that my parents had been unsuited long before she told me. Jack was happy enough, according to Beatrice, but it was a selfish contentment, a highly individual satisfaction from doing whatever he wanted. I got more information that I felt I could trust from Beatrice.

I told Matthew bits and pieces about my father and my mother over breakfast, but only after he had explained about the night before. It had taken me quite a long time to convince the police that I didn't want to press charges and that he wasn't an ex-husband or jilted lover out to kill me. They cautioned me about letting him off so lightly. They wanted Matthew to come back to the station with them, telling me that they could fix up somewhere for him to stay, but I insisted it was all right that he stayed, as long as he stayed in room one.

Matthew had dissolved into tears in front of the police and was so embarrassed that I didn't know quite what to say. I actually began to feel sorry for him. He cried and said he had nowhere else to go as he had run out of money. Over and over again, he kept apologising. The police were not moved by his tears and didn't seem too impressed about my decision to let him stay.

'I thought you said no one lived here,' Matthew said, anguished, when the police had departed. 'You said you were staying with friends.'

He assured me that if he had known I was here on my own, he would never have broken in and scared me. Don't call it breaking in, I told him. Thieves break in to steal, not the homeless to sleep. He sighed and gave a weak smile. It was midnight when the police finally left. Although I was curious to hear his reasons for staying upstairs, we were both very tired, so I told him I'd hear it all in the morning over breakfast. He nodded and sank back down on the bed and I made sure the bed had a mattress, clean sheets, a pillow, and a blanket before I said goodnight and firmly locked the interconnecting doors between the two buildings. Although I was exhausted, I couldn't sleep until around five in the morning.

He came down to breakfast a little after nine, looking worn out. I cooked eggs and bacon and made cup after cup of coffee. After he had showered, he dressed in the clothes I had seen hanging in room two, the blue shirt and jeans and brown jacket. I told him that he'd saved my sanity in some respects. I wouldn't have to go and seek out a shrink or buy any more self-help books—well, not right away. He listened with interest to what I had been going through in the past two days and he sat, looking sheepish.

'I've never squatted before,' he said. 'It's not something I'd recommend. I'll make it up to you somehow. I'm really sorry.'

Back in England, he'd had a good career with an income that allowed him to lead a comfortable middle-class lifestyle. He was paying off a mortgage, a car, and keeping up maintenance payments to his ex-wife for the upkeep of his son, whom he saw every second weekend. However, he was hiding a secret from all who knew him: he'd developed an addiction to gambling. He was in therapy when he left England, but without support in Australia he'd slipped back into old habits. He missed his son terribly. By the time he arrived in Rachley village, he was very low on money. All he possessed was his return ticket to England, one hundred and thirty-two dollars, and his credit card, which had reached its limit. He'd had to come clean, and he'd contacted his parents the day before. They deposited some money into his account. They weren't that shocked, he told me. They knew something was going on.

While he was talking, I suddenly had an idea that I thought could solve some problems for both of us.

'You can stay in the guesthouse rent free with all meals provided—that's if you want to stay here for a while—and in return, you help me paint and renovate so I can save money on tradespeople. Although now you've got some money, you might want to do something else.'

The arrangement would work for both of us. A part of me was reluctant to give up the solitary existence I had recently become accustomed to, but on the other hand, I needed some company and despite what had happened, my instincts told me to trust him.

'Well,' I said. 'What do you think?'

His face broke into relief. He looked at me and smiled.

'I need a place to just get my head together. I like it here. It's a deal,' he said.

It was good having someone to talk to and shop with. Matthew was so easy to live with, shop with and to talk with. We often sat out on the guesthouse veranda watching the stars. The distant sounds of the river boats floated up over the garden. We listened to the muted shouts from teenagers, who were obviously truanting school, jumping into the water and swinging from ropes. We drank Pinot Grigio and sorted out the world's problems. He liked listening to me read aloud from my diary and laughed at my eleven-year-old girlish perceptions of the world.

Dear Diary,

Lambs brains for dinner again! The bad thing about brains is that, firstly, you're eating a brain, and secondly, they taste awful. Boatman and I used to believe what Brenton told us about eating brains. He said eating brains makes you smarter. He said that when you swallow brains you should immediately stand on your head because the brains actually find their way into your own brain and make you more intelligent. Of course, I never stand on my head at the dinner table. My grandmother would never allow it. I sometimes drop something on the floor like a fork or spoon so that I can bend down and pick it up and have my head upside down for a few seconds so that the brains fall in the right direction.

The weather is so wet, it's terrible. The guesthouse cook looks completely red all over and she keeps saying the fans in the kitchen are not enough. She wants air-conditioning but my grandmother says it's too expensive.

The Hovel would be damp and mouldy in this weather. It stopped raining for a few hours, so Boatman and I went down to the river. We couldn't even get down there because everything is under water, even the picnic ground.

I like talking to Bernadette Brennan. She's fun and she even knows what songs are in the charts and stuff like that. Sunita said that we should cook some stuff to send over to the Boatmans because she doubted Dan and Josh would be doing much cooking. Brenton said that people on Rachley Island are parochial, paranoid, pathetic, and petty and it wasn't even Wordsday. Then he said that Sunita was showing more Christian charity than the Montrells and she's a Hindu. My grandmother didn't like being outdone, especially by a Hindu, so she made the guesthouse cook put stuff in containers for Dan. Elise loves putting red dots on everyone's foreheads. Mum is still saying weird stuff. I hate the Shelley's soft drink man. Hate him. Hate him. Hate him. I don't want him doing things with my mum like in those pictures that WH has in the tin. It's disgusting.

Yesterday Camilla rang. Matthew answered my mobile as my hands were covered in flour. I laughed as I listened to him trying to make conversation with her. When he passed the phone over, he rolled his eyes. She'd been asking about the cleanliness of the place and because I had prompted him, he went to great lengths to explain about spiders, cockroaches, dust, mould, and anything else he could think of that would put her off visiting.

'I can't even begin renovating,' I could hear him saying, 'until this place is thoroughly clean. You wouldn't believe the smell in the guesthouse.'

Camilla was not impressed that Matthew was staying.

'He's a stranger, Siobhan.'

I didn't tell her about him squatting. She said I had no common sense.

Matthew and I got a routine going, or rather, we just fell into it. After he'd been here for three weeks, he still showed no signs of wanting to move on. In the mornings after breakfast, he painted and I cleaned and sorted through cupboards. After lunch, we usually went down into the village to get supplies and paint from the hardware store. Sometimes we went to the pub, but when we did, we wouldn't get a lot done, so we decided to only do that on Fridays. We went to the Wi-Fi café and looked up renovating tips and watched YouTube clips on how to fix up mouldy bathrooms. The people at the hardware store were very helpful. I'm sure the old man who worked there recognised me as he looked at me intently, saying he had seen me somewhere before.

'You're the Boatman girl, aren't you?' he asked on my third visit.

I shook my head and left it at that. Correcting him would have meant explaining other things, and the time was not right.

Sometimes we took the car if there was going to be a big load, and sometimes we walked. We wandered along the riverbank several times. I showed him the tree where Billy hanged himself and the places where Boatman and I swam. He saw the flood poles with their markers, the boat shed, the new wooden tables and chairs at the picnic ground. We walked past the turnoff tree and he ran his fingers over the ageing bark. The Hovel, I kept for another day. I found myself telling him all sorts of things. I pointed out landmarks, I recounted events from my childhood. It felt like I'd known him for years. I told him small things about Elise; how she was adventurous with food, how she tried to get onto Esther's lap, how she couldn't yet pronounce her 'v' sounds. Wolkswagen. Wery nice. How her eyelashes were so long that Bernadette Brennan said she would never need mascara. How we became blood sisters.

Matthew seeped into my landscape, my past history. He had a good memory. Sometimes he'd look at something or touch something and then he'd say, 'So this is where you and Boatman parted ways and took separate routes home.' 'Is this where you sat when you helped behind the reception desk?' 'This is where Sunita grew the herbs?' He made me feel as though I perhaps had some sort of normal childhood, that I did things and my family did things that weren't so different from other families.

After the third week of his stay, I invited him to sleep in Esther's old room. At first, he seemed hesitant, but I explained that it was better for security reasons.

'In case of squatters,' I said, and we both laughed.

One night, we sat up talking about his addiction. I didn't

judge; I'd gone through periods when I knew I was drinking too much but couldn't stop. I had to block everything out. He started to gamble when his first wife left him. We compared therapists' strategies and swapped stories of our progress and setbacks. We fell asleep in our clothes.

The next morning, the first thing I saw on entering the kitchen was a huge bunch of flowers. Forgetting myself and because I was embarrassed, I chided him for spending money on me. He told me he wanted to say thanks for giving him a place to get himself together.

We went down to the village to buy champagne and smoked salmon, cream cheese and chocolate. We planned to go down to the riverbank as we had decided to take a rest day from renovation and writing.

The river was still. We found a shady spot a few hundred metres down from Billy's tree and we lay there for three hours, sometimes talking and sometimes just locked into our own private thoughts. He listened to the story of Billy's death, not saying much. Small row boats passed by, teenagers jumped and splashed and swung into the water from ropes, glad of school holidays. The river cruise floated by, followed a few minutes later by ducks swimming close to the bank. The sun was warm on our backs. Matthew put his hand in mine.

'I might just stay here forever,' he said.

'I might not object to that,' I replied.

He sensed my decision to take things slowly. Perhaps it was his decision as well.

After such a relaxed day, it surprised me when I had a nightmare that night. It seemed so real, it woke me up, shouting and sweating and I wondered if I had been not only talking but walking in my sleep as well. Matthew was there with his arms around me, telling me that everything was all right.

'Bad dream?' he asked.

'Was I talking?'

'You were shouting, not talking.'

I lay back down again, embarrassed. He rolled the blankets back and said I was too hot.

'What was I shouting about?'

He said not to worry, that people talk in their sleep all the time and most of what they say is nonsensical. However, I pressed him. I needed to know.

'You mentioned some of the people you've told me about, Elise and Bernadette Brennan.'

I said nothing for a few seconds. I needed some water and a shower. If ever someone invented a pill that would stop dreams, I would buy them in bulk, I thought as warm water cascaded over my head and down my body. Bad dreams have been with me all my life, but never a dream like that. After a cup of tea, I crawled back to bed. Matthew came to see if I was feeling all right. When I told him I was, he turned to go back to his bed in Esther's room, but I asked him whether he would sleep in the bed opposite mine.

'It's not 'cause I'm scared,' I told him. 'I just want some company.'

'Do you want to talk about it?'

I turned to face him in the dark. He shuffled under the sheets, and I knew he was waiting for me to say something. Back to childhood, Jamilla and I trading insults in the dark, Boatman and I lying across from one another, talking until late, facing each other in the dark. Matthew and I, facing each other in the dark. I don't even know him that well.

'It started on a rainy day. No, that's not correct. It started before I was born.'

The beginnings of the tragedy were forming before I was even thought of, but I played a part and this has always been my problem.

'It's a long story.'

'Go on,' he said.

Chapter Fourteen

I t is not difficult to remember even the finer details of that day, a day that began like any other, but within a few hours had twisted into tragedy, starting the beginning of the end for all of us. It was a day I would take back if I could. I'd start it differently, do it all again, right from the moment I opened my eyes on that fateful morning.

The rain had started after days of relentless heat that cast a still pall over the river. The water seemed sluggish, unable to move, not even to form a ripple on the surface, and then a light splatter of rain fell from the sky, so light it was barely noticeable. Bird life began to shriek and screech. The river creatures smelled the impending rain and roused themselves from lethargic sleep. Frogs leapt along the bank, fish came to the surface, and then the skies opened.

It had been raining for about a week. Occasionally, it stopped for a while, but not for long. The guests left the island every day to do inside things over on the mainland; shopping, the museum, beauty routines. Olivia wore gumboots as she trudged up the hill to the guesthouse. Large pools of mud lay swirling at the bottom of the slope. Olivia's sons careered down the hill on huge plastic incontinence sheets meant for Esther. They landed with a splash in the mud pools below.

Boatman and I were at the Hovel when the rain started the week before. Dan had picked up Elise and my mother said I was free to do what I liked for the rest of the afternoon. Boatman and I knew we should have made a move hours earlier. We had no raincoats or umbrellas and time was getting on. Our bike tyres would be filthy with mud by the time we crossed the fields and made it down into the village. The rain hit the roof of the Hovel with such force that I thought it would break. Riding home in the wet was looking more and more likely. An hour before the rain started, we thought we had heard someone outside, but saw only a sheet of old canvas twirling in the wind. It rose up and hit the side of the barracks with a thud before the wind moved it on again, scraping it over the ground till finally it rounded a corner.

We left the Hovel, venturing outside into an abyss of water. The wind had strengthened even in the last few minutes, tearing at branches, snapping them off and hurling them over our heads. Visibility was minimal. Boatman went first and I followed, slipping and getting back on my feet again. I thought perhaps it was hailing; I couldn't see in front of me and the rain seemed to hit us rather than fall on us. Our sandals were coated with mud. Small puddles quickly became large ones as we rode away from the barracks.

Our bikes splashed through the well-worn path from the barracks, over the large expanse of field. We crossed the field and came onto the track that led into the village. Soon the muddy track turned into a concrete path. Our bikes fared better once we were on concrete, but it was still difficult to see. Boatman was in front. At times, she'd yell something out, but her voice was swept up in the tumult. I knew I should keep my head up to see straight ahead, but the rain fell so hard it was better not to. Finally, we reached the turn-off tree where we separated. Boatman took the track down to the village while I began the fifteen-minute ride uphill, the rain pelting hard against my skin. After leaving the tree and heading the bike up the hill, I turned to shout something to Boatman, but she didn't hear me. It was then that I saw Walter Heather trudging through what had become a fierce storm. He was coming from the east, soaked through, his head down, watching the path so as not to slip. I wondered why he was coming from that direction and supposed he had been down to the village and had decided to take a longer route home. Still, it was odd and later it occurred to me that he had not been carrying shopping bags or the black plastic bags from the hardware store. Why would he be coming from that direction? There was nothing on the eastern side; a few farms, defunct army barracks, a rifle range. I forgot about Walter Heather and concentrated on getting home through the storm and thinking up an excuse for being so wet. Arriving home, I was chastised by my mother for being soaked and told to quickly change out of my sodden clothes and have a shower. My grandmother asked where I had been and I lied and said I had just been riding around.

I felt cooped up, frustrated. I was anxious to get back to our hideaway, as we had work to do on the door, but my grandmother would not let me go out in the rain. I built Lego houses with Elise; as soon as we'd finished one, we'd take it apart and do it again. I kept thinking about the Hovel, imagining the soggy floor and wet tablecloth, the sloping tin roof battered in the wind. The grey concrete of the ablutions block would shine in the wet.

Our House had a tin roof. We listened to the drumming as it grew louder and then to rolls of thunder, subtle, far off at first and then tumultuous, gathering momentum as the storm moved into the western part of the island. Lines of lightning cracked over the sky in zigzag patterns that sent the cat under the reception desk. Even Esther sensed the movement. She squirmed in her chair, her mouth open, her hands fluttering up and down. I gave her the drawing book, but it fell from her hands as if she couldn't bear to hold it. I picked it up from the floor and tried to make her take it, but she refused.

The sky darkened, a grey canopy covered the land, and lights went on in the daytime. A disappearing sun made the afternoon take on the colours of evening. My mother sat out on the veranda, right on the edge, dunking biscuits in milky tea, letting the rain fall over her. Her legs were up on the wooden railing, her sandals kicked off, revealing chipped nail polish we had painted on several weeks before. She put her head back, closed her eyes while the rain dripped onto her face, her dress, and her legs. The day before she had kissed the Shelley's soft drink man in full view of the guests. I saw her do it. When she came in for dinner she was drenched, her fringe plastered down on her forehead, her lipstick smeared on her chin. The rain hit the tin roof so hard we had to raise our voices to hear each other. My grandmother turned up the volume on the radio in the kitchen. We hardly spoke to each other that day until the afternoon when Brenton barged into the kitchen.

'An emergency vehicle complete with wailing device, medical attendants therein and the ability to bypass traffic laws and speed limits is urgently required as a female person of advanced years has succumbed to a most unfortunate lack of balance on the apparatus that allows one to move from one level to another.'

We all looked up, saying nothing. The psychiatrist had said to ignore Wordsday.

'Your lexical density is becoming excruciatingly boring,' Jamilla spat out, not even looking at my brother.

'What are you talking about?' I asked my brother.

'Get an ambulance, you idiots! The old lady in fourteen has fallen down the stairs. What are you waiting for?'

Following behind the others, who had rushed into the lobby,

I saw Walter Heather, completely drenched, this time coming into the guesthouse by the door at the front. He looked at me and he looked anxious. When we arrived at the bottom of the staircase, Bernadette Brennan, who seemed to know what to do, was attending to the woman who had fallen.

'Trained nurse here,' she said firmly and went on to explain that she thought the guest had a broken ankle. It was the first time I had considered that Bernadette Brennan had a profession; that she worked like everybody else, got up in the morning, dressed and ate a hurried breakfast before rushing out the door to catch grimy buses and trains that dropped her off at a badly lit building somewhere. I wondered why she had chosen Rachley Island as a holiday destination and was even more curious about why she was staying for so long. Not that I was unhappy about that.

Jamilla turned on Brenton, her eyes flashing.

'You deliver a smart-arsed message like that in a real emergency, and someone could die in the time it takes to deliver it,' she said. 'You're a moron.'

My grandmother yelled at both of them. My mother seemed to be in a daze. She was talking about being out of Shelley's soft drink, totally unconcerned about the accident on the stairs.

'It comes in different bottles now,' she said. 'There's more flavours. But it still tastes the same,' she told us.

After that incident, where Bernadette Brennan had seen my family at its worst, I found myself telling her more and more in the following days. I told her about how I wanted to talk to my mother but how impossible it seemed to be with her illness and preoccupations. I told her all about the conversation I'd over-heard, the one featuring 'you know who'. She was interested in everything I told her.

After a week of continuous heavy rain, the river rose, threat-ening to overflow. Brown, murky water swelled and rushed downstream, taking leaves, branches, and debris with it. Living on a hill, we weren't particularly bothered, but there was talk in the village of flooding. Boatman and I became more and more irritable at being cooped up. We were allowed to talk on the phone for fifteen minutes, but it was difficult to talk without being constantly interrupted by her brothers at her end and my grandmother at mine.

On the sixth day, the river flooded, sending Rachley Village into chaos. The flood affected us only in economic terms. Visitors from the mainland could not come across to the island, and deliveries and supplies ran short as the boats were cancelled. Guests who would have left were forced to stay longer, and they became annoyed and demanding, sometimes taking out their frustrations on the staff. From Esther's window on the southern side, we watched the brown water lying in a giant flat sheet at the bottom of the hill.

Seeing the rain stop on the seventh day was strange after days of grey. Guests gathered on the veranda as the sun appeared and threw bright light over the lawn. Olivia wheeled Esther out and positioned the chair under the Moreton Bay fig tree, facing the garden. She put the drawing book in Esther's hands and soon Esther was busy drawing and writing, while the guests took their seats nearby or wandered around, feeling the sun's heat. My mother and I both felt the need to get outside after days of being cooped up with a three-year-old. We didn't want to sit on the veranda with the guests, so Walter Heather put a groundsheet down for my mother, Elise, and me and we looked up at a clear, blue sky. Elise was surrounded by her toys: building blocks, crayon and paper, her doll with the missing eyes, and several books, some of which I had given to her on her birthday. Bob Patterson came up the gravel drive, regaling us with news of emergency teams who were helping with the storm damage and the latest on when the river crossings could resume. The Shelley's soft drink truck came into view, but my mother took no notice. He waved frantically at her. She turned her back. Birds wandered on the lawns, pecking at scraps from the guests' sandwiches.

My mother was drinking tea in the morning sun, her thin legs stretched out in front of her, her head thrown back, looking at the sky. She lazily lifted an eyelid now and then to check on Elise. Ants crawled over my legs and I flicked them off. No one spoke for several minutes. Birds warbled and chirped, occasionally swooping down to pick at some morsel on the ground. The shade cloth over the cook's herb garden shone a bright green in the light of mid-morning. Sunita passed by with the sound of a swishing sari, bangles jangling and glinting in the sunlight. She carried a potted plant in her hand, which she gently dislodged from its pot, setting the pot on the ground and unwinding the long hose. The smell of jasmine filled the air. The sounds of saucepans crashing to the floor in the guesthouse kitchen woke my mother for a second before she closed her eyes again and then there was quiet. Two of the guests strolled by, deep in conversation. A woman picked flowers from the garden, ignoring the sign that asked guests not to do this. The Shelley's soft drink truck rolled softly down the drive and the cook's assistant crossed the lawn in the direction of the skip bins at the back of the guesthouse. The smell of cherry tarts baking wafted from the guesthouse kitchen. Elise drew little girl pictures in green crayon. A slight, sudden breeze stirred the bushes momentarily, and then all was still. It was the perfect moment.

'Look!' Elise cried. 'An ant.'

My mother gave a slow smile and extended an arm to pat the top of Elise's head.

'Mum,' I said. 'Are you all right?'

She took my hand in hers, her eyes still closed, and nodded slowly, as if the mere effort of doing that had exhausted her.

'Look, Siobhan,' exclaimed Elise, holding up a dead ant she'd squashed with her book.

I nodded at Elise. It was my mother's attention I wanted. I

thought back to what Bernadette Brennan had said. She said the best way to get my mother talking was when there were just the two of us. I wanted to talk about something that she liked, something that made her happy. I sat thinking of topics. An image of a campervan rolled in my head.

'Do you remember when you said that one day we'd go round the whole country? Even Tasmania. Do you?'

She nodded and opened an eye. 'One day, we'll go.'

'I'd like that,' I said. 'Just you and I and no one else.'

'Your father went round Australia.'

I said nothing, not wanting to break the moment. She so rarely mentioned him in front of me that it took me by surprise and I wanted more.

'Where did he go?'

'Everywhere, he went everywhere. Up north where he worked as a contractor on building sites, Perth, Adelaide, everywhere.'

She lapsed into silence once again, and I did not say anything for a while. I closed my eyes and let the sun fall over me, drinking in the sounds of birds and Elise's crayon scratching across paper. I sat like that for several minutes, not speaking. I was aware of people passing by, of shadows and light and the smells of the garden. The faint sound of Sunita's bangles came from over near the shade house.

'Once,' my mother said, 'long before Jack, I was engaged to another person. He wanted to live abroad where he had business, but things didn't turn out as I expected. Your grandmother became very ill not long after the engagement and I had to stay. He waited for some time but he couldn't put his plans on hold forever.'

She related the information in a matter-of-fact tone, as if she were reeling off a list of ingredients for a new recipe. Perhaps it was so far removed and in the past that it hardly mattered anymore. I opened my eyes. The sun was bright and strong.

Elise had walked over to the shade house where Sunita was hosing plants.

'Come back here, Elise.'

'I want to stay with Nita,' Elise shouted. 'I want to water.'

I could hear Sunita telling Elise to go back.

'Go on, I must go inside. I have some herbs to cook.'

Elise hovered for a moment, then started to walk over in our direction.

'What happened after that?'

My mother sighed before she answered. 'Sometimes, Siobhan, life doesn't turn out the way you plan. When your grandmother got better, I decided to join him but unfortunately, she became sick again and so I stayed. I received a letter to say that he had married a woman from New York and after that I never heard from him again, nor did I want to.'

'And what about Jack?'

Jack. I called him Jack. I never really knew him, but saying his name out loud suddenly made him real.

'Jack was the life of the party. He had lots of girls after him. He was very intelligent.'

Again, she rattled the sentences off in a perfunctory manner. There was no particular tone that gave away any indication of feelings.

'He was schizophrenic, but I didn't know that when I married him. And neither did he. He also had a drug problem. You know what that is, don't you? You're almost twelve now so I can start telling you things I think you need to know.'

I thought for a while. Life of the party, she had said. I didn't really like parties, although I'd only ever been to a few. I never had boys after me and I didn't consider myself intelligent and I had heard that drug taking killed people.

'Will I be a schizophrenic too?'

For the first time that morning, she laughed out loud, patting my head and telling me I wouldn't and that I was very smart for my age. She was quiet for a moment before she spoke again about it not necessarily being hereditary and then had to explain to me what that all meant. She lit a cigarette and held the smoke down in her usual manner. The barrier had been crossed. I felt like I could ask her all the things I had always wanted to.

'Is that what's wrong with Brenton?'

'Perhaps.'

'I remember Jack's bright orange shirts.'

My mother started to laugh again, stretching out on the groundsheet like a lizard in the sun. 'He had yellow and purple ones too!' she exclaimed.

'Why don't you like Bernadette Brennan?'

My mother drew in her cigarette smoke and opened her mouth. Her bottom jaw dropped slightly before she blew a ring of smoke, so circular, its proportions so symmetrical and so perfect that I wanted to open my mouth and swallow it. It hung for a moment, a defiant O shape, before quivering and finally breaking up to drift over my head. She opened an eye, half turning to me. It seemed as if she was thinking before answering, but suddenly she said, 'Where's Elise?'

The sun had retreated; it seemed to close in on itself, seeming smaller, greyer, and cold. The guests had left the veranda. Grey clouds were massing overhead. It was suddenly very quiet. I looked around and started to say something, but my mother was up in a flash. She dropped her cigarette on the ground without bothering to stamp it out. Turning toward the driveway, she motioned to me to go in the other direction. A few minutes before, Elise had been with Sunita in the shade house, so that was the first place I looked. The shade house was empty. The smell of fresh water on plants and herbs hung in the air. A coiled-up hose was at my feet like a sleeping snake. I came out from the shade house and I looked over at Esther. She looked like she was having a fit; her mouth was working, forming words that did not come out, and her hands were fluttering in distress. Her eyes were moving strangely, and her head jerked. I had no time to call anyone about Esther.

'Elise!' I yelled. I ran back into the shade house, knowing she wasn't there. I screamed out her name. I ran out.

'Esther, I can't come now, I'm sorry,' I cried out as I ran to the hedge bordering the garden, thinking Elise might be behind it. No one was there.

My mother rushed into the house and was back in the garden a few moments later. Sunita followed behind. The cook emerged, followed by Brenton, and my grandmother and Bob Patterson trailing behind. My mother went up to guests on the verandah. She asked them if they had seen Elise, but no one had seen her.

'I sent her back to you. She was right there walking toward you two. I went inside the house, but she was almost there. I wouldn't have left her, you know that,' Sunita exclaimed, her voice rising in anxiety.

'Did you see her?' my grandmother asked me.

I told her I had seen her walking toward us, but then I had turned my head to speak to my mother and we had been carried away in conversation.

'It was only for a minute,' I kept saying, feeling sick.

'I'll go and get the others,' Sunita said.

'Yes,' my mother yelled. 'The more helpers, the better. Start looking.'

My mother and I instinctively ran for the slope down to the river. We saw Walter Heather running down the slope as well, but he came from the eastern side. Our feet had no traction on the grass, slick with rain. We ran downhill, slipping on the ground, mud covering our clothes. Others were already down at the river, shouting, their faces distorted in the torrent of water that battered down. Bob Patterson was yelling out directions.

He split people up into groups, directing them where to search so that everyone wasn't looking in the same place at once.

For the next hour, we searched, all of us, including the staff and a few of the guests who had heard me yelling Elise's name. Returning to Gables without any sign of her, I could tell by the look in my grandmother's eyes that the situation had not changed. She said Bob Patterson had rung the emergency services and the police and they were on their way. My grandmother sat by the phone.

No one manned the reception desk in the guesthouse. Walter Heather searched the gardens and the sheds. I was ordered to look in the house and guesthouse while the others did the gardens and the gravel drive, which was quite long, and the side of the house and garden that faced the village. The cook had taken the pick-up and driven down the hill to see if the child had wandered off into the village. Jamilla was ordered to look in cupboards and spaces in the guesthouse.

Someone had wheeled Esther into the house; now she was in a state of distress but Olivia had joined in the search and so couldn't attend to her. I called out to her, telling her I would help her after we had found Elise. My chest was hurting and my heart beating so fiercely I was afraid I would not be able to run, but I managed to keep running, shouting out her name. Sarah Boatman, who had been informed, rang and cried drunkenly into the phone, saying the police were looking all over the village. I couldn't imagine how a three-year-old could make it down the hill into the village by herself without someone noticing. I felt like I wanted to die.

Finally, one of the guests said something that I had been thinking about for hours but didn't dare give voice to. He said that perhaps Elise had wandered down to the riverbank and had gone into the water. I wanted to hit him. The thought was just too awful to contemplate. Outside the French windows, I could see the darkening sky and streaks of lightning stabbing down.

Large spears of rain hurled themselves against the windows. Please, no more rain, I kept saying. Then the sky split open, and the rain pounded harder than ever. I offered up childish bargains to the sky; I promised God I would not lie about going to the Boatmans' while I was really at the Hovel, that I wouldn't eavesdrop, never treat Jamilla unkindly ever again, throw away the heathen statue Sunita had given me, not talk to Bernadette Brennan when I had been expressly told not to. All this in return for Elise. The words of the guest burned under my skin.

Once again, I started for the slope toward the riverbank, calling frantically. My mother ran after me, shouting at me to go back. Slipping over on the lawn, I started to cry and then continued to run, my heart beating wildly, my lungs aching. My mother was still running after me. Walter Heather was running too, but he was coming up the slope from the riverbank. He shouted something to me, gesticulating like a madman, but I ignored him. Crying and in pain, I ran down the slope to the river where Brenton was out in the dinghy, soaked through. He was standing up in the small boat, paddling with one oar, yelling into the rain, trying to keep his balance. He kept shouting for me to go back inside, motioning in the direction of the house, but I stood, frozen and dripping on the slope.

'Elise!' I screamed.

Chapter Fifteen

The next morning when I walked into the kitchen, the sight of Sarah Boatman startled me so much that I promptly turned and walked back out again. My grandmother pushed me back inside the kitchen, insisting that I eat breakfast as usual. The only problem was that nothing was usual. The house seemed to groan under the weight of what had happened. The night before, I felt its bones shudder as though they might break, its walls expanding and contracting in a death rattle of unbearable grief.

The local police and officers from the mainland had come the night before. Emergency Services, Police Rescue, and local residents had braved the storm to look for Elise. The search was called off eventually; visibility was too poor.

My mother and Sarah sat at the table, a teapot in front of them, two half-filled cups set to the side. A plate of biscuits lay untouched in the centre. The antiseptic smell of alcohol hung in the air. The radio babbled softly in the background. It wasn't tuned properly and every now and then the rasping sound of white noise punctuated the silence of the kitchen. I rose from my seat and twisted the dial. I needed something to do. I twisted it back and forth. Scraps of songs punctured the still-ness. In short bursts, they mocked us. Oh, Happy Day, belted out the gospel choir. My grandmother turned the radio off. She told me that Olivia had called in sick, so there were going to be a few extra chores for me to do.

Sarah sat swathed in a light grey tunic that morning, a turban of the same material on her head. The material was the crushable type. Sarah was crushed, the whole effect making her look like a scrunched-up tissue. Huge gold loops dangled from her earlobes. I couldn't understand Sarah's presence in our house. It seemed wrong, abnormal. I had expected frozen rela-tions between the Boatmans and my family, anger and resent-ment, and yet I saw neither from Sarah. Her bloodshot eyes looked as though she hadn't slept; a bottle of brandy was on the sideboard and I knew she had been drinking. My mother's hunched shoulders and bleary eyes told me she had been crying. She was dressed in black. Her coral lipstick had been applied hastily and crept over her lip line, leaving a frosty smear. Her shoes were under the table and she rubbed one foot against the other continually. The cook lumbered in from the hallway and placed a new brandy bottle on the kitchen table. She looked in Sarah's direction and tears filled her eyes. She mumbled some-thing in Russian under her breath. She placed a plate of pryaniki biscuits, something she only made at Christmas time, next to the brandy bottle. The sight of any biscuit turned my stomach.

My head was spinning with the unreality of what we were going through, but even so, our conversations swung from fearful murmurings about Elise and standard talk about everyday matters.

Can you get me some Panadol please? Yes, Mum. Sarah is coming over so make sure the kitchen is tidy. Yes, Mum. Can you ask Cook to bring in more brandy? And make sure Esther has taken her tablets. Olivia has called in sick this morning so you'll have to take over. Some stomach thing, that's why she was sick in the garden.

My mother and Sarah sat in silence; this was what disturbed me the most. I would have preferred it if they had been arguing, yelling, apologising, criticising—anything but silence. Every now and then, one or the other would start a slow, quiet sniffle. After a few minutes, this would lead to loud tears and then they would put their arms around each other and sob hysterically. The ashtray overflowed, dead butts floated in an ash grey sea, and Sarah was now tapping her cigarette into her saucer.

Audrey Landers sat next to my mother. She flicked through the pages of the Bible, frantically searching for just the right verse, the fat under her arms swinging in time with the pages as they flicked over. I looked at her legs, close to my mother's, under the table. Scrunched-up fat spilled over the sides of Audrey's black shoes in small layers. Her feet reminded me of Hassellback potatoes. Her thick ankles in their brown socks grounded her like her beliefs: solid, salt of the earth. My mother's reed-thin legs looked as though they might snap at any moment. They were brittle, delicate, hairless. The Hassellback potato feet tapped out a rhythm on the pale carpet. Audrey rose once to open the window; a curtain of smoke escaped from the kitchen, and then she sat and flicked the pages over again.

Audrey spoke to my grandmother before she left. There was much to be done. A prayer circle for Olivia and Sarah. A working bee of cooking for both families, food that could be frozen as well. Prayer circles, frozen casseroles, and kindness, the hallmarks of tragedy. Audrey was an expert in this department, a veteran of funerals, wakes, and the aftercare of the family in the eye of the storm, and later, post funeral. She was needed. People looked to her for reassurance, for an explanation where there was none, for some kernel of hope when everything seemed hopeless. Audrey irritated my grandmother. My grandmother knew that Audrey's comments were meant only in a spirit of kindness, but they always had the result of making my grandmother feel quite not up to scratch.

'I've got the perfect patch to mend that hole in those curtains,' she'd say. 'I'll bring it over.'

'My word, that cistern doesn't sound like it's doing its job properly.'

'Goodness me, that's a huge stain. I've got just the thing to get rid of it.'

Moving around the kitchen, preparing food I couldn't stomach, I tried to be as quiet as possible. My mother looked up occasionally and relayed small, domestic details: I'd have to get milk from the guesthouse kitchen, the marmalade was almost empty, and Esther needed her breakfast. It seemed surreal. Elise was missing, feared drowned, abducted, or dead, and my mother was talking about marmalade. I was hoping that Sunita would stay in her room, as I was worried that perhaps Sarah would blame Sunita for walking into the house before Elise had actually reached my mother and me on that day.

However, when Sunita came into the kitchen to rummage through a shelf in the pantry, Sarah rose from her chair and they embraced each other for several minutes. The bangles on Sunita's arms jangled as she rubbed her arms up and down Sarah's back. I couldn't bear to look.

For the next few minutes, I busied myself blending up porridge and fruit for Esther, but she pushed it aside when I presented it to her and put her drawing book into my hands. Pretending to read the long scrawly writing, I stayed like that for several minutes and then tears came. It didn't matter what I said to Esther, she couldn't understand, and so I expressed my remorse and self-hatred out loud. Esther held out her gnarled hand and closed it over mine. Her head fell back and she appeared to sleep, so I carefully extracted her hand so as not to wake her. It touched me that she recognised tears, even if she did not understand the source of my misery.

Sunita noticed I wasn't eating when I returned to the kitchen. She didn't say anything but went again to the shelf of Indian medicines and herbs and took down several small packets. Being as quiet as she could, she pounded the ingredients with a mortar and pestle, boiled the jug, and made up a pungent smelling tea, which she placed in front of me. My grandmother came in and out of the room, poured herself a cup of tea, and took two biscuits from the plate on the table. The smell of the tea wafted round the kitchen, strong and brackish.

Sarah put her head in her hands and sighed. Audrey leaned forward and put her hand on Sarah's arm.

'Sarah, if the Lord has decided to take Elise home...'

'Audrey,' Sarah whispered, 'I want Elise to come home with me—now. She has a home. Do you understand?'

Audrey was not discouraged. Rather, she found new resolve. 'Listen, Sarah, to the words of the Lord,' she said. 'And when he cometh home, he calleth together his friends and neighbours, saying unto them: Rejoice with me, for I have found my sheep which was lost.'

Sarah poured more brandy into a cup. My mother followed suit.

Audrey placed her hand on Sarah's. 'You will see her in the next life, if you believe.'

'I want her in this life,' Sarah said, and drained her cup.

'We're having a special prayer service in the church at three,' Audrey said.

My grandmother had just finished pouring out more tea when Dot Patterson burst into the kitchen. Her hair was soaking, her body shaking, and for a while her incomprehensible babble hung in the air, waiting for someone to decipher it.

'It's Olivia,' she shouted. 'She put her head in the oven. She took the pie out. She took the pie out.'

Dot stood frozen on the spot. She had been so intent on her own mission of imparting the news about Olivia that she hadn't noticed who was in the kitchen and the reason they were there. She looked from Sarah to my mother and back to my grandmother, realising that she had walked into a room thick with grief, only to spread even more of it.

'What pie? Dot Patterson, get a hold of yourself!' said my grandmother.

My grandmother took Dot by the hand and led her into the lounge room away from the kitchen and indicated to her to sit. I followed them, expecting my grandmother to tell me to go away, but she didn't. Brenton walked in after me and then Sunita joined us as well.

'She took it out,' said Dot. She breathed heavily. 'And she put her head in and it was just lucky that the police came around and found her just in time because they wanted to ask John something, you know because of what happened with that little girl but...'

'You mean she tried to gas herself?' asked Brenton, his eyes widening.

Dot sat and closed her eyes until her breathing returned to normal. Sunita placed a glass of water in her hand and motioned everyone to stop asking questions. After a gulp of water that dripped down her dress, Dot sat back in her chair and sighed. She picked up her handbag from the floor and plucked out a sheet of paper, fanning herself.

'I knew she was having problems, but I didn't think she'd do that.'

'So, that's why she called in sick,' Brenton said. 'Where is she now?'

'At home. She refused to go to hospital. Reg Dalton came straight away. Anyway, John Newmark's been cleared. Had an alibi, backed up by people in the pub.'

'Who's going to look after Esther?' my grandmother asked.

'I will,' said Sunita.

My grandmother turned to Sunita, her face drained of colour. 'Thank you,' she said.

After Sarah and Audrey had gone, two detectives from the mainland arrived by seaplane to interview my mother and me. My mother insisted we sit in the back room, away from the kitchen. She took her highball glass and snatched up her cigarettes from the table. I took a tray of coffee and biscuits into the room. The detectives gave me a wan smile. They were questioning my mother as I entered.

'And your husband?' one of them was asking. 'Was he present?'

My mother sucked in her cigarette and touched her hair. She twisted the wedding band on her finger. She said nothing for a few seconds while I placed the tray on the table. She tugged at the hem of her skirt and crossed her legs.

'Separated,' she finally said.

She waited. The detectives felt her embarrassment. Then, as if to correct the impression that she was the inadequate one, she said, 'I could stand by my man, but he couldn't stand by me. Literally. He had both his legs amputated. It was just too difficult.'

I half expected my grandmother to pop her head round the door and explain that it didn't stop him from using his third leg, but no one appeared. My mother adjusted her skirt and fiddled with an earring. She looked from one detective to the other.

'These things happen,' the older detective murmured. The younger-looking detective, quite out of his depth, tried to look busy, scribbling into his notepad.

He motioned to me to sit, saying he had a few questions.

He questioned me about small details. Anything you can remember, no matter how small, he kept saying. He asked the same questions many times over, but in different ways. He asked if I'd seen anything unusual and then he asked if I'd seen anybody talking to Elise just before my mother and I realised she was not with us.

I answered the questions truthfully, but the truth was slippery. I thought about the perfect moment. It was Bernadette's fault. I thought about how wrong that moment was. It was my fault. No, it was my mother's fault for not paying attention. No, it was Sunita's fault. She should have walked Elise back from the shade house to my mother and me. Some part of my brain put several pieces together, and they collided, smashing into each other, making sense, making up a history that I wanted to be real. Biscuit tin images; he's overly fond of children. I opened my mouth. I spoke from the pit of my stomach.

'I saw Mr Heather with Elise.'

My mother sat forward with a jerk and frowned at me. 'That's not true,' she said. Her voice was sharp and anxious.

The detective held up a hand, motioning for my mother to be quiet. He nodded, waiting for me to continue. 'Go on,' he said.

'I saw him with Elise, I did. He had his biscuit tin with him.'

'When *exactly* did you see Mr Heather with Elise?'

I told him I had seen Walter Heather coming up the slope from the riverbank as I was running down.

My mother cleared her throat noisily.

'You said you saw Elise with him?' the detective asked me.

'I saw him running down with her and then he was running back by himself.'

'For God's sake, what's got into you?' my mother cried.

I looked at my mother. Her eyes were frozen and angry. She twisted an earring and squirmed in her chair. For the next half an hour, they questioned me while I sat, my heart racing as the lie got bigger and bigger until I felt like I could no longer control it; it seemed to have a life of its own. They were particularly interested in the biscuit tin pictures and told my mother that they were going to ask me some very delicate questions. Can you describe what you saw in the pictures, they asked. I sat for some moments. I couldn't say the names of the body parts. A red rash crept up my neck and spread all over my face, and then an idea came to me in a flash.

'Well, you know those pictures in the biscuit tin. It's the same thing, like what people do, you know what I mean, except one of them doesn't want to do it, so the other uses force. Understand?'

Both men nodded slowly.

'Siobhan, why didn't you tell us this yesterday?'

'I don't know,' I said. 'I was scared.'

They rose to leave, telling my mother that they may want to talk to me again, but I wanted them to stay. I wanted them to stay forever and listen to my stories and write it all down as though it was the most important thing in the world. I wanted my mother to understand what an astute observer I was. What an amazing, clever child she had. I wanted her to notice me. I wanted them all to notice me.

'It was an Arnott's tin,' I said desperately.

One of the men scribbled quickly on his notepad. My mother's face was set in hard lines and I told them I couldn't remember anything else. When they finally left, we heard them telling my grandmother they would need access to Walter Heather's storeroom. We watched as they took away the biscuit tin and some magazines. My mother turned to me. I expected an angry outburst, but her voice was low and calm. She looked straight at me, as though I was someone she didn't recognise.

'You are a *liar*,' she said.

I couldn't reply. She ripped a cigarette out of the packet and placed it in her mouth. Leaving it unlit, she spoke through tight lips, her arms crossed over her chest.

'Lies like that can ruin people's lives,' she said slowly.

'I saw the pictures in the biscuit tin,' I retorted.

'You may have. That's not what I'm talking about. You did not see Mr Heather with Elise.'

All of a sudden, tears were pricking at my eyes, but I tried to keep them back.

'He could have taken Elise down to the river. He could have followed her. You saw him coming up from the river, up the slope.'

My mother rose from her chair, stepped forward, and looked down at me.

'Yes, I did, but that was because he was *looking* for her, like the rest of us. That isn't the issue either. Yes, he could have and so could anyone else, a guest, a delivery man, a passer-by. We both saw him run down the slope. He was by himself. We both saw him come up the slope. By himself. The issue is that you lied. You did not *see* Elise with him because *I was there*.'

My mother enunciated the last three words as though she was teaching someone English and expected them to repeat the words back to her.

In that moment I hated her. She'd reduced me to something insignificant. My story was worthless. I was worthless.

'The Shelley's soft drink man took her. I saw him!' I cried.

My mother stepped toward me, her eyes wide. 'What did you just say?'

She stood over me, demanding I repeat what I had just said. I stood motionless, saying nothing. She slapped my face; the sting, shocking and sudden, burned into my cheek. She turned and walked out of the room.

That evening, Bob Patterson and Dot came over again. My grandmother busied herself with the drinks tray, trying to stay in control. She fussed over martinis and ordered me to get cakes and savouries from the kitchen. My mother was filling her high-ball glass like she was drinking water on a hot day. Her words grew more slurred, she dropped ash all over the carpet, and couldn't seem to walk properly in her high heels. My grand-mother ushered everyone into the formal dining room on the southern side of the house, which afforded them a view of the garden. She drew back the curtains.

My mother drew me aside. 'The police know you're lying,' she said.

She walked toward the tray of appetisers on the sideboard, loping and slurring her words. My grandmother watched her, her face giving nothing away. She smiled at Dot Patterson.

'We're all a bit under the weather,' she said.

I wondered if the news of Olivia's suicide attempt had made its way down to the village. I wondered if my best friend knew. I hadn't heard from Boatman and I was actually relieved. I didn't know what to say. Guilt flooded through me, the only feeling I was capable of producing. I sat drinking my awful tea, wishing I were dead. Bernadette Brennan had told me over and over again that it was no one's fault, but she didn't sound confident about it. Perhaps she apportioned some of the blame to herself for telling me to choose a moment and talk to my mother. Or perhaps she blamed my mother and just couldn't say it out loud. I thought about that much, much later.

I remember wishing that I could turn back the clock, just one day. Images floated through my head like a movie on a continuous loop, but they were heavily edited and the ending was quite pleasant. It was a sunny day; the rain had stopped for a while. My mother sat out on the lawn, in her cane chair from the veranda, her head thrown back to the sun, her legs stretched out. A cup of milky tea and two biscuits on a plate were beside her. I came and sat down next to her. The grass was still wet, but we sat on a groundsheet, picnic-like. She told me all about my father and we laughed and talked while Elise played with the hose, wetting Sunita. Sunita sent Elise back to us, where she played with her toys until it was lunchtime. We all went inside and had smoked ham sandwiches and tomatoes and chocolate milk. My mother put on Vivaldi's *Four Seasons*. She hummed at the top of her voice.

But it wasn't like that. Not at all.

Elise swam through my dreams at night, under water, perfectly dry. She glided through the mud and silt, pushing leaves and branches out of her way. She had a smile on her face. I'd wake, think about what day it was and what I had to do, and suddenly the reality would hit me a few seconds later. Elise was missing, feared abducted or drowned, and my stomach would start to tie itself in knots.

Jamilla woke me at three in the morning on the second night. 'Have they found her yet?'

I told her to go back to sleep.

'It's not my mother's fault,' she whispered.

'It's not my mother's fault either,' I hissed back at her.

'Why did Olivia try to kill herself?'

'Because her husband is overly fond of children. He went to jail.'

'Shit,' Jamilla said. 'So, you reckon he took Elise?'

'No. He didn't. Bob Patterson said Olivia's husband is in the clear.'

Jamilla gave a long groan and shuffled her bedspread. 'I hate this house,' she said.

'Then go back to bloody India,' I retorted.

Jamilla threw her pillow at me, but not before she reminded me that she was born in Australia. You're a bitch. You murdered Elise, she told me.

On the fourth day, I manned the reception desk, but there wasn't much to do. There were no new bookings for the guest-house because nobody could get on and off Rachley Island. In his spare moments, Brenton often poked his head around the kitchen door, offering to make tea or asking if there was anything he could do. Sunita frowned at him and her eyes widened, giving him the signal that he was not wanted in the room. He spent a lot of time looking lost and sighing, roaming around the house looking for something to do. Whenever the bell in reception rang, he would practically run into the guest-house, grateful for a distraction, no matter how small. At one point, he started knocking on the doors of the guests' rooms, asking if they needed anything, until my grandmother barked at him to leave the guests alone. Once he realised nobody needed him for anything, he sank into a torpor behind the desk and tried to read.

Sarah came that morning and after she left, my mother sat in the back room and played mournful country music. She sang along with Tammy Wynette. Stand by your man, they advised us, soulful sisters, bonded by pain and sacrifice. What man? My father with the amputated legs? The Shelley's soft drink man? Brenton tried to drown it out with Black Sabbath, but Tammy won out in the end. I tried to get my mother to play some classics. She blew smoke around the room, finished one cigarette and lit another with the butt of the last one. Her coughing hacked and slashed at the air, announcing her presence before she entered a room.

My mother had been over to the Boatmans' house, but I was not allowed to go with her. I heard her tell Sunita that Sarah couldn't bear going into Elise's room. Dan Boatman's conductor's ruler lay on top of Strauss's waltzes, untouched. At one of Audrey's prayer circles, we listened to Reverend Landers read verses about children from the Bible. I drifted off and thought about the Hovel. I had to hold Dot's clammy hand in mine while we joined hands to say the final prayer. When the singing started, my mother's voice rose above the others, competing and finally outdoing them. Audrey had said it wasn't good to end on a negative note and so we sang a totally inappropriate song with no connection to the missing girl. Evil is everywhere, Audrey told us. We must fight it with every bone in our bodies.

I'm in the Lord's army,
Yes, Sir!
I'm in the Lord's army,

Yes, Sir!

Jamilla sang loudly, only too happy to be in the Lord's army, the song and its rousing chorus cementing her rejection of her mother's Hindu beliefs. Yes, Sir! she shouted with enthusiasm. She had the stories about her father weaselling his way out of the regular army years ago and he was not eager to be re-conscripted into any army, even the Lord's, but Jamilla had found, even if was just for one night, a way of identifying even more with Anglo-Celtic mores. She happily put on the cloaks of righteousness and the shields of faith that Audrey was dolling out like costumes for extras in a Roman epic.

'You should have seen our little girl singing tonight,' my grandmother told Sunita when we arrived home.

My grandmother's tone told Sunita that Presbyterianism had triumphed.

'I'm in the Lord's arh-mee,' sang Jamilla, stuffing a biscuit into her mouth and giving her mother a pointed look.

'Good. Good. Spiritual warfare is important,' Sunita said. 'It doesn't matter what form it takes. Evil is everywhere. Now we must all say prayers for the safe return of Elise.'

'Fuck,' said Brenton and put his head in his hands.

It seemed the only thing to do was wait and so we waited, while the rain fell, heavier and heavier, as the hours dragged by and our hopes fell with it. Bob Patterson rang to say the police divers could not go into the river. It was too dangerous. The ferocity of the storm had turned the river into a seething, frothy serpent. Debris floated everywhere, churned up by the wind and rain. Visibility was poor in a storm and impossible under water in such conditions, the sergeant from the mainland informed us.

On that fourth morning, Josh arrived to take Sarah home. It was the first time he had been in our house for many years. He was agitated. He seemed impatient to go, refusing offers of food and drink and motioning to his mother to get her things so they could return home.

'Come on,' he kept saying.

I looked up at him once and was taken aback to find him staring at me with cold eyes. His mouth was set in a sneer. He knows, he knows it was my fault, I thought. Various things spun round in my head, things to say to him but, in the end, nothing seemed appropriate. I felt his hatred toward me.

A break in the rain raised hopes that the police divers could now go down to the river. Abduction had been ruled out. The wind was still up, whipping leaves off trees and sending empty Coke cans scudding across the grass. Walter Heather dashed out onto the lawn, chasing the cans and flying chip packets. The topiary bushes stood firm against the wind in a united hedge, unbending, while around them plants, trees, and bushes shuddered. Boatman arrived at the back door. She put her head into the kitchen; she saw the raw grief, the ashtray overflowing, the clink of ice-cubes in tall glasses, the smell of gin and despair.

'I'm really sorry,' I whispered. 'Please don't hate me.'

'Let's go out for a walk,' she said to me.

'Don't go too far,' Sunita said.

We only got as far as the front veranda. We stopped at the sight of the police pushing Walter Heather's head down into a police car.

The rain suddenly stopped. It didn't even ease off. There was no wind or light, just overcast dullness, grey clouds with thin strips of white underneath. We turned the radio up and waited for news and not about clouds or rain. We wanted to see for ourselves how far up the water had come. We wanted to see whether police divers were down at the river, but we had been told to keep away. The police had come to speak to my mother again, and we were all banished from the kitchen.

My mother was in there with them for two hours and three

minutes. I couldn't imagine what they had to talk about for that length of time. When she emerged, she didn't say anything. They asked me the same questions they had previously asked, and I gave them the same answers I had given them the first time. I couldn't go back on my lie. It was too big. The problem was that at times I was beginning to believe my own lie. Then confusion clouded my thinking. Had I seen Walter Heather? Was Elise with him? Or was it someone who looked like him? I could say that I thought it was Walter Heather but maybe it was just someone who looked like him. It was difficult to see in all that rain, I could say. I felt like putting the Shelley's soft drink man into the picture as well, but I didn't. My mother had not told my grandmother about my lie, and I was fearful that all would come out. Walter Heather had still not returned.

At three o'clock at the Boatmans' that afternoon, the phone rang and our world fell apart. Elise had been found. A police diver had found her body in the river a few hours earlier. Sarah had made a positive identification. My mother nodded slowly when the news was broken to her, her face expressionless. She lit a cigarette, went into the back room, and shut the door. Sunita knocked several times and then left her alone. Minutes later, we heard loud classical music coming from her room.

A dreadful hush fell over the house and guesthouse. The guests padded down the carpeted corridors upstairs, speaking in whispers. Sunita prayed in front of her statue.

'We have to keep going,' my grandmother said, but she didn't sound as though she believed it was possible. I went to find Bernadette Brennan to tell her, but she had already been told. A candle was burning in a small brown holder with a picture of a saint next to it.

'Candles and cigarettes aren't allowed in guest's rooms, they might cause a fire, that's my grandmother's rule,' I blurted out stupidly and then dissolved into tears.

Bernadette said sometimes rules have to be broken. We sat

on her bed and she asked me to tell her some of the beautiful things I remembered about Elise. I can't remember what I told her but I remember her saying, 'Yes, that's lovely. What else do you remember?'

At six o'clock, Brenton kicked in the door of my mother's room as she had not answered anyone calling on the other side. Sunita had said she was fearful of my mother taking too many sleeping pills and not being able to wake. Over a crashing cacophony of cymbals and cellos, Brenton was suddenly screaming for an ambulance. He emerged from the back room, panting, my mother in his arms, her wrists bound with socks, Brenton's Rachley Soccer Club sport socks with the blue stripes. Brenton carried my mother to the lounge, where he dropped her lifeless form. After what seemed an eternity, medical help arrived. The ambulance staff, one man and one woman, shooed everyone from the room. Eventually, the door opened. My mother was on a stretcher, her face pale grey. The ambulance staff lifted her inside their vehicle. My grandmother told me to pack a bag for my mother and to be quick about it.

'Don't pack too much,' she told me pointedly, as if my mother would be back the next day. 'Pack her grey dress with the stripes,' she told me, as if my mother would be attending a job interview in a corporate office.

Sunita grabbed my arm and pushed me into my mother's room, where we hastily wrenched clothes from cupboards and scrabbled through drawers, throwing assorted garments onto the bed before deciding what would go into a bag.

Sunita helped me pack toiletries, underclothes, a tracksuit, a pair of linen pants and three shirts. An ambulance was parked outside, right in front of the guesthouse. Naturally, an ambulance drew the guests' attention and within a short time, a crowd had assembled on the lawn and out on the veranda. Some of the guests were drinking cocktails as they watched, the brightly coloured liquid and the gaudy cocktail umbrellas at odds with what was unfolding before them. I wanted to scream at them all to go inside. The staff came out from the kitchen, the cook and her assistant sobbing uncontrollably. My grand-mother stood, tight-lipped, her arms folded across her chest. She looked defiant, but I was standing next to her and she was shaking.

'We're ruined,' she said.

The ambulance turned sharply on the gravel drive. I lingered a bit longer than the rest of the crowd until my grandmother finally told me to go inside.

'Go get Esther her dinner,' she said.

If it weren't for Sunita and Bernadette Brennan, I would have been lost in confusion over the following days. Both took time to explain that my mother was suffering from guilt over Elise's death and that she blamed herself. Both told me that guilt can muck up stuff in people's heads.

'But it wasn't her fault,' I said.

'Of course, it wasn't,' Sunita said.

'It was my fault.'

'It wasn't your fault. It was an accident,' Bernadette Brennan said.

I wanted my mother back, that's all I knew.

That night when I took Esther her dinner, she didn't want to eat. I stood, the spoon poised in mid-air, then dropped it onto the plate and started to cry.

'Esther,' I whispered. 'I've done something awful.'

Telling Esther was not difficult; she wouldn't understand anything I said. Boatman had told me that when she did some-thing awful, she went to confession at her church. Our church didn't have confession, but I understood what Boatman meant when she said she came out feeling better. I poured out my story to Esther. I told her about how I distracted my mother and Elise wandered off. I told her about blaming Walter Heather because I'd seen dirty photographs in the storeroom. She listened while I described how Brenton examined the photographs, looking for any that had children in them. I told her how everything came together in my head. I put my head in Esther's lap and cried. When I had no more tears left, I sat up.

Esther sat in her chair, shaking her head from side to side.

We were allowed to visit my mother in hospital on the mainland. The room was dark and smelled of mould. Brenton tried to make light banter with the nurses, while I cringed in embarrassment. He spoke to the doctor, but their conversation was about things I couldn't follow. My mother told us she was feeling better, and that Sarah had visited that morning and Elise's funeral would be arranged as soon as her body was released by the coroner. Sarah said she wanted my mother and the family to be there for the funeral. I didn't like listening to talk of funerals. It didn't seem real. They had played rock music at Billy's send off. It's what he would have wanted, they said. How could they know what Elise would have wanted?

The next time I saw my mother was a few days later in a psychiatric unit attached to a hospital on the mainland. Sunita, Brenton, and I walked down endless corridors of white until we turned into a wing called the Turner Centre. It was most un-hospital-like. The centre housed a games room, a kitchen where patients could make their own tea and coffee, and gardens not unlike those at Gables. No one would tell me why, but they would only say it was for the best that she did not come home for a while. A doctor, who spoke at length to Sunita, said there was a chance she would be able to attend Elise's funeral but would have to come back as soon as the funeral was over. My mother was not in bed. She sat in a chair in her room, watching television. Looking tired and struggling to keep her eyes open, she was nevertheless glad to see us.

'What about the coroner's report?' she asked Sunita.

Sunita took my mother's hand. 'She drowned, Margaret. She wasn't interfered with. The autopsy confirmed it. The river took her.'

When Sunita bent over to kiss her goodbye, my mother whispered that there'd be certain things she'd take with her to her grave. Let's not talk about that now, Sunita told her.

I was stunned to hear that my mother would be going to Elise's funeral; it somehow didn't seem right. I knew that Sarah had insisted on it, but I didn't think it would actually happen. Deep down, I felt that it was my mother's fault; her fault for being distracted while distracting her was my fault. Mother and daughter, bound together in negligence.

The day of Elise's funeral was a blur. I knew how difficult it was for my grandmother, Sunita, and Brenton to attend, but they could hardly have done anything else. Sarah had insisted on their attendance. She had rung two nights before the funeral to speak to my grandmother and had reminded her that it was important for us to go. I still couldn't believe that the Boatmans harboured no malice toward us, and I was waiting for it all to blow up in our faces. The cold look that Josh Boatman had given me wasn't an indication of the feelings of the rest of his family. On several occasions before the day of the funeral, I'd had bad dreams where Josh strode through the rain and stood at the top of garden. Fucking murderers, he screamed. The Montrells are murderers.

Esther wasn't going to the funeral. A temp nurse had been employed to wash, dress, and medicate her for that day. On the morning of the funeral, the nurse informed my grandmother that in her professional opinion, Esther should be put in a nursing home. My grandmother replied that if all people like

Esther were put in special homes, then people like the nurse would be out of a job.

It seemed to take all morning to prepare for the church service. My grandmother made me change clothes at least four times. She said the blue skirt and white top were too happy looking, the pinafore dress had red checks in it—inappropriate for a funeral, she said—and the pale blue was unsuitable. Not serious enough, she told me.

'Sombre colours,' she snapped.

I had to ask Brenton what sombre meant. I found a brown dress that I hadn't worn for several seasons in the back of the cupboard. It was too small for me because I was growing in the chest, but it was the only dark colour I had. It was so tight I felt like I was going to faint in the church. Jamilla wore a brown dress too. We looked like a pair of dead leaves. Brenton had to borrow a suit from someone in the village at the last minute, which caused a terrible argument. My grandmother kept muttering under her breath about him not organising himself a suit for a funeral, so how could he possibly organise a soup business. The day started badly; tension was in the air from the minute we rose in the morning.

My family sat at the back of the church with some of the staff. My mother sat next to me, all in black, and Jamilla sat on the other side. Sunita was not wearing a sari. A navy-blue suit was in its place and her hair was pinned up in a roll. Brenton sat next to Sunita, and Olivia was next to her. I was surprised that Sunita knew all the words to the hymns without looking once in the hymnbook. My mother seemed vague and disoriented and at one point asked me where we were. Bernadette Brennan sat in the pew in front of us, her hair in a simple ponytail with a black bow. The heat was unbearable, pushed around the tiny church by two large fans that made little difference to the humidity. I used a piece of paper as a fan, folding it over and over until I had achieved perfect creases, then realised it was the Order of

Service. There was a picture of Elise on the front. The creases ran all over Elise's face. I crumpled it up and hoped no one had noticed.

Bob Patterson and Dot sat in the middle of the room, the mayor flanking them on one side with Audrey and Dave Landers on the other. The boys from my school were well behaved that day. Miss Abercrombie, principal of the school, sat near some of them, as if her presence was enough to cast a school-like atmosphere of order. From time to time, she would crane her neck around and cast her eyes over the congregation, picking out students, noting their presence. People sat with stiff backs and eyes to the front.

As the Boatmans made their way up to the front, the congregation rose from their seats in respect. My best friend looked at me and gave a sad smile, and I felt my legs give way underneath me. My mother pulled me up and took a butterscotch lolly out of her purse. I sat back down again, softly crunching, watching the backs of the Boatmans as they took their seats. Sarah was swathed in black; a black dress with a large overlay of netting, completed with a wide-brimmed black hat with a veil coming down to her chin. For once, her pale face was devoid of make-up. Dan Boatman didn't look right in a suit. I was so used to seeing him in overalls and work boots with grease-covered hands that at first I didn't recognise him. I almost expected him to stand up with his conductor's ruler when the music began. I didn't dare look at Josh. His cold eyes had frightened me that night in the kitchen. I had asked Jamilla if she thought he was good-looking. She told me he was nothing special. The Boatman children trailed behind their parents. Their faces gave nothing away; they had done this three years earlier. They knew what to do.

While the priest was talking, I tried to remember Elise's face and found that I could not. I closed my eyes and concentrated. Still, I could not conjure up her image and when I kept failing to do so, I began to quietly panic. I knew the crumpled Order of Service with the picture of Elise was on the seat beside me, but I couldn't bear to look at it again. I kept my eyes closed and concentrated. A blurry image appeared in my mind, like a photo developing in the tray. I waited for sharpness and clarity and after a while I saw the blonde curls, the dimples, the blue eyes, and then I wanted the service to be over. Dread filled me up, thinking about what would happen after the church service ended.

The priest told us the Lord was with Elise on the day she died. He read from Isaiah 43:2. 'When you pass through the waters, I will be with you. And when you pass through the rivers, they will not overflow you.'

I turned to Brenton and frowned. He understood immediately.

'It only overflowed her literally,' he whispered. 'It didn't overflow her soul.'

Before the service ended, Sarah rose from her pew. She walked slowly up to the front. When she had composed herself, she thanked the congregation, the community, everyone who had joined in the search. She didn't cry. She stood still, looked out at the mourners, and told them she would be reunited with her lost sheep one day.

'Both of them,' she said.

Reverend Landers and Audrey nodded with approval. Stifled sobs wafted up from those in the pews. My mother uncharacteristically took my hand and squeezed it so hard I almost cried out in pain. Brenton closed his eyes.

I didn't know what to expect, how people would react after we came out of the church. The thought of my mother staying to mingle with the mourners after the service was something I didn't want to see, and the thought of Sunita doing the same compounded my fear. I had visions of the mourners standing in small groups saying, 'That's her, that's the one,' and pointing at my mother or at Sunita. And at me.

When we emerged into the sunlight, Boatman came straight over. Distressed relatives were hugging Sarah and Dan. The girls from school stood in tight groups. I felt their stares from a distance. People's faces were contorted with grief. Josh Boatman stood to one side with a sour expression on his face, the same expression I had seen when he came to pick up Sarah from our house. For a split second, I had a fantasy of going over and hugging Josh Boatman, of him saying all was forgiven, that it was just one of those things that happen, that it was an accident.

When Bernadette Brennan emerged from the church, my first impulse was a feeling of anger. If you hadn't told me to pick the perfect moment, I wouldn't have talked to my mother and distracted her. If my mother hadn't been distracted, she would have been concentrating on Elise. It's all your fault. I knew this wasn't true. I needed someone to blame.

Then guilt and shame washed over me. Thinking those thoughts on the day of Elise's funeral.

Outside, after the service, no one was pointing fingers or staring. Boatman and I looked at each other, not knowing what to say.

'Mum made her own outfit,' she finally said.

'It's nice,' I replied.

There were a few seconds of silence.

'Do you hate me?' I asked.

'Don't be silly,' she said. 'Mum said it was an accident.'

Josh called Boatman over.

'See you at the Hovel,' she whispered.

I tugged at my mother's sleeve, wanting desperately to go. She stood, resolute, until most of the mourners had drifted away, and when she saw that Sarah was finally alone, she walked over. I turned away, feeling apprehensive, and sought out Jamilla, who was standing outside the church door, eager to go. In the next few minutes, Jamilla and I talked to fill up space, talked to overcome the shame, averting our eyes from the scene in front of us. Boatman's words were spinning in my head. It was an accident. Was it, really? Part of me didn't believe my best friend. I was waiting; waiting for the moment when she'd unleash the full fury of her anger on the girl who'd distracted her mother, who had in turn not paid attention to a child in her care. It was an accident. It was an accident. I repeated the words under my breath. I was shaking.

Jamilla and I had nothing left to say to each other. We turned to face the two women, both of us nervous. There was nothing to be afraid of, however. Sarah and my mother conversed for a few minutes and then Sunita joined them. To this day, I have no idea what was said, but I know there was no animosity as they parted with hugs and weak smiles. It was the last my mother and Sarah ever saw of each other. Before my mother left to go back to Gables before returning to hospital, there was one last person she wanted to speak to. Again, I have no idea what she and Bernadette Brennan discussed, but I imagined it was not something pleasant, judging by the look on my mother's face. I remember feeling terribly sad that the two people I loved most in the world didn't seem to like each other at all. At one point, their voices were raised. Bernadette put her hand on my mother's arm, but my mother shook it off.

When we arrived back home, my grandmother told us to change our clothes. My mother said she wanted to stay as she was. Out of respect, she told us.

'We're not donning sackcloth and ashes for the next week or even for a day. Life must go on.'

'But it doesn't have to go on straight away,' I blurted out.

'I'm staying in my black,' my mother said. She went to the sideboard, opened the bottle of gin, and poured a generous amount into her glass.

That night I couldn't sleep. I thrashed around in my bed, trying not to think about Elise in that small brown box. It seemed unreal that Elise lay inside it.

'Your mother shouldn't smoke at a funeral. It's not respectful,' Jamilla suddenly said.

'Shut up. You don't know anything. What's wrong with your eyelashes?'

Jamilla suddenly leaned over from her bed across the room. 'I'm sorry about the smoking thing. I'd smoke too if it helped.'

'It's all right. Go to sleep,' I said.

'I can't sleep. I keep thinking about Elise's ghost. Mr Heather said there is no such thing. He said there's not even a God.'

Now it was me who leaned across. 'You shouldn't go talking to him. I'm not allowed to, so neither should you.'

'Why not? He's just an old man.'

'He isn't,' I said.

'Rubbish,' said Jamilla. 'He wouldn't hurt a fly. He's all right.'

'He isn't,' I insisted furiously.

'Well, what is he then? Give me a reason.'

And suddenly I wanted something to fill up the space where so much grief and guilt were taking up room, something so huge it would push the events of the last few days aside and make way for something else. And on top of that, I wanted authority over Jamilla.

'He really did kill the peacock. I saw him.'

Jamilla was silent for a few seconds. 'You're lying,' she said.

'Don't believe me then, I don't care,' I said and ruffled the sheets noisily. I turned to the wall and feigned sleep. The act of aborting the conversation had the effect I wanted it to.

'Really? You really saw it? What happened?'

'He caught it when he was feeding it down near the hedge.

He grabbed hold of it and wrung its neck. Real quick. Snap, just like that. It didn't even make a sound.'

'But why? Why would he kill such a beautiful bird?'

Now I was on a roll. I couldn't stop. Jamilla sat up in bed, hanging on my every utterance.

'He needed the blood. He drinks animal blood. He does occult stuff. Remember how I told you about the dirty photos he has? Well, he used the blood and the photos in a ritual.'

I dragged out the word. Rit-u-al. I'd only learned it that morning.

'He rubs himself with the blood, he gets excited and he looks at the photos.'

'You're making me feel sick,' said Jamilla. 'And how come you haven't told anyone?'

A note of suspicion crept into her voice. I had to think quickly. The world of everyday routine fell away as I plunged into fantasy. I was having fun. Jamilla was now sitting on my bed.

'Because he said that if I told anyone, I would disappear like Elise.'

'You really saw him playing with himself?'

'Yes.'

'And then what happened?'

'Stuff came out when he was rubbing himself.'

Jamilla made an impatient huffing noise in the back of her throat. Yes, I know *that*, she told me. It was the sort of information that Boatman knew about and I didn't, and now Jamilla knew about it too. I felt as though I knew nothing.

'He said if you're not careful on window cleaning days, he'll try and look through to see you in your underwear. That's why we close the curtains. You can ask my mother or my grandmother or Olivia about the curtains, but don't ask about anything else, all right?'

Jamilla accepted everything that I told her. I asked her again about her eyebrows; she said she'd been pulling them out, but she didn't know why.

After the funeral, life returned to routine as much as possible, but things had changed. My mother was far away on the mainland. At night, I lay in bed checking off the nightly routine, but the sounds and smells seemed different, as if they belonged to another place. Nothing was the same.

Every day and every night, my mother's words burned in my brain. *You are a liar.* My appetite was at an all-time low. I had trouble sleeping, imagining Elise disintegrating bit by bit under the cool earth. It was an accident. An accident. The mantra did me little good. I was consumed by guilt. I'd wrecked everything. Elise and Walter Heather. I had a scene on a loop going around in my head; I imagined Walter Heather in the police interview room, just like the interview rooms on television. There'd be two detectives sitting across a table from him, the room thick with cigarette smoke, a tape recorder on the desk. Walter Heather's lawyer in a pin-stripe suit sat next to him, tapping his pen on a lined pad. The short detective leaned forward. He flipped a switch on the recorder.

'It's 4.37pm. Detective Charles Hayes here to interview Mr Walter Heather. Present with me are Detective Mullen and Mr Walter's solicitor, Mr Keith Cottrell. Right, let's get started. Mr Heather, are you overly fond of children?'

'You don't have to answer that, you know,' the pin-striped lawyer said.

My imaginings didn't stop there. Walter Heather locked in a cell. Walter Heather in a courtroom packed with people who looked like the Shelley's soft drink man and my mother with her bad Audrey Hepburn haircut. The judge looking at a pile of dirty photographs. Walter Heather sentenced to jail, eating stale bread and drinking tepid water. I wondered where my lie had taken him and where it was going to take me. I was consumed with dread.

I told Bernadette how I was feeling. She told me that Elise's physical body may be decaying, but her soul was in heaven. Think of her there, she told me. It made me feel slightly better. As for Walter Heather, she predicted he'd be back. She told me that what I had seen that night with Boatman and what I had seen in the biscuit tin didn't mean that people who did those things abducted children. Walter Heather didn't do anything to Elise, she told me.

'So, he's not like Mr Newmark?'

'No, not as far as I know.'

The next morning, Walter Heather returned to work. No one had said anything to me about the lie I'd told. Perhaps my mother hadn't told the rest of the family.

A few days later, Walter Heather came to the back door looking for Brenton to help him with a job. I opened the door and was startled at the sight of him. He didn't look angry. The look on his face was hard to read at first.

'It's all right, child,' he said. 'You made a mistake. Let it lie now.'

I felt like I was going to cry, but instead I nodded and went to find my brother.

I couldn't stop thinking about what Walter Heather had said and I couldn't stop thinking about Elise in a box under the cold, hard earth. In a split second, I had picked a time to talk to my mother, a good time, I had thought, the perfect moment. In a split second, she had been distracted and Elise had wandered off. In a split second, my one lie took on a life of its own and may have ruined a man's life. A small unit of time, a fragment, not even enough time for a single thought, that's all it took.

Chapter Sixteen

Matthew listened as I read aloud.

He was a good listener. Except for the therapist, I'd kept it all to myself for so long that at times, even as I was telling him, it was as though the story belonged to someone else. Sometimes he'd ask questions, but mostly he just stayed silent. It was he who suggested that I take a look at Esther's drawing book, and when I finally had the courage to open it, I was completely stunned.

There were a few pictures, but most of the pages were covered with handwriting. Esther's writing was awkward at times, but her flow of the English language was remarkable, succinct, concise, and accurate. Randomly, I had opened the book on a page describing my grandmother's dislike of Clara Borges and her concern over my being sent to Turridge House when my mother was recovering in the psychiatric hospital. I could hardly believe what I was reading.

On seeing my name and the names of all the others, I scanned the pages and then there was the synaptic snap when I knew what I was holding. I was holding Esther's own family history, chronicled in hundreds of pages with occasional rough sketches at the bottom of some pages. On first glance, I thought she must have started it before the dementia set in, but as I read on, I realised that most of it was written long after that.

I didn't open it on the first page. On a random flick through it, I saw my name and started reading. It was all there, the time I stayed at Turridge House after Elise's funeral.

My grandmother thought it best that I go somewhere for a while. People are talking, she told me. You shouldn't have to listen to what some people say. You can have a holiday with Beatrice at Turridge House.

Turridge House and the surrounding estate was not that far from Rachley Island. When I was a child, however, the ferry crossing seemed to take forever and the drive after that seemed never ending as well. The house stood on three hundred acres, a huge Georgian mansion on the outskirts of one of the major centres on the mainland.

Arthur Turridge, owner and philanthropist, collector of art and antiques, and an artist himself, was a man of few words. In his seventies, and in ill health, he had engaged the help of a housekeeper-come-cook by the name of Clara Borges. She was an eccentric, artistic woman who claimed to have links to European royalty, although my grandmother said that anybody could buy a title if they had the money. Brenton told me and Beatrice the Clara story on the night before I left to go to Turridge House. He had suddenly decided to treat me as an equal, discussing things with me that my grandmother definitely wouldn't have approved of.

Beatrice had met Clara one summer on the French Riviera and had scandalised decent society by becoming Clara's lover. Clara, at the time, had just ended her fourth marriage. She took up a job as personal assistant to the recently widowed Arthur Turridge. My grandmother said we could read personal assistant as housekeeper and cook and a provider of 'other services'. She made it quite clear what she thought of Clara Borges.

As a result of her relationship with Clara, Beatrice was cut off from the rest of my grandmother's family for a while, but in the end, my grandmother didn't have the energy to keep Beatrice at bay. Far more tragic events had happened at home and the 'problem' of Beatrice had little priority. Beatrice, on the other hand, took absolutely no notice of what anybody thought. She phoned and wrote and visited whenever she could, making reference to Clara as her companion, and after some time my grandmother's only comment was that she was glad her father was in his grave and didn't have to suffer through the humiliation.

The day Beatrice came to collect me, she was wearing a maroon nineteen-twenties' drop-waisted dress and a huge straw hat with fresh flowers stuck in it. Her long tortoise-shell cigarette holder was never out of her hand. She wore her trademark strings of beads in different colours. Blood-red nails and the same coloured lipstick, her hair dyed a shocking bright purple, she tumbled out of the car in a clash of colour.

'As if there hasn't been a tragedy in the family at all,' my grandmother said to her.

'Dressing in black won't bring anybody back,' Beatrice replied.

'Make Siobhan eat,' my grandmother said. 'Get her mind off things.'

Beatrice and Clara tried to lighten my mood, tried to make me see that things were not so bad. But they weren't there. They played no part. I had caused Elise's death and perhaps had accused Walter Heather of a crime he hadn't committed.

Beatrice laughed a lot, regaling us with stories of her and Clara's adventures in Europe, living in caravans, being invited to castles and balls in proper ballrooms. She said that Clara had tried to entice old Turridge into marriage because her finances were low, but he wasn't interested. Clara was certainly not an attractive woman. Short and squat, she dressed like a bohemian.

drink man or the Boatmans, and my instincts told me that these were unsuitable topics to bring up.

Clara continued to make so many jokes about putting poison in Mr Turridge's food that I asked Beatrice whether Clara intended to kill him.

'Not before he changes his will,' Beatrice replied with a laugh.

I rode horses with Beatrice and Clara, went to a movie, and visited my mother. I sat in the rotunda and read my favourite books. Beatrice let me stay up late every night and watch movies with her and Clara. We'd eat toast and jam and ice-cream. Clara, who said she was on a diet, ate miniscule amounts at dinner-time but could eat half a tub of ice-cream watching a movie and half a packet of Iced VoVos. Vodka was her favourite drink, and a glass was rarely out of her hand. Beatrice sipped at a sherry and I had lemonade and ice-cream drinks. At night, I'd think about Elise and wonder if her soul had reached heaven yet. Sometimes I'd get up, not long after going to bed, to get a drink or go to the bathroom. Beatrice and Clara would be in the kitchen, speaking softly. At times, I overheard. Sometimes, what I heard made me feel better and at other times, worse.

'It's not her fault,' Beatrice said. 'It's Margaret's fault.'

'Sounds like she drinks too much. Then again, who I am to judge? I drink too much as well.'

'You didn't sign on to look after a child.'

'Do you think she understands how ill Margaret really is?' Clara asked.

'Probably not,' Beatrice said.

I heard the *clink* of the vodka bottle against the glass.

Clara sighed. 'It's all so fucked up.'

One afternoon, after lunch, Clara was preparing an afternoon tea tray for Mr T, as she called him, when the phone rang. A friend of Clara's was sick and Clara was summoned to the hospital. Beatrice insisted on going with her. Clara asked me to take Mr T's tray up as she and Beatrice had to leave straight away. In half an hour, take it up, she told me. I thought about writing a letter to Boatman, but I didn't know what to say. I couldn't tell her that I was staying at a place where there were horses and a swimming pool, where I could stay up and eat ice-cream. After countless attempts, I gave up and by that time half an hour had passed and it was time to take the tray upstairs.

The tea tray was heavier than Esther's tray. Mr T liked a whole pot of tea, not just a cup. I was careful on the staircase, treading each step as though I might slip and fall any minute. When I reached the landing on the second floor, I realised that I didn't know which room was his. The doors were all shut and there was no sound coming from anywhere. Quietness in such a big house was something I was unaccustomed to. I imagined the guesthouse, how busy it could get. I thought of what I would tell Boatman—that the Turridge house had sixty rooms, not counting the quarters where Clara and my aunt lived.

Knowing that I really shouldn't have been using the pretence of taking up tea to see the house, I comforted myself with the knowledge that I was doing Clara a favour. As I crept along the dark hallway, I thought about Bernadette Brennan behind her door in room one on the second floor, back at Gables. I wondered what she would be doing. I pictured her putting her hair up in a French roll, placing each pin in carefully so they were completely hidden. She'd put pancake make-up over the freckles and line her eyes in dark black liner, then a smudge of lipstick and she'd be ready to start the day. What she did all day, I have no idea. Somehow Rachley Island provided enough interest for her to stay and fill in the hours.

The tray was getting heavy. I put it down gently on the soft, green carpet and wondered what to do. In the next few minutes, I gently knocked and turned the handle of every door in the hall-way, but all were locked. Then a sudden, sharp, throaty cough startled me. It hadn't come from any of the rooms lining the

'Elise to come back,' he said, and made a large sweeping movement with his brush.

'Yes,' I said.

'I see.' He held the brush in mid-air and turned to look at me. 'Yes, ghastly business. I was expecting you to say a new doll or a bike or a trip to Queensland. She will not be coming back, but if you will permit me to paint her, she can live forever.'

Asking my permission threw me completely. I nodded dumbly.

'Bring me a picture of her,' he said. 'You can go now.'

I had no pictures of Elise, but I knew if I asked Beatrice she would somehow be able to get me one and ask no questions. As it turned out, she didn't have a picture of Elise and I wouldn't have expected her to have one, but she suggested we go through the stack of newspapers in the kitchen that Clara hadn't thrown out yet. Between the three of us, it didn't take long to locate the article. Beatrice cut out the picture and handed it to me. I couldn't look at it right then, but later, in my room, I looked at it.

When I next visited my mother, I told her that Arthur Turridge was doing a painting of Elise.

'A portrait,' Beatrice corrected.

My mother patted me on the head. She seemed pleased that I had had a good time with my aunt and her friend. Beatrice filled my mother in with the news of Clara's friend's hospitalisation while I sat and wondered how a portrait of Elise might look.

I didn't want to disturb Arthur Turridge again, so I slid the picture under the door of his studio and tiptoed quietly away. I didn't see him again for the rest of my visit. The end of my sojourn at Turridge House came, and I said goodbye to Clara. She gave me a scarf from Romania and told me to be a free spirit. Beatrice saw me safely back to the ferry crossing to Rachley Island and then roared off in Arthur's car. Brenton met me on the other side. I hadn't seen him for two weeks and he looked older and weighed down with worry.

As the car rounded the bend in the driveway up to Gables, I found my hands were clenched in tight fists.

I forgot about Arthur Turridge for a few weeks, until a package arrived for me. On unwrapping it, Sunita burst into tears, while the others looked upon it, stunned. Elise Boatman was more beautiful than I had ever seen her. The portrait was signed A Turridge. The colours were those of the sunlit room where I had sat, thinking about the one wish in the world, should it be granted to me. Arthur had seemed surprised that I hadn't wanted a doll or a new bike or a holiday. I didn't have to think twice about what I wanted most in the world.

Chapter Seventeen

Begin at the beginning. I'd decided to read Esther's writings from the start, rather than just flick through and read at random. Curiosity had turned into an absolute need to have a panoramic view of the family, to understand what was at its core. I wanted to be able to look at it the way it really was.

Esther's observations about our family were incredible. Her perceptions of Beatrice, Clara, Arthur Turridge, and my grandmother were absolutely accurate. But what really struck me was that those entries were written in the years that we treated her like a child. It was almost unbelievable. Esther had never met Clara or Arthur, but she had obviously formed her own opinions from listening to Beatrice and me speaking about my time at Arthur's estate. I found it comforting that she did not take on my grandmother's impressions of them, but rather formed her own opinions from what she had heard. She wrote about them as I would have.

Brenton had always said Esther understood much more than people gave her credit for, and Olivia always told us to treat Esther as though she were no different to one of us, and I am only just beginning to see why. All those times I spoke aloud or cried or voiced my frustration, she understood. All those times she sat behind the reception desk listening to guests complain and staff whisper to each other, she understood. All the time I spent in regret and guilt over Elise, she understood.

At first, I didn't want to share Esther's writing with Matthew; there was still that whole thing about family history and airing dirty linen, and there was enough in mine to fill a laundromat. He said he was interested in my past and I told him I was interested in his and I suppose we were going through that whole thing that happens when people are first attracted; they want to see baby photos and your first school report and pictures of you in flares and terrible haircuts. And then wedding photos of your ex's so they can compare themselves and feel good.

'A lot of skeletons in my family closet,' he said.

The more thought I gave to it, the more I felt that an outside opinion would be a good thing—an objective onlooker, someone to bounce ideas off and someone with whom to compare skeletons. When I opened the first page of the drawing book, my eyes filled with tears. Esther had written a small prefacing paragraph.

Dear Siobhan Margaret,

An aunt does not usually have as important a role as a mother or a grandmother, but I know that I have had some role in your life even though it has been as a burden. You have certainly had a place in my life. I was born without the gift of speech, but I have spent a lifetime observing and listening. I am writing this for you because you deserve only the best and that includes the truth. You have looked after me in a spirit of kindness and patience and I am sure at times you would rather have been out playing than preparing food and feeding an old lady. I am grateful for your help all these years and this is my way of saying thank you. I am nearing the end of my life, but you are just at the beginning. It does not

she would say with a dismissive wave of the hand. As it turned out, Margaret did not get to travel. A few weeks before she was due to leave, my grandmother came down with an illness that confined her to bed. Dr Dalton administered every test under the sun but could find nothing wrong with her.

She lay in her bed, telling Margaret not to cancel the trip away. Of course, Esther wrote, Margaret cancelled her trip with Beatrice and stayed to nurse her mother through the mystery illness that went away soon after. Beatrice, who hadn't taken her sister's illness very seriously at all, went to Europe by herself.

'She's a Montrell,' Beatrice had said. 'Strong as an ox. She'll live.'

And she did.

By this time, my grandmother had been running the guesthouse for some time with the help of Henry Morse, my grandfather. A heavy drinker, Henry was not like Edward Montrell, however. He was a happy-go-lucky drunk who sang and put his arms around the nearest person available, telling them his life story. He had genuine affection for my grandmother's sisters. Beatie and Essy, he called them. When he was drunk, it was Eatie and Bessy. Brenton and I thought that was very funny. I remember my grandfather as a boisterous, loud, laughing man who had nicknames for everyone. Famous in the village for his humour and his ability to drink more than anyone else and still be standing, he was known on the mainland as well by the traders and suppliers to the island. When he died, the whole village turned out for his funeral.

'His heart,' my grandmother said.

'The drink,' Reg Dalton said to everybody when her back was turned.

After his death, my grandmother, in a radical move for the times, went back to her maiden name of Montrell. I'm glad she did. My mother followed suit and changing my name back to Montrell was the first thing I did after my first divorce. I kept the name Montrell when I married for the second time and couldn't think of myself as anything else. Siobhan Montrell—that's who I was, and no matter what the future brought, that's how I was going to stay.

After Elise's funeral, I didn't want to be a Montrell for quite some time, as I imagined everybody knew the circumstances of Elise's death. I lay on my bed and made up names. Christy Brown, Mary Buckley, Julia Johnson. I liked Julia Johnson. The trouble was I didn't feel like a Julia or a Mary. I felt like a Montrell. I also felt somehow less like a child after Elise died. Prior to her death, I had favoured the colour pink, but I didn't want pink anymore. I asked my grandmother if my bedroom could be repainted purple, and she simply agreed without an inquisition. I realised I could have asked for a lot of things that day and they would have been granted. I wanted my mother to come home, but the doctors had told us that she needed more time.

I wanted the Hovel to look different too, for Boatman; a fresh, new look for when she finally returned. I was convinced she would return. Secrecy about the Hovel made it impossible for me to ask anyone about painting, but I knew that if I asked Brenton he would, after some questioning, tell me what I wanted to know. One morning, he poured paint into two cans for me, gave me a brush, some cleaner, and a meaningful look.

'I promise, it's all right,' I said as I rode away with the basket on the handlebars full of equipment.

The wallpaper, which hadn't been put on properly in the first place, came off easily. Standing on a chair, I painted three quarters of the way up the walls. The top quarter, where I couldn't reach, was left as it was. The next morning, an idea occurred to me, but I had to again seek Brenton's help, as I wasn't sure my idea was a feasible one.

'Brilliant,' he said. 'But you'll need a groundsheet so that when you dip the mop into the paint, it won't drip on the purple you've already done or on the floor.'

He offered to come and help me, but I shook my head. That afternoon, I dipped an old mop into lime-green paint and splotched it on the remaining quarter of the walls. It had an interesting effect. Where the purple met the green was messy, so I mixed the two colours together and splotched a line across. The next problem was the floor. Brenton told me that there were rolls of old linoleum ready to be thrown out on the second floor. He retrieved one for me, cut it down to size, and wiped it over with methylated spirits.

The Hovel was transformed. I knew I could not ring the Boatman house, but I needed to speak to Boatman to tell her about the newly painted Hovel. After some thought, I came to the conclusion that I would like to surprise her, so I dropped a note with instructions for a meeting in the Hovel at an appointed date and time into the Boatmans' letterbox, and as I did so, I imagined her wide smile, her blue eyes lighting up as she danced around the purple and green room. She'd bring the radio, sing and show me new dance steps, and tell me that Sarah was having another baby to replace Elise; it's a girl, she'd tell me, and everything would go back to the way it once was.

'Did she like it?' Matthew almost whispered, touching the flaking, mouldy walls. He looked around, taking in the decay.

Something about the deserted army barracks made people want to whisper. Matthew ran his hand over the walls, flakes of paint falling onto the floor. I closed my eyes against the light and heat, breathing in what I imagine was leftover air. Coca-Cola cans and chip packets and a grey condom packet, looking new, littered the floor, evidence of others coming here. Graffiti and crude drawings covered the walls where I once splotched paint. The colour was still there, faded. The linoleum was no longer on the floor; there were bare boards with a badly drawn pentagonal star in yellow chalk. Rachley teenagers with their Ouija boards and ghost stories, told on days when they were supposed to be at school. Still, it made me shudder slightly.

Matthew walked around the room that was once the Hovel. He started to say something about the wood, demolition, and brickwork and how to tell if white ants were eating something but I was not listening. He said his uncle was in the army, then his voice trailed off as he saw I was distracted.

I wanted him to be silent so that I could speak, so I could tell him about the humidity on that day, about finishing my project, making a list of things to bring to my mother on my next visit. I had asked if I could bring her highball glass to make her feel at home. I wanted to bring her the things that made her happy. I wanted to tell him how I rode over to the eastern side in gumboots, how the mud squelched under my feet, how I almost fell several times. The grass was slippery, silvery green and wet. I had been glad to be alone. I wanted to sit and think.

Inside the Hovel, I'd fallen asleep, I told him, waking because of a noise outside. Several possibilities crossed my mind: a dog, the wind, branches falling on the roof. Boatman was late, but I knew she'd come. But she didn't come barging through the door like she usually did. Silent and still, I had watched the door handle turn, my heart pounding.

'Oh, it's you,' I'd said, breathing a sigh of relief as a face came into view from behind the door.

I remember my last thought before my head was smashed against the bedhead. I'll see Elise again, I thought, in heaven. We'll be together, playing in the sun.

Chapter Eighteen

When Camilla came through the door, I couldn't help but stare.

'Don't ask,' she said in a very definite tone, her hands held up, palms facing outward in a gesture of assertiveness. 'And from now on, I want you to call me Jamilla. Just like the old days.'

The shalwar kameez was a rich blue with subtle dots of gold along the edges. In the middle of her forehead, slightly off centre, sat a tikka. Kohl rimmed her eyes, widening them, making them appear very dramatic. She looked beautiful. She looked like her mother. I imagined her as a starlet from Bombay, dancing and singing in a Bollywood film with fountains and ornate gardens in the background and men on sitars and drums. Her eyelashes were missing, so I knew she was still struggling with her compulsion.

I shuddered. For a second, I saw Sunita, the bangles jangling, her feet encased in worn patent leather sandals. I saw the sun, the damp grass, the hose, Elise's smile. I was eleven years old. A lump was in my throat and I turned to the sink on the pretext of filling a glass of water. I had often wondered, if later on in her life, she might want to explore her Indian background, but I never thought I would see it embraced so quickly, perhaps extremely. It wasn't quick, she told me later. It had been brewing for a long time.

Matthew was slightly nervous about Jamilla coming and I realised I had probably painted a negative picture of her from the past. He looked as surprised as I was to see Jamilla dressed as she was. I left them to get acquainted and told them they could start on dinner. I rang Sydney and spoke to a friend for about twenty minutes, one ear on the kitchen conversation. Jamilla was extolling the virtues of a gluten-free diet to Matthew, who was pretending to be fascinated. After a while, the smell of vegetable curry wafted through the house and I heard laughing, so I figured they were getting along nicely. Dinner over with, we played cards and drank wine until midnight.

The morning after, Jamilla wanted to see the village. Matthew and I, sitting out on the guesthouse veranda, watched her walk down the slope, pass the turn-off tree, and continue on the track to Rachley. The grass on the hill was brown and dried out. It hadn't rained for a long time. The track to the village was covered in leaves and stones, baked brown by the sun. I looked out. My gaze travelled the length of the familiar landscape. I took it all in: the hill, the track, the-turn-off tree, the tops of the buildings in the village.

'She's quite attractive, that Jamilla,' Matthew said.

I felt myself grow hot in the face. I shrugged in reply.

While Jamilla was out, Matthew and I started on the storerooms in the guesthouse. Beatrice had not left any keys to those rooms and none of the other keys fit the locks, so we ended up breaking them. The cupboards didn't contain anything of interest, mostly financial records, bills, order forms for food, deliveries and invoices. A Shelley's soft drink invoice, thin with age. Most were signed by Federico. Poor Beatrice. There were pamphlets about Rachley Island that used to sit on a stand in the reception area, brochures about the Gables Guesthouse, unused supplies of stationery and piles of old newspapers. Two old computers sat on a table. I couldn't get them working. On the top shelf, I found some plans for extensions that Beatrice had had drawn up. She'd obviously planned to extend the guest dining room and put in a covered courtyard with tables for outside dining. An artist had sketched how the scene might look. The palm trees in pots between the tables were drawn in fastidious detail. There were candles on the tables and a bar off to the right. I imagined Beatrice and Federico sitting out there, smoking long cigarettes and drinking imported champagne. Not a bad idea for future reference, I thought, but then again, like Beatrice, I have no head for business.

Matthew sorted through the shelves on the left, and I did the right. He didn't seem to notice that after a while I had stopped looking for records and had fallen silent and still. The thud of my fist coming down hard on the floor startled him. As I looked at the picture of Elise on the front page of an old, yellowing local paper, I felt a stab of grief long buried, rising to the surface, spreading up toward my lungs, throat, and eyes. The words on the page blurred into each other.

'She's pretty,' Matthew said quietly. I gave a slight jump, not realising he'd been looking over my shoulder.

'Was. Was pretty,' I spat back.

He put his hand on my shoulder. I let it stay there as tears rolled down and dripped onto the newspaper. A lone tear fell onto the word 'died'. The word became suddenly huge, swimming in its own salty pool. Drowning. I wiped off the tear, stabbing at the place where it sat on the page. More tears fell until the black and white newsprint was splotched and soggy. Reaching for a cleaning rag, I wiped the page over and then wiped my face.

'Bloody stupid family never threw anything out.' I opened another newspaper and another, turning the pages with anger. 'Especially this. Why keep this?'

Matthew read aloud, his hand still on my shoulder.

Vicious crime rocks local community.

'You didn't finish your story the other night. What happened, Siobhan?'

I took a deep breath, closed my eyes and I told him.

After I returned from Turridge House, life on the surface was back to normal, but in reality, much had changed. Brenton had gone quiet. No more jokes. No more Wordsdays or any other idiosyncratic behaviour. I found him curled up in the shade house one afternoon, weeping inconsolably, the guinea pig clutched tightly against his chest. A while later, Brenton threw himself into his schemes with new energy. His latest was a health drink made from Sunita's herbs and soft drink combined with honey and a secret ingredient that he would not discuss with anyone. The kitchen stank of boiling pots of brown stew, but my grandmother said little about it. Sunita urged him every day to contact the authorities about marketing, health restrictions, the legalities, and other essentials before he wasted time and money, but he said he'd think about those things later.

'I'm really onto something this time,' he kept saying, while behind his back Sunita looked worried, lowering her voice, saying that her nephew did not really know what he was doing.

My grandmother kept to her routine of church, rosters, charities, doctors' visits, conferring with Olivia about Esther and running the guesthouse. Her visitors sat around eating cupcakes and drinking tea.

Dreadful business, they'd say, shaking their heads.

through the door, and I sat up even straighter when he sat down beside me. I didn't know what to say next; my heart was beating fast.

'Kerrie-Anne will be here any moment,' I said.

'No, she won't,' he replied. He reached into his pocket and took out a crumpled yellow envelope. The envelope that I had dropped in the Boatmans' letterbox containing the note that asked my best friend to meet me at the Hovel.

He moved toward me and sat down, putting out his hand to touch my face. I flinched back in surprise and then he slapped me hard right across the cheek. I fell back on the bed and started to cry.

'You tell anyone, you're dead,' he said.

He pushed himself on top of me. I could smell the heavy aftershave, a smell I have never forgotten. Kicking and screaming, I tried to bite him, but he put his hand over my mouth, stifling my cries. I pulled at his hair, but he reached up and pinned my arms down with his hands. My mouth was now freed of his hand and I screamed, so he covered it again. I bit his hand hard and tasted blood in my mouth. He yelled with the pain and then he sat up and hit me again, even harder. I felt all the energy drain out of me; my legs went weak. I remember thinking about Catherine. The same thing happened to her. Urine dribbled out onto the bed, soaking the back of my skirt. He was staring at the hand I had bitten, and in that short moment I found the energy to spring up from the bed and try to make an escape.

He was too quick for me. He grabbed my leg, and I fell heavily to the floor. I started to scream again, and then he picked me up and threw me onto the bed. My head hit the back of the bedhead, coming down on the metal rail with a sickening thud. I hit out wildly, without aim, my legs flailing in the air. He came closer, and I managed to strike out just once with my foot, kicking him in the stomach. It only served to make him angrier. Swearing loudly, he hit me in the face and then grabbed me by the hair, his fist pulling at every inch of my scalp. He lifted my head up by the hair and banged it down on the rail. I knew what was about to happen, but I was too weak and exhausted to do anything. His hands were halfway up my thigh. I closed my eyes. I am going to die, I kept thinking. It is my punishment for Elise.

A loud banging on the door and shouting from outside made him stop for a second. I must have had my eyes closed very tightly because when I opened them again, my vision was blurred for a split second. A huge piece of wood came down on his head. He fell off the bed, but still I couldn't move. For a moment, I imagined that the roof was about to cave in, but then I saw her, the wood still in her hands, and I registered what was happening. He rose from the floor, holding his head, anger boiling in his eyes.

Bernadette Brennan waited, breathing hard. Without warning, he lunged at her and she hit him again. Being taller and stronger, he managed to take the wood from her hands, but not without a struggle. He swung the piece of wood at her body, but she ducked out of the way, knocking over a chair.

'Go outside,' she shouted at me, but I stayed, paralysed, on the bed. 'Outside,' she screamed.

Years later, when I was able to talk about what happened, I used to go over all the things I could have done. I could have picked up a chair and hit him, but I didn't. I could have run for help, but I didn't. My legs wouldn't work. I couldn't scream anymore; my throat was hoarse. Urine dripped down my legs. I was useless.

He stood, the wood in his hands, looking at both of us, shaking in anger. Bernadette Brennan did not seem afraid. In fact, she spoke calmly.

'Let the girl go,' she said. 'Siobhan, go outside and wait.'

I did as I was told, and as soon as the door was closed, I could hear her struggling with him. Covering my ears, I sat on the step, humming as loud as I could, but even my loud humming was not enough to block out the sounds of him hitting her. I was sick, the vomit splashing all over my new shoes. Because I was vomiting, I hadn't noticed Walter Heather come around the corner. He stopped when he saw me, and then, seeing the vomit and my dishevelled state, he ran over.

'Quick, it's Bernadette Brennan,' was all I managed to get out before I was sick again.

He looked bewildered for a second, but on hearing the chaos inside, he barged through the door and I crawled and hid in the toilet block. It seemed like I was there for hours. I sat shivering against the cold concrete, every bone, every nerve shuddering uncontrollably. When I came back out into the sunlight, there was no sound coming from the Hovel. I sat some distance away from the steps, carefully avoiding the vomit. I desperately wanted to know if Bernadette Brennan was all right, but I was too afraid to even knock on the door. Finally, she appeared, again seeming calm, sitting down beside me and putting her arm around my shoulders. She smoothed down her dress and patted her hair, which was all messed up. We sat like that for ages, saying nothing. I wanted to ask her what he'd done to her, but I couldn't even form the words. I was shaking.

'Where's Mr Heather?' I asked after a long period of silence.

'Inside. He'll be out in a minute.'

'He saved us,' I said.

'He did,' she said.

'How come you were here?' I finally asked.

Bernadette Brennan sat and put her head in her hands. She looked exhausted. Her French roll had come undone. Two fingernails were broken. Her dress was dirty. When she spoke, it was an effort to get the words out.

'I've watched you for a long time. You're rarely out of my sight. Everywhere you go, I make it my habit to know. I've known you for a very long time.'

'How long?'

She reached inside her blouse and took out a thin chain and there, on the end, was a tiny ballerina, gold and zirconia.

I told her that I had one too.

I was quiet for a while before I made sense of it. The lady with the jet-black hair who had left the present under the tree all those years ago. I had seen Bernadette Brennan before; I had been right all along.

'You had black hair!'

'It's blonde now. From a bottle,' she said with a tired laugh.

'Have you stayed at the guesthouse many times before?'

'Every summer. Part of the bargain,' she said quietly.

I was about to ask her about that, but Walter Heather came out of the Hovel and interrupted us. He had blood on his head and was holding his arm as though it hurt. He said he was going down to the village to get the police. Bernadette Brennan nodded, and we watched him disappear beyond the wire fence.

'What was he doing here?'

'Looking after you,' she said.

'Did you get hurt? Did he, you know…'

'I'm all right,' she said.

'What bargain?'

A pained expression crossed her face. She picked up my hand and held it in hers, then straightened up her posture as if she were about to give an important speech.

'Never mind about that. I just want to protect you.'

She waited for my reply, but I didn't really understand, so I said nothing. A few seconds later, I asked, 'Why do you have to protect me?'

'Because that's what mothers do.'

She looked at me and I stared back.

'My mother is in hospital,' I said, feeling confused.

Bernadette Brennan looked suddenly exhausted. 'Yes, she is. Now, let's get home and cleaned up,' she said.

'What about him in there?' I asked.

She pulled my hand to stop me from going in, but I jumped up from the steps and looked through the grimy glass of the window. The table was broken, the chair as well, and Josh Boatman was lying on the floor, unconscious, covered in blood.

Chapter Nineteen

The river was still and quiet.

The last of the day's clouds scudded quickly across a dark evening sky. We moved together under the water. I felt his skin against mine and when we broke the surface, we wrapped around each other. I was faintly aware of the sounds of crickets and the occasional flutter of a bird, and then our own breathing drowned out everything, filling up the blackness. Later we lay on the riverbank looking up at bright stars. The last boat to the mainland would have just left.

'It always leaves at seven-thirty, just as it did in Elise's time,' I told him.

I lay with my head on Matthew's chest, going over the day in my head.

'When did Jamilla begin pulling out her eyelashes and eyebrows?' Matthew asked.

'When Elise disappeared, according to Esther. I didn't notice till the day of the funeral. It's a condition called Trichotillomania, where people pull out all the hair on their bodies. It's to do with impulse control and anxiety, I think. She still does it, but at least there are therapists and a support group now, which she says helps.'

Her habit got worse just after the service when people were still dazed with grief and my grandmother was speaking in hushed tones about washing and guest lists and leaking showers, desperate to impose order. It was a time of surreal motion, speech and action. Feelings leapt up and consumed us, and we didn't know what to do with them. Three weeks later there was a fresh tragedy to deal with. What Josh Boatman did to me made headlines, and not just on the island. There were no counsellors and therapists in those days, and even if there had been, I doubt my grandmother would have sent me to one. She finally breathed a sigh of relief when it became clear that I hadn't suffered the same fate as Catherine Parker. After a hospital visit and two sessions with the police, we walked up to the milkbar where she bought me chocolate ice-cream and potato straws as if to congratulate me on my narrow escape.

There had been no contact between the Boatmans and the Montrells since Josh's attack on me. I asked if there would be charges laid against him and my grandmother told me I was never to mention his name ever again. One afternoon, about a week after the incident at the Hovel, I crept upstairs to visit Bernadette Brennan. When I stepped up onto the landing, I saw that the door to room one was open. I could hear raised voices, my grandmother's and the guest's. The cleaning trolley was at the side of the door, so I crouched down beside it. In the next few minutes, my world, as I had known it, changed without warning, growing larger and more complicated than I could have ever imagined.

'...long enough and it's time for you to go.'

'And you think you can look after her, do you? She could have been killed,' Bernadette Brennan shouted. 'If Walter Heather hadn't come along, God knows what would have happened.'

'The worst is over. Siobhan won't be going out on her own again,' my grandmother said.

'Josh Boatman drilled a hole in the wall of their cubbyhouse at the old barracks,' Bernadette Brennan screamed. 'He'd been watching them in there and getting off on it. Walter Heather was onto him and had been going there too to make sure those girls were safe.'

Bernadette paused before she spoke again.

'You're not fit to look after her.'

'How dare you!'

'I want her back.'

'Impossible.'

'I am her mother and I want her back,' Bernadette Brennan shouted. 'I can take it to a court,' she said. 'I'll see a lawyer. Times are changing and people don't care whether mothers are married or not. And I'm pressing charges against Josh Boatman for assault. And the police can press charges for Siobhan. Walter Heather has agreed to be a witness.'

The door slammed shut. I could hear their voices, angry and loud, but it was difficult to understand what was being said. I thought about my mother lying in the stale-smelling hospital ward on the mainland. If Bernadette Brennan was my mother, then who was Margaret Montrell?

It was the look on Sunita's face when I asked her who my mother was that gave it away. That afternoon, I sat under the turn-off tree nursing the shock and wondering how to reconstruct a normal world again. The longer I sat, the more I realised that they had all kept the knowledge from me. Every single one of them. My grandmother was mortified that I had overheard the argument in room one and doubly so when I locked myself in my room and refused to come out. She kept telling me that she could explain everything. In the end, I had to open the door because Esther was locked in as well.

Trying one by one to talk to me, they came, each with a different approach, but I sent them away, screaming that they had betrayed me. Relations between Bernadette Brennan and my grandmother were temporarily unfrozen as they united with different strategies. A tortured Bernadette Brennan would cry and try to talk to me through the door, but I pushed her away too, telling her that I hated her and I wished Josh Boatman had killed her. I didn't mean it, of course, but couldn't believe she had given me away as a baby; she had not wanted me.

She kept on talking about a bargain.

'Sometimes we have to break promises,' she repeated.

I had no idea what she was talking about.

'I want to see my mother,' I said. 'I want to see my mother.'

I didn't know what to do about my mother. I had always thought of her as my mother and still did. Anger and outrage and total confusion made it impossible for me to talk to any of them. They had kept a secret from me for all those years. A few years later, I asked my grandmother if they had planned to tell me one day and she uncharacteristically broke down and cried, saying that they had planned to one day, but the years kept slipping by and they thought it was for the best. When I turned sixteen, I wanted to see my birth certificate and my grandmother handed it over without a fuss.

Esther had written that Bernadette Brennan came to Rachley Island in the summer of 1963, presumably for the same reasons anybody came to the island, to have a holiday. She was strikingly beautiful. With shoulder length jet-black shiny hair, pale skin and tiny freckles, she turned heads. At nineteen and from a sheltered background, she was still quite naïve but not totally unaware of the effect she had on men.

'I knew, as soon as I saw her, that there'd be trouble. Not because she was trouble in itself, but because she was beautiful and what surrounded her was not,' Esther wrote.

Brought up in a town not far from Belfast, she was the product of an educated Catholic family, well known in the district for their work within the church and religious organisations. Her father was a university lecturer, her mother stayed home, and her two elder brothers were both parish priests. At the time of her visit to the island, one of her uncles on her mother's side was on his way to becoming a bishop.

Both parents held egalitarian values where education for women was concerned and Bernadette was encouraged to study hard in order to attain university entrance. Her mother had a prospective husband picked out, a boy from an equally esteemed family, whom Bernadette seemed mildly interested in. After she had finished her final year at school, at her father's suggestion, she took a year off before commencing university study and teamed up to travel with the sister of the boy her mother was so fond of. Both sets of parents wanted the girls to 'get it out of their systems' before study, marriage, and children. Contacts with relatives and friends were set up in England, Europe, and Australia. The initial plan was for the girls to stay with these contacts, but it didn't work out that way all the time. By the time the girls had reached Australia, they had had a falling out and decided to go their separate ways.

When Bernadette's parents were informed of the falling out, they urged their daughter to come home, but Bernadette had attained a degree of self-confidence and independence. The mild interest she had in the boy her mother liked so much had dissipated into total ambivalence. She knew that there were plenty of men who looked her way and she would have no problems finding one if that's what she wanted. Another traveller from Ireland had given her a brochure about Rachley Island and suggested it as a travel destination. What interested her most were the pictures of the gardens, the trees and plants along the riverbank, the promise of water and willows. Gables Guesthouse beckoned with champagne sunsets, river cruises, dinner served at dusk on crisp, white linen. She would lie in a wicker chair stuffed with soft pillows and read novels, only rousing to order another Paradise Cocktail.

'She was a kind girl,' Esther recalled.

Every morning, the guests would come down to breakfast and then go back up, collect their belongings and come down again to start their day of leisure. They passed me several times a day, sitting in the reception area in my chair. Rarely did anyone acknowledge my presence until Bernadette came and she was like a breath of fresh air.

'Morning, Miss Esther,' she would say. 'It is a lovely day. Would you like me to take you out on the veranda?' She knew I couldn't speak, but she treated me as if I could. Sometimes she would wheel me out onto the veranda without asking anyone's permission. We would sit together, she reading or writing letters home, while I listened and watched. She made sure I was always in the shade and always facing the garden. Every few days I would watch her walk down into the village in her broderie anglaise dresses and flat sandals, her straw sunhat and light pink lipstick. The village cake shop was a popular haunt; she had a sweet tooth. Sometimes I would doze off, and upon waking would find small delicacies left on the portable tray on my chair, a tiny pink cake with frosting, a lamington, a lemon butter tart. When the cook's son, who was four at the time, came down with an illness not long after Bernadette arrived, Bernadette often assisted in the kitchen. Sarah Boatman, who would occasionally fill in as the cook, was pregnant, suffering from nausea.

Margaret had other duties in laundry, linen, cleaning, and general organisation and Jack was busy with the outside maintenance. My grand-

mother even sent for Beatrice, but received a reply from somewhere in South America saying it was impossible for her to come home. My grandmother was not pleased to find a guest in the kitchen and told Bernadette that she could not afford to pay her and therefore she should cease assisting. Bernadette, however, was not interested in being paid; she worked in the kitchen for three days before another cook was employed for a while so Mrs Schliapnikova could go back to the mainland and look after her son. My grandmother even told Bernadette not to bother me when she saw her wheeling me out on to the veranda. Bother me, for heaven's sake!

No one had time for an old lady in a wheelchair who could not converse, and a fresh face and a compassionate nature certainly did not upset me. The garden was one of Bernadette's favourite places while she was at Gables. She'd wander amongst the plants and bushes, touching the fronds and petals delicately as if she were a student of botany. Behind breakfast newspapers or dark glasses, the slow gaze of the male guests on the veranda quietly followed her every move. After their wives and girlfriends had returned upstairs to gather hats and bags for the day, some would take a walk in the garden on the pretext of interest in the greenery. Many men approached her as she walked amongst the flowers. She conversed politely but showed no particular interest in any of them.

Then Bernadette met Jack. I cannot be sure what this particular union had as its attraction, other than the obvious. I never married or had lovers or experienced what it was to share a life with someone, but I have watched and learned a lot. Bernadette was a serious girl. Your father, forgive me for saying this, was a fly by night, opportunistic, selfish man. Not unintelligent, he had an undisciplined mind which, had he been of a different temperament, might have held him in good stead. He was diagnosed late with a mental illness. I suppose she fell for his charm, a characteristic in which he was not lacking. Women were very attracted to him. He had charisma. Bernadette was young, and she did not have the experience to be discerning in matters of the heart. I did not dislike Jack; there was something quite likeable about him. He was possible to like as long as one was aware that he was irresponsible and fickle and could never fully be trusted.

From the start, your parents' marriage was a troubled one. Margaret, I believed, always knew of Jack's infidelities but chose to ignore them, and there was a reason she did this; she truly believed that once she had a child, her marriage would be all that it was supposed to be. Jack had no trouble reconciling his affairs with his other life as the family man; the two worlds simply did not collide. He crossed the line from one world to the next as neatly and with as much precision as a tennis ball bouncing from one boundary into another. Sarah had two children already and another on the way by the time Bernadette arrived and I knew, every time that Margaret held Sarah's children, she longed for one of her own. Children hadn't brought Sarah the happiness that the women's magazines promised, but Margaret made a choice not to see this. It was about this time that Margaret started to show signs of a personality change. Her mental health deteriorated as a result of depression and frustration at not being able to produce a child of her own. She saw doctors on the mainland, specialists in Sydney, a dietician. Nothing worked.

While Margaret was making every effort to fall pregnant, Jack was seeing several women at the same time. At one time, he was sleeping with the cook. Margaret held no ill feelings toward the cook because the cook despised your father within a short time. Added to this, Margaret did not subscribe to the unwritten law of loathing the woman who seduced another woman's husband; she knew what Jack was like. She sheeted the blame directly at him and saw the cook as more of a helpless victim. They banded together, in fact. I felt sorry for the cook myself. She understood perfectly that Jack had no love for her whatsoever. And there lay the difference; Jack's women meant nothing to him—until Bernadette came along.

When Margaret and Jack's first child, Brenton, was born, Margaret believed that now Jack had become a father, his philandering would stop. She finally had the baby she wanted, but even this did not stop Jack from having other women. Outwardly, she put on a brave face, but underneath she was full of sadness and existing in this constant state started to take a toll on her health. Jack's other women had never driven Margaret to the point where she couldn't stand it anymore, only because she knew he didn't care for any of them. His love for Bernadette changed all that.

When Bernadette fell pregnant to Jack, Margaret was shattered. Bernadette could not return home at nineteen, unmarried and with a baby. The disgrace would have been too much, and so the family worked out something that would satisfy them all to some extent.

My grandmother made the decision. Margaret was not in a fit condition to do anything. I hope, Siobhan, in years to come, that people's attitudes will change regarding women having children out of wedlock.

You were very much loved by Margaret and by your grandmother, in as much as she could demonstrate affection to anyone. Jack, I know, doted on you. After Jack's death, things settled down. As time went by, Margaret's hatred for Bernadette increased. Unlike the cook, who had no love for Jack and who was forever after full of regret and remorse, Bernadette demanded her part of the bargain and was granted what she wanted.

Every year, she would come as a guest. She was to have no part in your life but could observe, from a distance. She could make no demands or interfere with any aspect of your upbringing. My grandmother had Bernadette over a barrel; one false move and she would make sure Bernadette would be disgraced in the eyes of her family, and even worse, would never see her child again. After you were born, Bernadette returned to Ireland, where she studied to become a nurse.

Esther remembered the day Bernadette visited in 1971, the chaos with the men doing an inspection, my grandmother on the phone, Brenton's terrible humour, my mother showing signs of strangeness. Esther was in her chair in the reception area, watching through half-closed eyes, though everyone presumed she was asleep. It was a Wednesday—Wordsday, Esther had written. Not the best morning for her to arrive, Esther noted in brackets. She went on to say that it was school holidays and I was helping at the front desk. The cook was in one of her moods as her assistant was ill and something had gone wrong with the soufflés.

She recalled Brenton sitting on the reception desk, the staff barging in to ask when Walter Heather was returning as a pipe had broken in the laundry. The two men doing a hotel inspection had arrived and then Bernadette arrived in reception in the middle of it all.

I read on until I came to the events of 1971. I read about the rain, the river rising, Elise walking off.

Siobhan, I saw Elise wander off. I tried to get your attention. I was waving, trying to point in the direction she had walked off in. I was trying to get sounds to come out of my throat. I tried, but I understand why you ignored me.

I had to stop reading for a while. I was numb. So, Esther knew that day. She'd seen everything. I'd ignored her, but how could I have known?

I read on, about Olivia being sick in the garden and then trying to end her life, the speculation about whether Elise had drowned or had been abducted, my mother being unwell and blaming herself and then trying to suicide. And then there it was. My confession to Esther the night I cried and told her about how I'd distracted my mother and lied about Walter Heather. Josh Boatman's attack and the roles of Bernadette Brennan and Walter Heather were chronicled as well. My time out at Turridge House. Everything. Esther had understood everything I had ever said to her.

I couldn't read any further. I had to ring Brenton. There was something I needed to talk to him about.

'I've found Esther's old writing book,' I said to Brenton on the phone. 'She's written some things that are very disturbing.'

'Esther *was* disturbed,' he said pointedly, and then he laughed.

'Physically, yes,' I told him. 'Remember how you used to feed her and tell her that you knew she was a shrewd old bird that noticed things?'

Esther was smart, Brenton said. Probably the smartest out of everyone.

I apologised to him for not believing him all those years ago.

'Well, I was right about Esther all along,' he said.

Chapter Twenty

I have always measured time quite unlike anybody else I know.

Elise's life and her death have been my reference points for as long as I can remember. I know I do it, this strange, perverse measuring; my friends, at least the ones who know, have told me I do it. No matter what the event, it has always been in the context of that fateful day.

I finished school five years after Elise died. It was a few years after Elise died when I went to university. I got married sixteen years after Elise died. It was as if there had never been any other yardstick with which to chart the course of a life.

I grew up in a few weeks, crossing the neat, safe boundary of childhood into adulthood. There was no gradual process, no gentle sliding into an older, worldlier place, no preparation. Sharp and shocking, girlhood vanished the day Elise disappeared and the adult world came into force with the look on Josh Boatman's face as he came through the door that day in the Hovel. It vanished in a conversation between a daughter and a mother who sat on the grimy steps of a little girl's hideaway.

The knowledge washed over me, thick and nauseous, too raw to digest.

I couldn't take it all in for a number of years; it was just too much at once. The events that took place all those years ago and the knowledge that was imparted to me as a child have had their consequences. They have seeped in and out of my marriages, relationships, career, my friendships with others, colouring every decision I have ever made. Over the years, I've sifted and shifted through what happened, analysed it from every point of view, gone into therapy, and there are times when I think it has settled into layers of acceptance. It fools me every time though, sneaking up on me when I least expect it, when I think that I've got it all worked out. In the pea-green carpeted therapist's room, I revisited the lie I told for the first time since I told it.

What happened back then is the reason my life has turned out as it has. It is the reason why I never had children myself. I have always felt I could never trust myself with them. I think of my childhood as a cake, a layer on top, icing-sugar sweet; picnics on the riverbank; Brenton's jokes; a secret place with a best friend; an older woman who was like a sister. She painted my nails and showed me how to wrap up my hair. Nascent, naïve, and wanting to be loved, I wanted to be just like her. I see the irony of it; I was just like her. I came from her lifeblood. I just didn't know it at the time. Little girl reality, sandwiched in the middle, was not aware of bargains and past histories at the bottom layer, mired in secrets and bribes and mental illness. Beneath the respectability of the household, there were lies so deep I doubt that anyone could have remembered who told what to whom and why.

I lived like that until I was almost twelve, a life under a life, another world operating below the one that was real to me. Then a few false moves and it all came undone. At times, the top and middle layer of the cake were in danger of melting into each other. My grandmother and my mother must have lived on tenterhooks when Bernadette Brennan visited. The top layer would have been in danger of seeping into the middle.

They would have breathed a sigh of relief when she left again, not to be seen for another year. The danger period passed, the cake would be resurrected in perfect form, a beautiful, treacherous lie, and a lie that stretched over a decade. I have forgiven Brenton for not telling me that Bernadette was my mother. He knew, but, like me when I found out, was confused. I've realised lately just how like me Brenton really is, a keeper of secrets, a Montrell through and through. He knew the circumstances of my birth and yet he never said anything.

I was the lucky one, really. Brenton ended up with the bad seed, Jack's genetic material, unstable chemicals. It's not a pleasant thought; frantic sperm propelling themselves into a new existence, carrying enough dangerous genetic material to ruin a life or two.

Brenton tried to escape his prison of madness in 1981, taking an overdose. He was found in time by his first wife, who saw him hospitalised, medicated and finally stable. His medication keeps him functioning, enables him to hold down a job, and he has recently been awarded a promotion at work. He is in charge of personnel at a well-known hotel in Sydney. At night, he is studying hospitality management and is planning to undertake a Master's degree. Married for the second time, he has two children, none of whom have shown signs of anything out of the ordinary. His doctor has said that there may be a chance that the children will inherit the illness and so they're watched closely. The eldest child, Michael, showed a remarkable command of the English language from a very early age. Once, when we took the children to the lake on a very windy day, I said to him: 'Look Michael, that boat has turned upside down.' He looked at me and said: 'Auntie Siobhan, it didn't turn upside down, it capsized.' He was two.

I asked Sunita years ago about how much she had known.

She told me that she and Robert had argued quite a bit about keeping secret the circumstances of my birth. I didn't blame her. It wasn't her story to tell. Sunita, being the astute person she was, knew what I was thinking. She tossed her head and said that it was not her place to tell me, and I replied that I would not have expected her to.

I went to her naturalisation ceremony a few years ago. She had lived in Australia on a permanent status for years and finally decided to take out citizenship. We went to a party after the official ceremony, where a choir sang a song from the musical *Oliver*. 'Consider yourself one of us,' they sang and Sunita looked so proud I thought she was going to cry. My grandmother should have been there to see it. She liked *Oliver*, even if she never totally accepted Sunita. Jamilla started to laugh under her breath and so did Brenton, and I had to give them both a look to silence them. It was, all in all, a very Montrell moment. Brenton had far too much to drink and rolled around the room telling anyone who'd listen about Sunita's university degrees, her cooking, how Hinduism has thirty million gods and whatever else he could think of.

Not long after that, Sunita bought a house in Queensland and opened up as a naturopath on completing a course in Sydney. She still lives in Queensland and comes down to see Jamilla twice a year. She had a cat that she named Elise. It lived until the age of fourteen. It was her way of remembering and I don't find it disrespectful at all.

These days, Jamilla and her mother are close. I don't mind talking to Sunita about the past because she never skirts around the issue of my mother or Bernadette Brennan.

Before she took her own life, my mother said something to me I will never forget.

'You didn't grow inside me,' she said, 'but you grew in my heart and to me it is just the same.'

As I approach my forties, I have thought a lot about the two women who played major roles in my life. One of my darkest, saddest thoughts is that they really never liked each other.

At times, over the long years of my mother's confinement to psychiatric hospitals and getting to know and spend time with Bernadette, I would find out small things about one or the other that led me to believe they may have had things in common. Or perhaps I desperately wanted them to have things in common. They had both, at one point in their lives, loved Jack and maybe that was the only connecting link.

I spent years ignoring Bernadette's letters and phone calls, pretending to hate her, but after my mother died, I relented. Years later, I listened while she told me stories of how she watched over me. She related incidents that I remember well and yet I had no knowledge of her presence at the time. She told me about the time she saw me fall off my bike near the turn-off tree and scrape a large patch of skin off my elbow.

It was my mother, in the end, who encouraged me to make peace with her. The day I found out that Bernadette had been diagnosed with breast cancer, I shut myself in my room for two days and didn't come out, numb with shock and grief and whatever else was left over. I held her hand for weeks as she lay dying in hospital in Ireland. She told me on the morning she died that she had really loved Jack and all I could do was nod dumbly and squeeze her hand. It was so long ago, I didn't care if she did or didn't and yet she still felt the need to justify herself to me. She slipped away while an insect on the flower arrangement held my attention momentarily. I looked back at her and she was gone. Distraction at crucial moments seems to be the hallmark of my life. She had watched over me for years, watched from a distance, impotent and regretful but there, nevertheless. She was there when childhood collided with the adult world with only seconds in between. Even my grandmother had a change of heart about her toward the end.

My mother raised me and looked after me as much as a

mother in a chronic state of mental illness could. She spent her remaining years in a psychiatric unit in a hospital on the mainland; vague, quiet, and remote from her own tragedy. I have no particular feelings for Jack either way as I never really knew him, but my memories of my mother are still the ones I've taken with me from girlhood. In a covered box I bought at a Melbourne market lie her blue beads, her hat, and her pincushion in the shape of a cat.

The day I related the details of that terrible week Elise disappeared to the therapist, I could hardly get my words out. My lie about Walter Heather came tumbling out, my mother's words following close behind. *I was there.* But she wasn't, the therapist said. For a moment, I was confused. No, she was there, I told the therapist. She saw Walter Heather go down to the river and return up the slope. And then I realised what the therapist had implied; she wasn't there emotionally for me. Absent mother. Detached from the world. She didn't really raise me. I did that myself.

And then there was Esther.

Esther, the filter, through which all information passed; large slabs of information, bodies of dialogue, fragments of gossip, rumour, innuendo, stories of misfortune and triumph as well, secrets whispered in hallways. Behind those impassive eyes and a body that would not obey, she was sorting through it all, sifting and sorting, housing what she saw as the truth and editing it the way she felt it was meant to be. Her mind had been clear and sharp, her observations so astute it was as if she had plunged her head into ice-cold water, looked up, and recorded what she saw. She summed up character, understanding motive and the darker psychological nuances of behaviour. There are still questions I will never know the answers to. When did she start it? There are no dates on any part of it. This is what she wanted me to read at the time I was feeding and cleaning her. I had missed it completely. In the short note at the beginning of the writing, she had spoken of taking responsibility for the consequences of me finding the document, and this has led me to believe that she wanted it to be found.

This year, Elise would have turned thirty-three. I still wonder what would have become of her had she survived. Last year on television, I saw a documentary called *The Face*. A photograph of a very young person was scanned into a machine that had the technology to project the image years into the future. And I thought about Elise, thought about the lost years and opportunities. Those thoughts about where a soul goes have kept me awake at night. I've often thought about the poem by Bruce Dawe, 'Elegy for Drowned Children', in which he wonders where the old king of the sea takes the children.

Why else would they be taken out of the sweet sun,
Drowning towards him, water plaiting their hair?

It was all so random, so unfair.

In the therapist's office, I cried for weeks until my face felt raw from wiping it with the tissues I ripped from the box on the therapist's table. I know it wasn't my fault. I was only eleven. A child looking after a child. Even with the most attentive mothers, accidents can happen, the therapist told me.

'You have to forgive yourself. Not for being distracted when you were a child. You have to forgive yourself for taking on the burden of responsibility you felt. Margaret Montrell paid the price for that. You don't have to.'

'But what about my lie?'

Children lie sometimes, she said. Later, we worked out why I lied. I was just Siobhan, fending for myself, with no one really looking after me. Everything was jumbled in my head; Elise missing, my guilt about distracting my mother, dirty photographs, what Boatman and I saw Walter Heather doing in his kitchen, the Heather Files, Brenton looking through the photographs for those with children in them, my anger toward my mother over her affair with the Shelley's soft drink man, and the fact that on some level I was desperate for my mother to notice me. You wanted your mother's attention, the therapist told me. You wanted her approval.

Now, for the first time, the burden of responsibility I've felt for years is slowly lifting. I learned a hard lesson about maligning people on the basis of rumour and innuendo. I shifted the blame on to an innocent man because I couldn't bear to acknowledge that I had played a part in Elise's disappearance.

Recently, I've been able to think about Elise without reaching for the wine bottle. During those months when I was fixing up Gables, I went back and forth to therapy. I made some decisions, one of which was to try to find the portrait Arthur Turridge did. I went into the large storeroom at the back of the guesthouse, the place from which I'd stolen the larger items Boatman and I needed in the Hovel. Beatrice had left instructions about the portrait's whereabouts. As I peeled off layers of bubble wrap and tape, I broke out in a sweat. I was down to the last layer when I stopped. Then I ripped the layer off and held it at arm's length. There was Elise, again, trapped in time. Arthur Turridge was right; she would live forever in people's memories.

Would she have been like Sarah and Kerrie-Anne: carefree, impulsive? Or would she have been more serious, like Dan Boatman? No one will ever know, and it is quite a fruitless exercise thinking about it. I've fantasised about running into Kerrie-Anne in the street, in George Street, Sydney, far from Rachley Island; we'd have one of those conversations: 'Well, that's life, it's all in the past. So how are you these days?'

I know in reality it wouldn't happen like that. I know that I could perhaps find her on Facebook, but would she want me to make contact? What would be the point? I told the therapist how sad I was back then that Boatman never saw the renovated Hovel.

Boatman and I have both probably rolled up our pain in a tight ball; contact with each other may puncture it after decades of making sure it is contained. The leaks might just be too great and undo whatever we have done to make sure those leaks don't spill out into our relationships, careers, and the way we manage our lives. It is too great a risk.

Sarah Boatman drank herself into oblivion after the death of Elise and her son's attack on me. Assaulting me was Josh Boatman's revenge on the Montrell family, and she knew it. She couldn't face anyone in my family after that, but once again she showed no anger. I suspect she was shattered that any child she had raised could do such a thing. Josh was incarcerated, Billy was dead, Elise dead too.

I lived with Beatrice and Clara on the mainland for some time after the events of 1971. When Clara and Beatrice finally did end their friendship, it was because Turridge proposed to Clara and she accepted. Beatrice had no objections at all. She had always said she was a free spirit and did not believe in possessing another person.

My grandmother's health deteriorated to the point where she was incapable of running a guesthouse and she succumbed to lung problems in the remaining years. Esther died quietly in her sleep, upright in her chair a few years before my grandmother, neither ever to receive a telegram from the Queen. On my grandmother's death, Sunita and Beatrice cleaned out the house and threw out three thousand handy little boxes and handy little pins before Beatrice took control of the house and the business, threw the rest out, and started again.

Beatrice tried for a while to run the guesthouse with Federico. They argued constantly, and neither really had any idea how to properly conduct a business.

Now I live on the other side of the past, on the other side of Elise, who was suddenly there and suddenly not, of my mother and my grandmother and Beatrice and Esther. And of Bernadette Brennan, my mother, the one who watched over me, who protected me without my ever knowing.

They were certainly not perfect, but they were family none-theless, a strange motley collection of people who never quite fit together, acting out their parts in a surrealist drama fuelled by madness, lies, and alcohol that provided a fertile breeding ground for disaster. We all drowned the day Elise was taken from us, but now, looking at the view from my aunt's old room where I write every day, I am not, like Esther, turning my back on the view but cleaning the windows so the water is always the first thing I see.

The sun is going down, the river is full and at peace. It lies like a shining ribbon of silk under a sky streaked with pink and pale mauve clouds. Our boat glides across the water. We pass Billy's tree where the willows bend low to kiss the water. Soft laughter evaporates on the breeze; the taste of cold champagne hits the back of my throat and warmth floods over my cheeks, down into my body, right to the ends of my fingers. A pale pearl of a moon backlights the trees so they are silhouetted in dark shapes that reach for the sky above. On a floating branch, a waterfowl sits, dipping its beak, looking for food. We don't speak, spellbound by the serene nature of the river at dusk.

Matthew spins the boat in slow circles and the ripples spread outward across the smooth, green-brown surface. Birds are calling each other. Their light tones ring out over the dusk. Water creatures settle in for the night, small crabs dart in and out of their homes. Fish jump out of the water occasionally and the crickets are singing a quiet monotone symphony. Tomorrow my arms will ache from rowing.

The boat is small, but the three of us fit in comfortably. The gold edging on Jamilla's shalwar kameez catches the last rays of the sun. She keeps an eye on the river cruise boat; she thinks it will swamp us even though I have assured her it won't. The people on the cruise boat lean over the railing, tipping their glasses to us as they sail on by. Muted jazz music washes over us and quietly fades away. Jamilla has a citronella candle burning on the seat beside her. From time to time, it hisses gently as droplets of water splash over it.

We pass the place where they found her. Those who do not know the river could not distinguish it from any other place along this stretch. There is nothing to mark it, but I know it well. I remember back to the day Olivia prayed to St Hyacinth. She told me that the footprints of the saint remained on the water, even after he had crossed the river, and that when the water was calm, they could be seen for centuries afterward. Here are Elise's last imprints, her tiny footprints are here, shining on the surface of the river; her very short journey ended here. I let my hand drop down, feeling the sensation of cold water running through my fingers. I've carried her in my heart, my blood sister, for all these years. She was a part of my life, a bigger part than I ever could have imagined, but now it is time to let her go. My fingers move slowly underneath the water, spreading apart, and as the boat drifts on they move closer together, touching each other to bend in a wave, a final goodbye to Elise, the river child.

About the Author

Jo Tuscano is an author of both fiction and non-fiction. Jo taught English and ESL for twenty years in schools, colleges and community centres and then went on to write full-time and do professional editing. Her co-authored book, *Back on the Block: Bill Simon's Story* was published in 2009 and is the first memoir by a member of the Stolen Generations incarcerated in the notorious Kinchella Boys' Home. Jo has a long history of working with multicultural communities and with First Nations people.

Jo is a content creator for imagineer.me, an organisation that provides courses for building the imagination and accessing creativity, and which is underpinned by neuroscience. She is the creator of The Peach Project, a course that uses visual learning to access figurative language. She works with First Nations creators at imagineer.me creating programs that utilise Aboriginal and cross-cultural learning methods that teachers can use in their classrooms.

Jo has had articles published in the *Westerly Journal, New England Review,* the *NSW History Teachers' Association* journal, the *Newswrite* journal and various other journals. She has had excerpts from *Back on the Block* published in the *Sydney Morning Herald* and in Indigenous publications. She has done media interviews with the ABC's *Stateline* and various radio programs in Sydney and Melbourne about writing with Indigenous Australians and bringing their stories to publication. She has been a presenter for Reconciliation Western Sydney on issues of mandatory sentencing in the Northern Territory and the Stolen

Generations. Her work has been performed by the Voices of Women Project. Her co-authored non-fiction book, *This is Where You Have to Go,* written with Biripi elder Lynda Holden is coming in the future.

Her next novel, *Under Andromeda,* will be published by Odyssey Books in 2022.

facebook.com/Jo-Tuscano-Writer-108506167651543
instagram.com/jotuscanowriter